THE LOCK-UP

John Banville was born in Wexford, Ireland, in 1945. He is the author of many novels, including *The Book of Evidence*, *The Sea*, winner of the 2005 Man Booker Prize, and, more recently, the bestselling crime novels *Snow* and *April in Spain*, both of which were shortlisted for the CWA Historical Dagger.

by the same author

NIGHTSPAWN

BIRCHWOOD

DOCTOR COPERNICUS

KEPLER

THE NEWTON LETTER

MEFISTO

THE BOOK OF EVIDENCE

GHOSTS

ATHENA

THE UNTOUCHABLE

ECLIPSE

SHROUD

THE SEA

THE INFINITIES

ANCIENT LIGHT

THE BLUE GUITAR

MRS OSMOND

SNOW

APRIL IN SPAIN

THE LOCK-UP

JOHN
BANVILLE

faber

First published in 2023
by Faber & Faber Ltd
Bloomsbury House
74–77 Great Russell Street
London WC1B 3DA

This export edition published in 2023

Typeset by Typo•glyphix, Burton-on-Trent DE14 3HE
Printed and bound by CPI Group (UK) Ltd, Croydon, CR0 4YY

An extract from T. S. Eliot's 'Fragment of an Agon', from *Collected Poems
1909–1962*, reproduced by permission of the publisher, Faber & Faber Ltd

*This is a work of fiction. All of the characters, organisations and
events portrayed in this novel are either products of the author's
imagination or are used fictitiously*

A CIP record for this book
is available from the British Library

ISBN 978-0-571-37098-6

2 4 6 8 10 9 7 5 3 1

alla mia cara amica
Beatrice Monti della Corte

They flee from me that sometime did me seek
With naked foot, stalking in my chamber.

Sir Thomas Wyatt

ALTO ADIGE

after the war

1

Brother Damian stood with a hand held up to shield his eyes against the sun and watched the man, still far off, making his slow way up the steep track towards the monastery. It was April, but ragged patches of snow still clung on in the lee of drystone walls and in the blue-shadowed hollows under over-hanging rocks. Below, the village nestled in the valley floor. The grass down there seemed unnaturally green, after the ice and storms of a long winter. The village, with its timbered houses and steeply slanted roofs, its narrow streets, its clock tower and steeple, was as quaint and timeless as a picture on a postcard.

Faint sounds of village life could be heard on the clear, chill air: the chatter of housewives, the voices of children at play, the ringing notes of a blacksmith's hammer. From the far side of the valley came the distant dinning of cowbells, and the soft, querulous bleating of unseen sheep.

All round the skyline stood the soaring Alpine peaks, glassy and glittering, silver-blue, indifferent. Although he had been here for more than twenty years, at the monastery of Sankt-Fiacre, Brother Damian still found it hard sometimes to believe in the reality of this vast ring of mountains. In spring sunlight, as now, they looked flat and semi-transparent, as if they had been painted onto the sky in washes of watercolour.

Strange, he thought, not for the first time, that a place that had seen so much history, that had watched so many armies surging across its rocky landscape, should look so much like a chocolate-box picture of itself.

Everything in the valley spoke of old days, old ways. The men of the village dressed in braided jackets and knee breeches and carried alpenstocks, while the girls wore dirndl dresses and arranged their wheat-coloured or inky-black hair – here was where the blonde north met the dark-eyed south – in long, gleaming plaits that they shaped into flat coils and pinned against their ears like big spiral-shaped pastries.

Often, encircled here in the high Dolomites, the friar found himself longing for the soft grey rain and heaving purple seas of the far west of Ireland, his birthplace, his lost land, the home he had forsaken when, as a young student, he decided to pledge his life to God.

The man wending his way up the dusty path had to stop frequently and mop his brow with a blue bandana. Then he would stand a while to rest, looking back down at the village, or upwards to the snow-capped peaks.

He wore a faded green loden jacket, twill trousers, stout boots and a battered black hat with a yellow feather in the band. His stick was a shepherd's crook. A small canvas knapsack was strapped to his back. He also seemed too convincing to be true. He might be a figure out of one of the tales of the Grimm Brothers, or a lone wayfarer in a story by Stifter or E. T. A. Hoffmann.

But Brother Damian knew who he was. The man was expected. He should have been here three days ago. The delay was worrying. Had he been stopped at the border? Had he

4

been noted and identified, and tracked, perhaps, as he made his perilous way south and up to this high place?

The man arrived now at the top of the track.

They met under the arched stone entranceway to the courtyard, around the four sides of which the ancient monastery was built. It had originally been a stopping place for Crusaders on their way to the Italian ports to board ship for the Holy Land. The Franciscan Order had taken it over in the fourteenth century, under the benefice of one of the Avignon popes, and had occupied it ever since. It was a self-sufficient establishment, with its own herds of cattle and sheep and flocks of poultry, its piggery, its bakery and brewery, its dairy, its orchards and extensive vineyards.

Brother Damian had been Minister Provincial here for a decade now. His duties lay heavy upon him. In his heart he felt he wasn't fitted for a position of authority. However, God had willed it that he should be raised up, and who was he to object to or complain of the Creator's agency?

The man had a wedge-shaped face, tapering from a broad, unlined brow to a thin-lipped mouth and small, sharp chin. His eyes were remarkable, the irises a shade of pale, translucent grey and the lids as fine as folds of crêpe paper. They were never still. He kept darting quick glances this way and that, as if he felt himself surrounded on all sides by unseen foes. He looked exhausted, and his breathing was shallow and rapid, as if he had been running for a long time, running hard. Which, in a way, he had.

'The air up here is so thin,' he said, panting, and fixed his distressed gaze for a second on the heavy iron cross the friar wore on a chain around his neck. 'I feel light-headed.'

5

'You'll soon get used to it,' Brother Damian said. They spoke in English. The man was fluent in the language, with hardly a trace of an accent. He had lived for some years in London, the friar recalled.

They set off across the courtyard. When they had got halfway, the man had to stop again and stand a moment to catch his breath, one hand holding on to the friar's arm and the other pressed to his heaving chest.

'Forgive me,' he said. 'It has been a long journey.'

'Were you stopped?'

'Stopped?'

'At the border.'

The man took his hand from the friar's arm and wiped the back of it across his almost colourless lips. He shook his head.

'No, no. No one stopped me. But twice I had to leave the road and take shelter. It was all very difficult, very dangerous. There are soldiers everywhere, their insignia torn off and discarded but still carrying their weapons. Worse than them are the bands of children, young boys and girls alike, starving and lost. They are like wolves, roaming the countryside and the streets of the ruined towns, searching for food.' He looked aside, nodding. 'The world has become mad.'

'Yes,' Brother Damian agreed, 'it has been mad for some time.'

They walked on, and entered through a studded doorway into the refectory, a long, high-ceilinged room with a massive oak table running the length of it.

'I'm hungry,' the man said, in a tone of mild surprise, as if he had just that moment realised what it was that had been nagging at him for so long. 'My store of food ran out very quickly. I stole two pancakes in one of the villages I passed through. And yesterday a child, a little girl, gave me half of an apple she was eating.'

'What will you take?' the friar asked. 'Some bread, and a dish of coffee? Our bread is very good, baked fresh every day. And there might be a bit of soup left over from last evening. I'll go and see. Sit down there. I won't be long.'

The man nodded dully. He had become childlike suddenly. The mention of food seemed to have unmanned him.

He sat down carefully on one of the backless stools that were lined up at both sides of the table. He laid his shepherd's crook on the floor at his feet and unbuckled his knapsack. He looked about almost timidly. The silence buzzed in his ears. The air was so light and featureless it hardly seemed air at all, but some far thinner, hardly substantial medium.

'You're in luck,' Brother Damian said on his return. 'There is vegetable broth left over, it will probably be better today.'

Another friar appeared now, a tiny, wizened creature, his face burnt to a leathery brown by countless years of exposure to the Alpine sun. His arthritic hands were gnarled and claw-like. He bore before him a wooden tray on which were set a bowl of greyish soup with wobbly lozenges of fat floating on it, a plate with rolls, butter in a dish, a coffee pot and an earthen bowl. He set the tray on the table in front of the man, murmuring unintelligibly and smiling. His front teeth were almost entirely worn away; all that was left of them were sharp, yellowish spikes.

'Thank you, Brother Anselm,' the Minister Provincial said. '*Ja ja, danke schön, heiliger Bruder*,' the man joined in quickly.

He sounded like a little boy remembering his manners a shade too late.

The old friar retreated backwards, bowing and mumbling and smiling his gap-toothed smile.

Brother Damian ladled soup into the clay bowl.

'Eat,' he said to the man, and added, in the easy tone in which he would have commented on the weather, 'God is good.'

The man ate with conscious restraint, willing himself not to gobble down the food. It must have been a long time since his last proper meal, the friar thought, watching him as he crumbled a bread roll into the soup with unsteady fingers. What things he must have seen, what horrors he must have witnessed. The country he had come from had been devastated, bombed back to the Dark Ages. Such vast destruction, such a merciless avenging. Its people had been told they had brought their troubles on themselves. Perhaps they had, without meaning to. Yet God is good.

'Your family,' the friar said, 'your wife, your son, are they safe?'

'Yes. At least, they were, when I left them. They are with a family, in the countryside. The farm is far from the city, no one comes there.'

'Have you made arrangements for—?'

The man was hunched over the bowl, spooning up the soup, unwilling, it seemed, to let even the vapour rising from it go to waste. He nodded.

'Yes, there is a plan to bring them out through Holland. A ship will call at Rotterdam in three weeks' time. The captain is a friend from former times, and besides' – the man made a small, sharp sound that it took the friar a moment to recognise as laughter – 'he has been well bribed. My wife managed to sell a diamond brooch to a dealer in Munich.'

'And the boy?'

'He's seventeen. A man, almost.'

'What is his name?'

'Franz.' The man gazed before him, with the spoon suspended over the bowl. 'He's a good boy. Brave, you know, but not very strong, not very vigorous. Yet he will take good care of his mother.'

When he had finished, the man pushed the empty bowl and the bread plate away and crossed his arms on the table and rested his forehead on them, closing his eyes.

'A moment,' he said softly. 'I must rest for just a moment.'

Brother Damian waited, sitting with his hands on his knees, gazing up at the sunlight in the row of small, barred windows high up under the ceiling beams.

The tide of war had not reached the valley. They had been spared, in this high haven. Strange to think how tranquil the last five years had been, while not far to the north such terrible battles had been waged, the armies first surging westwards, then other armies eastwards, and then, after the tide of battle had turned and become a flood, the terrible convergence in the centre, the shrinking centre, as the German lands were taken and laid waste.

God in his goodness had willed it should be so. Sometimes it was hard to hold fast to belief in man's fate, as the dream of rightness and destiny died, foundering in a welter of blood.

The friar went away again, into a little room off the kitchens, and quickly returned with a straw-covered flask and two small glasses. The man at the table lifted his head with an effort. His eyes were bloodshot.

'Take a little of this muscatel,' Brother Damian said. 'We make it here at the monastery.' He poured two measures of the thick, tawny wine into the glasses, pushed one along the table to the man and lifted his own to make a toast. 'To the fallen.'

They drank, and smacked their lips.

'It's good, yes?' Brother Damian said. 'The grapes are left on the vine until the first frosts have come, to concentrate the sugar.'

In silence they drank. The man blinked rapidly. The flavour of the wine seemed to distress him – perhaps it had brought back memories of other, happier times – yet he kept on drinking until he had finished the last drop in the glass. The friar refilled it. They drank again, both gazing before them in silence, each contemplating in his way the dream that had failed so disastrously.

'Come on with me now,' Brother Damian said, 'you'll want to have a proper rest.'

They walked along flagstoned corridors. The man seemed wearier now than he was before he had eaten. It was as if the food had been not sustenance but yet another burden laid upon him.

Brother Damian carried his stick for him, and his knapsack. The knapsack weighed almost nothing, and seemed to be empty, except for something heavy in the bottom of it. A weapon? The man had lost everything, except his resourceful wife and his good, brave son, and a pistol with which to protect himself, or – God forbid – to put an end to his travails.

Yet perhaps the dream was not entirely dead. Who could say what might rise from the ashes of war?

'This is your room,' he said to the man, and smiled wryly. 'Or maybe I should say, your cell. We lead simple lives, here.'

It was a small stone chamber with a narrow bed, a rush-seated chair, and a commode on which stood an enamel jug and basin.

The man looked about intently, as if to take note of everything, to memorise everything.

'Like Vincent's room,' he murmured.

'Vincent?'

'The painter. The Dutchman.'

'Ah. Yes. The bed, the chair. I see.'

'When I take off my boots and set them here, the picture will be complete.'

Brother Damian put the man's knapsack on the bed and propped the shepherd's crook against the wall behind the chair.

'I won't disturb you until it's time for supper. Is there something more I can get for you now?'

'No, no, thank you. You've been very kind. All this' – he looked about, and made a gesture with his right hand – 'I can't tell you.' He seemed on the edge of tears.

'Oh, you'll have a chance to pay your way,' the friar said, smiling broadly. 'We'll put you to work while you're here.'

There was a brief, strained silence. The levity of the friar's tone had struck a discordant note.

'You've endured so much,' he said apologetically. 'But work,' he went on, brightening, 'work will lift your burden from you. Work will set you free.'

The man looked at him, his grey eyes narrowing.

'Those are words I've heard before,' he said.

The friar's big square Irish face reddened to the line of his scant, sandy hair.

'Forgive me,' he said. 'It's always been the way with me, no sooner do I open my big bloody mouth than I put my bigger bloody foot in it!'

'*Entschuldigen Sie*,' the man said. 'I didn't mean to rebuke you. God knows—'

He made again that gesture with his hand, expressive of gratitude yet also of futility. Theirs was an exhausted world, for all the greenness of this mountain valley, for all the purity of its thin, chill air.

'I'll leave you now,' the friar said. He turned to the door, then paused. 'When the time comes, you'll be going south again,' he said. 'To Rome, then by sea to Gibraltar, and up through Spain and France to the Channel. Safe houses all the way. There's always a monastery, a convent. We have our routes, we've had them since the days of Fiacra, the Celtic monk our monastery is named after. Fiacra is the patron saint of gardeners, did you know that?'

'Is that what I will work at while I'm here, as a gardener?'

'The labourer in the vineyard, yes.'

The man nodded.

'"The last shall be first, and the first shall be last",' he quoted.

'Ah, you know your Bible.'

'How would I not?'

So began his stay at the monastery on the hillside.

The days went on, then the weeks, and the sun rose a little

higher in the sky every day and shone a little more strongly. He worked among the vines and in the apple orchards. His hands and his thinned-out face turned brown, but his troubles were not lifted from him, as the friar had suggested.

He worried ceaselessly about his wife, and their boy. He worried about himself. He had been a part of such horrors, and why should he think they were ended now, just because the war had ended? War never ends, he knew, only the armies step back at intervals from the fray, to tend to the wounded and sharpen and polish their blunted, blood-encrusted weapons.

No, he thought, willing himself to hope, the struggle was not over. The phoenix would rise again in glory.

Presently, the day came when his wife and son were due to board the SS *Meermin* at Rotterdam, but still he had heard nothing from them.

De Grote was the ship's captain, Karl De Grote. The man had known him in the camps, first in Theresienstadt, then Dachau. He was one of the few who had got away free. It was from Dachau the man himself had set out southwards six weeks ago. Six weeks! It felt like six months, six years – a lifetime.

Could De Grote be trusted? He owed the man everything – he owed him his survival. But the man knew the world, knew the people in it and what they were capable of, even the best of them, even those who seemed the soundest, the most trustworthy.

Maybe Hilde and the boy had not made it to Rotterdam. Maybe someone had betrayed them, maybe they had been seized at the place where they were hiding. Maybe one of the farmhands had denounced them, or the farmer himself had got tired of sheltering them, or taken fright at the thought that they might be discovered and that he would be held responsible. These fears and worries kept the man awake at night, kept him tossing and turning on the narrow bed in a sweat of uncertainty and dread.

Then at last, miraculously, as it seemed, a letter arrived.

It was from the farmer, Ullmann, dated the previous week. In half a dozen lines, it told him his wife and son had left for Holland, that they had been well and in good spirits when they went, and full of confidence that they would get through and make it to safety. The people in Rome had made the arrangements – they would lodge in a convent until the man joined them.

The man read the letter again, twice, more slowly each time. He had a store of gold hidden away, he would find a place for the three of them, they would start a new life.

He sat on the side of the bed, breathless with relief, and smiling at Ullmann's comical Plattdeutsch. Then his vision blurred, and he rubbed at his eyes with the heel of his hand. It took him a moment to realise that he was weeping. When was the last time he had wept? In the world he had lived in, there had been no place for tears.

But how had the letter got through?

A young man on a motorbike had brought it up from the valley, Brother Damian told him.

What young man?

'I don't know,' the friar said, and shrugged. 'He gave me the letter, said to hand it to you in person, then turned his machine and rode away and that's the last I saw of him.'

This made the man anxious all over again. Could he be

sure it was Ullmann who had written the letter? It might be a forgery, meant to trick him, and lead him to slacken his guard.

'Have faith,' Brother Damian urged him. 'You've suffered enough, God is not so cruel that he'd try to deceive you in such a way.'

The man said nothing. If the friar mentioned God one more time, he would smash a fist into his big pink freckled grinning face. Hadn't he heard the news yet? There is no God, there never was. There is only this mindless sphere spinning in infinite darkness among countless other spheres. What this fool thinks of as the mysterious ways of an ever-attendant deity is in fact no more than *das Schicksal*, fate, blind fate, and we are its victims.

At last, the day came for him to leave the monastery and set out on the long loop of his journey to safety and freedom. Yes, a new life.

Brother Damian changed from his brown woollen habit into a layman's dark suit, and walked with him down the long track to the village. They entered the inn, Im Zeichen der Ziege, and sat down at a scarred wooden table in the pot room.

The place was deserted; even the innkeeper didn't make an appearance. This was the arrangement that had been agreed, that no one would see the man, in case he might be recognised, in case someone might report him. The man knew that others before him had come this way, along this route. Not all had made it through.

And so they waited.

The only sounds were the creaking of the friar's boots when he shifted his feet and the sighing of a draught in some chink in a door or window. The man felt an odd kind of melancholy.

Odd, yet he recognised it. Even as a child, he had felt every departure as a premonition of death, a little sip of the waters of the black river of oblivion.

A man appeared at last, a peasant, rough-looking, with a bushy beard and a surly manner. He was driving an old wooden cart drawn by a half-starved nag. The only seating was a square bale of straw set at the front, close behind the horse's rump. In this contraption the man was borne away, on the next leg of his long journey to a rainy island at the edge of what he thought of as the known world, his world, which now he was about to leave forever.

The friar stood in the doorway of the inn, waving a lifted hand slowly from side to side in a mechanical-seeming farewell.

'*Auf Wiedersehen*,' the man called back.

Above the friar's head, on a wooden sign, a painted goat with huge curled horns stood on its hind legs, lewdly smirking.

DUBLIN

twelve years later

2

Strafford was always surprised to find that when people learned he was a detective, they tended to become either nervous, or truculent, or both. Of course, it wasn't that they all had cause to feel guilty, or that they were anarchists and objected to a police force on principle. The reason was more subtle than that.

The country had been colonised by the English for eight hundred years, give or take – the first gang of Anglo-Norman robber barons had made landfall on these shores in the twelfth century – and the liberated Irish state, now stuck fast in the doldrums of the 1950s, was not much older than Strafford himself. The people had long memories, and bitterness against their former oppressors was corrosive. They had only to hear him speak to know him for a Protestant, and therefore, inevitably, to know he was not one of them.

What was he doing in the Garda force? they would ask – in *their* Garda force. And furthermore, how had he got to be a detective?

It seemed to them a scandal, in a way.

After independence, his people, his kind, the so-called Ascendancy, had, with a few exceptions, washed their hands of the new, self-governing Ireland and retreated into their demesnes and the solace of their accustomed, genteel pursuits.

The Ireland, or the twenty-six counties of it that constituted the Republic, that had been born of rebellion, and of the subsequent hard fight for freedom and the inevitable civil war that followed, might now be a rougher place, with rougher men in charge, but it was their own place, free and independent, if you didn't count the controlling power of the Catholic Church, which the majority accepted as right and proper anyway. Rome was the Republic's second, ultramontane, capital. Or the first, as some would say.

Detective Inspector St John Strafford was an anomaly, as he well knew, and if for an instant he should chance to forget that fact, there was no lack of those ready and eager to remind him, by a cold stare or a sardonic word, of precisely who and what he was.

But not, to his relief, Perry Otway.

Perry and Strafford were both members of the same rarefied tribe. Perry was, as he said of himself with rueful amusement, a son of the manse. His father was the rector of a far-flung country parish, who had sent his son across the water to be educated at Winchester College, one of England's grand public schools – not quite as grand as Eton or Harrow, perhaps, but grander than most. This made Perry, by another of the many peculiarities of English nomenclature, a Wykehamist.

He found this, too, mildly risible.

Perry was large and fair, with a baby's large unblemished face and guileless eyes of palest cornflower blue. He wore an oil-caked boiler suit the colour, and by now probably the consistency, of moist putty, and his fingernails were splintered and black from years of rootling in the innards of ailing and recalcitrant engines.

He ran a tiny workshop and filling station in a mews off Mount Street Crescent.

The premises consisted of a dim, windowless cube with many shelves along the walls, and a rectangular, grave-shaped hole sunk into the floor to allow for the inspection and repair of undercarriages. At the front, high-shouldered and toylike, there stood a single, crimson-painted petrol pump with a robot's head and a glass face. Everything in the workshop was neat and tidy, the tools, the spare parts, the stacked tyres, but thoroughly filthy and smeared all over with oil and engine grease.

The two men, meeting at the petrol pump, had sized each other up and on the instant each had recognised the other as one of his own. In the finely gradated social structure of the Ireland of the day, Peregrine Otway the begrimed car mechanic was every bit as anomalous as St John Strafford the Garda detective.

'Awful business,' Perry said, slowly shaking his big round head and looking off down the lane. 'A young woman like that.'

It was a day in late September. The air had a damp, silvery shine, and intermittent flushes of wind were tousling the already greying tops of the stunted trees in the railed-off wedge of waste ground at the back of the Pepper Canister Church.

Strafford slipped his hands into the pockets of his gaberdine raincoat and considered the toecaps of his shoes, which, he noted, were badly in need of a polish. He had been letting things go somewhat, of late, and he thought vaguely now, not for the first time, that he really must make an effort and bring some order back into his life. Shoes could be old, yes, in fact they only came into their own with the years, but they must be kept polished. It was the rule, unwritten of course, but a rule all the same.

'Where was she when you found her?' he asked.

'Come on, I'll show you.'

Perry led the way along the lane to another of the numerous garages that he owned in the area.

This one was a lock-up, for rent on short lets to suburban motorists in need of a secure place near the city centre in which to keep their cars. Another converted mews, it was a good deal smaller than the one where he had his workshop. He drew open the double doors and pushed them back flush against the walls on either side.

The space that he revealed was empty, and smelled, like the workshop, of grease and motor oil and tyres. There was also, today, a strong reek of exhaust fumes.

'I don't think there's much left that hasn't been investigated,' Perry said. 'Your forensics chaps went over the place pretty thoroughly.'

Strafford stepped into the lock-up and stood in the middle of the oil-stained floor and looked about. He sighed. Was it only his morbid fancy, or did death, especially when it was as sad and wasteful as this one, leave an imprint on the surroundings in which it had occurred?

And what a place this was to die in, a bare, blackened hole in the wall down a shabby back lane.

He took off his hat and held it at his side. He never quite knew what to do with things that were not actually attached to him, hats, umbrellas, scarves, handkerchiefs and the like. In the past month, he had misplaced or lost no fewer than three fountain pens.

'It was the smell of the exhaust that caught my attention,' Perry said, 'otherwise I mightn't have looked in at all. Funny, it always reminds me of ground coffee.'

Strafford frowned.

'What does?'

'Car exhaust. When I'm passing by Bewley's and the big roaster in the window is going and the smoke from the beans is billowing out into the street, I could well be at Brands Hatch.'

Strafford said nothing, having nothing to say. Grafton Street, narrow and choked with traffic from morning till night, and with coffee smoke or without, always smelled like a racetrack to him. He didn't drive. It was another anomaly.

'Lovely little motor, too,' Perry said wistfully. 'Austin A40 Sports convertible. You don't see many of that model over here.'

'Where is it now?'

'Oh, they towed it away.'

Perry drew shut the double doors and they walked back together to the workshop.

'What was she?' Perry asked. 'I mean, what did she do? Was she married?'

'No, she was single. An academic. History, I believe. Yes, history.'

'UCD, or—?'

'Trinity.'

'Uh-hm.'

This was a significant distinction. University College was where the Catholics went, while Trinity was for Prods and those of other, rarer, persuasions.

'Nice name, too,' Perry said, 'Rosa Jacobs.'

He repeated the surname quietly, and mused. Then they were silent. Many things in this country went without saying. Both knew that a person named Jacobs was bound to be of a rarer persuasion even than theirs.

Strafford reapplied his hat to his narrow skull with its smattering of thin fair hair, a lock of which tended to fall limply across his forehead. He didn't feel comfortable wearing a hat, but everyone else wore one, and it was either a hat or a flat cap, and a flat cap was out of the question.

Perry had picked up a spanner and was wiping it thoughtfully with an oily cloth.

'Do you come across Doctor Quirke at all, these days?' he asked. He frowned at the spanner's shiny head. The thing had the look of an animal waiting for something to seize on with its fierce, serrated jaws.

'Yes, I do,' Strafford said. 'In fact, I was with him in Spain when—' He let his voice trail off.

Perry nodded. 'Ah, yes. Read about it in the papers. Very shocking, that.'

'Yes.'

'To lose a wife, and in such an awful way – well.'

Now they both looked at their toecaps. Perry wore Dutch clogs with thick wooden soles.

Strafford had been present when Quirke's wife was shot. He had fired shots himself, and had killed her killer. He began to say something, but Perry interrupted him.

'In fact, he kept a car himself in that very lock-up, for a while, years ago.'

'Who did?'

'Doctor Quirke.'

'The same garage—?'

He gestured back up the lane. Perry nodded.

'Coincidence, all right. An Alvis, it was, and you certainly don't see many of *those*. Tremendous machine. Drove like a dream, smooth as silk.' The mechanic chuckled. 'Wasted on him, of course. He never even learned to drive properly. A car like that needs to be loved. I think he was a bit frightened of her.'

Strafford wasn't listening.

'Tell me again, about finding the young woman.'

'I was just closing up the shop for the day when I smelled the exhaust smoke drifting down the lane and went up to have a look. The padlock wasn't on, I remember noticing that. When I opened the doors, the fumes nearly knocked me over.'

'Was the engine still going?'

'No, no. It had run out of juice.'

'And the girl, where was she, in the front seat or—?'

'Yes, she was sitting behind the wheel, lying against the seat with her head thrown back and her hands in her lap. I'll never forget her throat, stretched out like that, the skin a lovely pale pink. Pink under her fingernails, too, but a deeper shade. She didn't look dead, though I knew she was.'

'Was the car locked? I mean, was it locked from the inside?'

Perry thought for a moment.

'No, no, all the doors were unlocked. But the hood was pulled up, of course, and the windows were up too, except the one beside her. Pretty well airtight, those models, though you wouldn't think it, with the canvas roof.'

'And how had she—?'

'Oh, she did a thorough job. Rubber hose wrapped in an oiled rag and wedged in the exhaust pipe, the other end fed through the window beside her with more rags to seal it up.'

'She went to a lot of trouble.'

'Showed determination, all right.' He shook his head. 'What was the matter, for her to do such a thing?'

Strafford shrugged.

'That's what we're trying to find out. There wasn't a note, or anything like that?'

'No. There was no note. Just her, with her head lying that way on the back of the seat and her hands linked together in her lap. She was pretty, even in death, with that wonderful pale skin, and the long black hair.'

'You must have met her already. You must have talked to her.'

'No, I didn't. Couldn't even be sure it was her, though I don't know who else it might have been.'

'But how did she arrange to leave the car?'

'She rang me, and asked if the lock-up was still available – she'd seen the ad. She said to leave the doors open and put the padlock and the key somewhere where she could find them.'

'How long was she going to keep the car here for?'

'She was to phone again, and we'd fix the details. She seemed in a hurry.'

'Yes? Why? Did she sound agitated?'

Perry considered.

'No, just in a rush, and sort of – strange.'

'How do you mean, strange?'

'Her voice was muffled, but squeaky, too. As if she had laryngitis, or there was something wrong with her mouth. Or maybe it was just that the phone line was bad. She spoke very quickly, and seemed to be getting ready to go off somewhere.' He paused, nibbling at a babyish lower lip. 'I suppose she was upset, if she had already decided what she was going to do.' Strafford said nothing. 'What age was she?' Perry asked.

'Twenty-seven.'

Now Perry pursed his mouth into a whistling shape, and shook his head again.

'What a waste.'

'Yes,' Strafford said, and, before he could stop himself, added, 'like Doctor Quirke's Alvis.'

This brought another, awkward silence. It was a question as to which of the two men was the more disconcerted. Strafford cleared his throat. He hadn't meant to say what he'd said.

'Well,' he murmured, 'I'll let you go.' He was turning away. 'If anything occurs to you—that's to say, if you remember something—anything, let me know, will you? You have my number. Or anyone at the Pearse Street Garda station.'

A gust of wind swept along the lane, smelling of autumn, of the dust of pavements, of coming rain. This was the season Strafford liked the most. He found it far more thrilling than spring, thrilling but melancholy, or thrilling because melancholy.

'I wonder why she chose to do it here,' Perry said.

Strafford paused, turned back.

'Why?'

'I don't know. It just seems strange.'

'Where do you advertise it, the lock-up?'

'In the *Evening Mail*, once a week.'

Not the *Irish Times*, then. Their paper.

'So she saw it and rang you up, even though she was in a rush.'

'Yes. Strange, as I say.' Perry turned aside and squinted at the sky. 'I suppose I'll have to sell it now. The garage. I'd keep seeing her, every time I open the doors.' He nodded slowly. 'A shame.'

Strafford wasn't sure which he was regretting, the young woman's death or the unwilling sacrifice of the lock-up.

3

Strafford had shut up the family home – or house, as he supposed he should say, since it had never been much of a home – and was living in a rented room in one of the handsome villas on Mespil Road.

The room was on the first floor. It was a little cramped, since it was half of a larger room, one wall having been put up as a partition. It irritated him that the ornamental plaster moulding under the ceiling only ran around three sides. Though he tried not to look at the bare fourth side, his eye would keep drifting upwards.

But all in all, the place suited him well enough. He didn't need much space, and the single window, a fine, tall Victorian affair with large and elegantly proportioned panes, let in a good light, and afforded a nice view of the front garden and, across the road, a sedgy stretch of the Grand Canal.

The owners of the house, an English family named Claridge, occupied the ground floor and three of the bedrooms upstairs. They were portly Mr and Mrs Claridge and their two teenage daughters, whose names Strafford didn't know, and probably never would, since by now he felt it was too late to ask. They had a sulky, dissatisfied air, the Claridge girls. It was hard to know whether this was the result of their being spoilt, or harshly oppressed.

One had tired, lank blonde hair, but the other, the older of the two, he judged, sported a mass of gleaming black curls that would have been attractive if her general demeanour had been less unattractive.

They were old enough to have finished school, but he didn't think they were at university either. They might be training to be shorthand typists, or perhaps they already had office jobs, for they often carried what looked like ledgers, or sheaves of documents, under their arms. They were both tight-lipped and had unnervingly calculating stares.

From the start, he had sensed their aversion to him, though so far as he knew he had done nothing to merit it. When he encountered one or other of them, coming in at the front door or making their way out through the hall, they would lower their eyes and turn sideways and squirm past him, as though they were afraid he might make a grab at them, or molest them in some other way.

What Mr Claridge did, or had done, for a living was something else Strafford didn't know – again, too late to ask. It seemed he must be retired. He was always about the house, often in shirtsleeves, and often with some implement or other in his hand, a screwdriver, or a hammer or the like, and once, memorably, a blowtorch, the snout of which was blackened from much use.

His wife was of an indolent disposition, and Strafford had only the rarest glimpses of her. She would on occasion open the door of their flat a little way and stand tentatively on the threshold, watching the hall, though when anyone other than her husband or daughters appeared she would draw back quickly and close the door soundlessly.

The room next to Strafford's, the other half of the original room, was occupied by a young man by the name of Singh, an Indian or a Pakistani, Strafford wasn't sure what the difference was. Despite his youth, Mr Singh was almost as portly as Mr and Mrs Claridge, and managed also to seem to be almost of an age with them. He carried himself regally, with his plump chest thrust out and his head and shoulders drawn far back. He was a student at the College of Surgeons.

Strafford shared a bathroom with him. Mr Singh always left behind in the narrow little space a sharp, warm tang. Though perhaps too immediately intimate, it was not unpleasant. At any rate, Strafford didn't find it so, despite the fact that he had what was probably an overly keen sense of smell.

The source of this aura was possibly an aftershave that Mr Singh wore, or some other body lotion. However, Strafford preferred to think it was his own, personal odour, a special aura in which he moved, an afterglow of the rich foods he had fed on since childhood, and which, as telltale aromas attested, he still sometimes cooked up for himself clandestinely in his room of an evening.

They were not on speaking terms, Strafford and Mr Singh. There was no animosity between them, only from the start they had confined their exchanges to brief nods and spare smiles. Both were happy to continue in this way, since Strafford was retiring by nature, and so, it was clear, was Mr Singh.

One day, Strafford's wife had gone to visit her mother and had not come back. Nor would she, it seemed, given the considerable length of time she had been away. There had been no fight or argument between them, no falling-out, or at least not so far as Strafford had noticed.

Marguerite could be odd, on occasion, and her moods had

31

always been hard to interpret. Strafford did sometimes wonder, feeling a vague disquiet, if there might have been some bone of contention of which he had been unaware all along. Perhaps he had driven her away, by a thoughtless word or action. But if so, he didn't know what action or word it could have been.

They spoke on the telephone once a week. These calls were not easy, and left Strafford feeling dissatisfied and obscurely in the wrong, and to blame for something, somehow.

The only telephone in the house, the only one he and Mr Singh had use of, was a large black rectangular coin-operated machine bolted to the wall just inside the front door. The hall was high-ceilinged and reverberant, and it was next to impossible, when on the phone, not to be over-heard by anyone who happened to be in the house, even by Mr Singh, in his half of a room upstairs, though he kept his door always shut.

Anyway, it hardly mattered, since Strafford limited his side of these conversations, such as they were, mainly to mono-syllables, and Marguerite, though in person she tended to shrillness, would never raise her voice on the phone above a level that accorded with the dictates of her, and Strafford's, class and upbringing.

He might have called her from one of the phones in the Pearse Street barracks where he was based, but for some reason he didn't, and she didn't suggest that he should. It wouldn't do to mix the personal and the professional. Although Strafford was not at all sure there remained a personal side to their union – if indeed they were still united, which seemed increas-ingly unlikely with each day that passed and Marguerite had still not returned.

They never mentioned any of this in their constricted weekly exchanges on the phone. Which of them would have dared introduce it, and what would he or she have said? Instead, they chatted desultorily of this and that.

The weather was a safe and dependable topic, and they discussed it a lot. Also, Marguerite made frequent mention of the state of health of the animals – three elderly horses, two dogs, even older, and a mouldering cat – that her mother kept on the family estate outside Abbeyleix. It wasn't really an estate, more a farm, but Marguerite's people had pretensions.

Sometimes the couple spoke of friends, or acquaintances rather, since Strafford didn't go in much for friendship, and the people whom Marguerite knew were a shadowy lot going mainly by nicknames. There was a Tinker, and a Waffles, and a Trudy-Bell.

One of them, most mysteriously, was known as Chins. Whether Chins was male or female Strafford did not know, or had forgotten, and now, as with the question of the names of the Claridge girls and whether Mr Claridge was retired, it was too late to bring it up. And anyway, he didn't care. It didn't in the least matter to him if Chins was man, woman, or neither. It might be a horse, for the daughter had inherited her mother's equine attachments.

The fact was, one could never quite be sure, with Marguerite.

Was the marriage at an end? If it was, Strafford felt no guilt, and of course this made him feel guilty. But the present arrangement, or absence of one, was fine with him, better indeed than he dared to admit, even to himself. He had always been a solitary soul, and was content to be so. Solitude, as he would tell you, is not at all the same thing as loneliness, and was certainly not so in his case.

In general, then, he was content.

The big, airy room above the canal was peculiarly to his taste – or to his peculiar taste, Marguerite would say, doing her thin little smile – with its chintz-covered sofa and comfortably dilapidated armchair, its faded Axminster carpet, its pair of spindly pedestal tables that stood one on either side of the white-painted door, each with its identical, scallop-edged circular lace doily.

His surroundings were especially congenial at evening time, with the traffic stilled, and the greenish-grey light coming up from the canal and filling the deep embrasure of the window with its mild effulgence.

Recently, after long hesitation and with many misgivings, he had dipped into his savings and purchased a gramophone.

Manufactured by HMV, it was the very latest model. It was housed in a large square wooden case, or casket, covered with stippled, burgundy-coloured leather, and lined with a synthetic stuff like stiff velvet, also deep red, the bristly nap of which gave him a little shiver of pleasure when he ran his fingertips over it.

After it was delivered and set up on one of the little tables by the door and he was left alone with it, he couldn't but be shocked at his own daring in having acquired such an outlandish plaything.

This sleek, complicated machine at first intimidated him, with its brash, insistent smells of wood and leather and jeweller's oil. What it reeked of most strongly, of course, was newness. This was, perhaps, the real scandal. In the world in

34

which he had been brought up, only those things burnished by time were fully acceptable, while novelty was looked on as vulgar and to be spurned as such.

Besides, he didn't know what to do with the doily, which he had to remove from the little table before the machine was installed. He wasn't sure what was disturbing about it, this redundant scrap of lace. Perhaps it was something to do with its having been separated from its twin on the other table, leaving behind a broken symmetry. Strafford had always been of a tidy cast of mind.

The shop where he bought the gramophone had given him a complimentary long-playing record of marches by John Philip Sousa, which would show off most strikingly the power and range of the inbuilt speaker. When he put the record on and set it going, the volume was set much too high and the blast of noise – it could hardly be called music – that came out at him made him start back in fright.

Since then, he had accumulated a small but choice library of glossy black discs, their scarlet-and-black labels stamped with the image of a puzzled little dog, the name of which he knew to be Nipper – for he had, somewhat superstitiously, remained loyal to HMV.

Maybe it was the dog on the label that led him to regard the instrument itself as a kind of household pet, one that would keep him company during the long nights, those nights when, before the coming of His Master's Voice, he would have tired of reading or of looking down from the window and become fretful and out of sorts. All he had to do now was to put on a record and settle back into the armchair's familiar and only faintly smelly embrace and close his eyes and stretch out his legs before him and allow himself to be borne away on the soupy sonorities of Brahms, or Mahler, or Richard Strauss.

This evening, he was listening to the sublime trio at the close of *Rosenkavalier* – the sopranos were Lotte Lehmann, Elisabeth Schumann, and the hardly pronounceable Maria Olszewska, all going full belt – when the doorbell rang. It gave him a start, his alarm intensified by the fraught acrobatic weavings of the three straining divas.

Who would be visiting him at twilight on a tranquil Tuesday evening?

It was, he reflected with a twinge of foreboding, the first time anyone had called on him since he had moved in. It was also, therefore, the first time he had heard the bell ring. He hadn't even noticed the apparatus itself, attached to the wall above the door. It was, he saw now, a shallow, black metal cup surmounted by a shiny steel nipple. He was a little shocked at himself for being so unobservant. But why would he have registered the thing? Even the postman hadn't rung yet, not even once.

He went to the window and stood behind the curtain and peered down carefully. However, the view afforded him was not angled steeply enough, and he couldn't see who it was on the step, even if he put his nose right up to the glass.

The bell sounded again, and he tiptoed across the room and lifted the needle from the record. The silence that fell was like the silence in the first seconds after a traffic accident, or after a bomb has gone off.

Had the music been loud enough to be heard outside the house? If so, it would have been heard abruptly stopping too.

In that case, he could hardly not go down and answer the door, since the caller would know he was at home.

Maybe whoever it was had made a mistake, and pressed the wrong bell. But no, his name was printed clearly on a piece of card stuck below the button, and besides, Mr Singh was the only other lodger in the house.

He stood very still, holding the record aloft with his middle finger hooked through the little hole in the centre and his thumb braced on the rim. He hardly dared to breathe. It was absurd. It was as if he were the intruder, and not the intruded-upon.

The grooves of the record were so fine, how could they contain such tremendous storms of sound?

He stepped out on to the landing and paused. Mr Singh was cooking a particularly pungent curry this evening.

Inside the room the bell rang again, more insistently this time, or so it seemed to him.

Quirke also had moved out of what had been his home, and was staying, temporarily, at his daughter's flat in Lower Mount Street. It was not an entirely convenient or relaxed arrangement, although they both did their best to adjust to each other's ways and moods.

Quirke loved his daughter, in his fashion, and he believed she loved him, in her fashion, despite the injustices he had inflicted on her when she was young. For the first nineteen years of her life, he had maintained the fiction that he was not her father but her uncle. Still, if she resented his presence, or found it, and him, irksome, she kept up a convincing pretence.

She could hardly have refused him shelter, after the events in Spain the previous spring that had left him a widower for the second time. Since his return, he hadn't spoken of his wife's death to Phoebe, or to anyone else. It was, as he gave people to understand, a forbidden topic. Phoebe didn't even dare to mention her stepmother's name. Someday they would talk about the tragedy, perhaps, but not now, not yet.

Phoebe had not been living for long in Mount Street, and the fact that the place was almost as new to her as it was to him made it easier for him to move in and not feel that his presence was too much of a burden on her.

Anyway, it was a big flat, too big certainly for one person. It had three bright and airy main rooms, or as bright and airy as the run-down condition of the Georgian house and the vagaries of the Irish climate would allow. She had used some of the money she had inherited from her grandfather to purchase a long lease.

But she had done so somewhat to her own surprise. Did it mean she was thinking of settling down? She hoped not. It would be all too easy to become a sad old spinster like the ones to be seen about the streets here of a morning, with their woolly hats and zippered black felt bootees, gripping their gamps and their shapeless handbags. She pitied them, but the thought that she might someday become one of them horrified her.

She was young still, or youngish at least, and while she had suffered more than her share of injuries and misfortunes, it seemed to her that she had achieved a newfound equilibrium, by what means she wasn't sure. She felt compassion for her grieving father, and mourned with him his lost wife, whom she too had loved, at some level. But in her deepest heart she was convinced, for no good reason, that a change was coming, that it would come soon, and that it would be for the better.

Evelyn, Quirke's late wife, having been a psychiatrist, would have assured her that what she was feeling was not a happy presentiment, but a subconscious determination to change things by herself, for herself. She would be right, the young woman supposed, although she was sceptical of such neat formulas. Yet she told herself, *I have seized my life*, though what the result of this bold seizure was likely to be she wasn't at all sure. She was content to wait for the great new coming day to dawn.

If it ever should. She had few illusions. Life always had some nasty little joke up its sleeve, itching to be played.

The maintenance of harmony between father and daughter was helped by the fact that Quirke spent very little of his time in the flat. For most of the week he only slept there. He would rise early, eat a quick breakfast and be gone, and on some nights she would be already asleep before he returned. He tried not to make a sound, but as often as not he managed to wake her, by his very stealthiness – over the years, Phoebe had developed a sharp ear for danger.

She wondered how he filled so many hours of the day abroad in the not very wide world of Dublin. He had his work, of course, in the pathology lab at the Hospital of the Holy Family. Probably he stayed on at his desk, chain-smoking and brooding on his loss, long after everyone else had gone home.

When they had first returned from Spain, she had urged him to take time off. In present circumstances, surely even a man as accustomed as he was to dealing with the dead would be justified in granting himself parole from the underworld, if only for a few weeks. But she knew her father. Something in him had always yearned towards the land of the dead.

Lately, he had joined the Stephen's Green Club. Dick FitzMaurice, a government minister, had put him up for membership. He dined there most evenings, alone, usually, though on occasion Dick stayed in town and joined him in the unexpected splendour of the members' dining room.

She knew he didn't pass his time in the pubs, since on most nights she was still up when he came home. They would sit together at the kitchen table for a while, drinking tea and talking about their day, or what they had read in the newspapers or heard on the wireless. However, on a few occasions she caught him creeping in after midnight, with the glazed and slightly desperate look that told her he had been drinking. Otherwise, he was sober, or as near to sober as could be expected of a man who in the past had been so frequently and so comprehensively drunk. Anyway, it was hard to tell with him, for he had the habitual drinker's knack of masking his condition behind a murmured word, a shrug, and a slow, lazy smile.

As it happened, his new-found temperance was as much a matter of surprise to him as it was to her.

He had thought, that ashen day when he flew back from Spain with Evelyn's coffin stowed below in the aeroplane's hold, that this time he would surely lose himself in drink, and lose himself for good. He would run to the bottle as to an indulgent mother's breast, and drink deep there, wallowing in his sorrows.

But he found that alcohol didn't deaden the pain of

bereavement, only dissipated it, in a curious way. After three or four glasses of whiskey he would sense a vague discomfort everywhere, on his skin and under his flesh, and deep within his poor, pummelled heart. He felt, ruefully, that at last he understood what the word meant that he had come across so often in Shakespeare: ague.

The thing about grief was that you could press upon it at its sharpest points and blunt them, only for the bluntness to spread throughout the system and make it ache like one vast bruise.

He walked and walked, striking off into areas of the city he had never been in before, the dingier the better. He derived little pleasure from these grim excursions. They were less like walks than forced marches. He was, as the saying is, driven. That was what he was: a driven man.

Yet he never let himself hurry. It was imperative to maintain a steady, even pace, putting one foot in front of the other in time with the tick-tocking of an inner metronome. This steady, slow, long-stepping stride, once he had settled into it, did have a calming effect, of a sort. It settled his mind, it blurred his thoughts, it kept the monsters of remembrance at bay, or almost.

He recalled the framed engraving that his predecessor in the pathology lab, Doctor Jeavons, old Billy Jeavons, had hung on the wall facing his desk. It showed an elderly but obviously still vigorous knight, in full armour, his visor lifted, astride a rope-veined, exaggeratedly muscular horse, with his sword at his side and his lance at his shoulder, indifferent to both a grotesque Death springing up beside him, hourglass in hand and mounted on a broken-down pony, and, bringing up the rear, the hideous figure of a cross-eyed Devil, snouted and horned and bearing a long-handled axe.

That was how Quirke would have to be now, the knight who has been in the wars and survived and who bestrides his horse and walks it calmly through a wintry world, with the sacked castle left far behind and grotesques crowding around him. But could he be that? Was he cut out to be a craggy hero in a helmet?

He wondered what had become of that print. Who had removed it, and why?

Sometimes he would stop in the street, late in the night, at closing time, outside a pub filled with roistering drinkers and beseeching barmen – 'Come on, lads, come on, have yiz no homes to go to!' – and would stand there for some minutes, listening to the half-drunk hubbub inside and breathing deep the sour reek of alcohol and sweat and cigarette smoke that washed out from the doorway and down from the shallow louvres open at the tops of the painted-over windows.

It wasn't the false, back-slapping, spittle-spraying bon-homie within that he hankered after. He was like a prospector panning for gold, searching for the never-to-be-found nugget the size of his fist that would release him for good from his labours and send him home a rich man. No, it was the smell of drink he was after, or not the smell of drink but the shining pure impossible amber drop that is its essence.

He was fortunate in the weather. The summer had been warm and exceptionally dry – for some weeks there was talk of water rationing – and September didn't seem to under-stand that it is supposed to be dull and foggy and redolent of sadness and smoke, not glorying in itself sunnily as if it were June in its full juvenescence.

This evening was particularly mellow, the air calm and the sun hazily ablaze in a low sky. He had walked up the canal from Mount Street bridge, and at Mespil Road had crossed over to the far side of the water and walked back down to Mount Street, where he had crossed again and retraced his steps.

Why was he so hesitant? What was holding him back? After all, it was only Strafford he was going to see.

He recalled the day, long ago, when he had gone up to Belfast to buy French letters. He was still a medical student at the time. The previous night he had met a woman at a party in a flat on Adelaide Road that she shared with two other nurses. The party was still in full swing when she took him into a darkened bedroom and they lay down together on a bed piled with coats and scarves and she kissed him and let him fondle her.

On Belfast's Glengall Street he had walked up and down in the rain for twenty minutes outside a chemist's shop, trying to work up the nerve to go in. At last, he forced himself to push open the door – the bell pinged so loudly he almost turned tail and fled. He made his purchase, and hurried off to the railway station with three packets of Durex hot in his hand and his face on fire.

After all that, of course, it turned out to have been a wasted journey. At the party the nurse had seemed willing enough, but it was a dangerous time of the month for her and she wouldn't go all the way without protection. When he arrived back from Belfast, he waylaid her in a corridor at the Hospital of the Holy Family – outside the natal ward, as it happened – and told her where he had been and what he had brought back with him.

Stella, was her name. Stella Partridge. Strange he should remember, after all these years. She was a Protestant, which was what had got his hopes up. But ah, how quickly those hopes collapsed when, in the hospital corridor smelling of ether and babies, she looked him up and down and shook her head and laughed and walked away, waggling her bottom derisively.

'I was drunk last night,' she called back over her shoulder, 'but today I'm sober.'

And now here he was, standing outside the front door of the house where St John Strafford had his digs, and he felt almost as reluctant as he had that day in the grey drizzle on Glengall Street.

4

It was all very awkward and difficult. For a start, Strafford had no idea what to offer Quirke to drink. After the tragic business in Spain, everyone had expected him to go on a self-destructive bender, one from which he would never straighten himself out. That he hadn't done so, and apparently wasn't going to, left people not so much relieved as nervous. They circled around him as if on tiptoe, fearing that a wrong word, or even a right one, would jolt him into recalling his awful predicament, and send him diving into the nearest pub.

For all the tragic weight of his presence, he had become somehow – *faded*, was the word Strafford thought of. Faded, yes. Reduced in substance. He seemed not entirely there, to others or to himself. He was preoccupied, absent-minded, always distracted. His manner was that of a man constantly patting his pockets in search of something he had lost, or misplaced, or only imagined had been there in the first place.

When Strafford went down and opened the door to him and led him up the stairs and into the bedsitting room, he stood and looked about him with a puzzled frown. It was as though he thought he should know the place yet didn't recognise it. This was how he looked on everything, now.

He's lost to the world, Strafford thought, or the world is lost to him, or both. Strafford had been listening to Mahler.

He might suggest tea? Tea was neutral, certainly. Tea was blameless. But that was the thing: offering tea to Quirke would seem as ridiculous as offering a glass of raspberry cordial to a vampire. Coffee, then? He had a percolator that he heated on a Primus stove in what Mr Claridge had coyly described as a galley kitchen, but which was only an alcove hidden behind a flimsy curtain hung on a brass rail. The coffee that the thing made always had a scorched taste, and left him with a swollen tongue and a parched throat. So, not coffee, then, either.

Quirke must have sensed his host's dilemma, since he solved it for him after a moment by saying he would take a glass of whiskey. Strafford had an immediate sense of dread. Was that the reason Quirke was here, to get drunk on ground not his own, or his daughter's?

Strafford himself rarely drank, but he did keep a bottle of Jameson on hand, in case of emergencies, and surely this was one of those.

He took down a couple of cheap, oversized tumblers from a shelf, gave them a wipe with a tea towel, and poured the whiskey. He saw the cold eye Quirke threw at the small measures he had doled out, and topped up one of the glasses with what even for Quirke would surely be a generous dose. Quirke took the drink without comment, and swallowed half of it in one go. He grimaced and shook his head like a horse, making his cheeks wobble.

They stood together in the middle of the room.

'I had a professor in the old days,' Quirke said, 'name of Shrewsbury, believe it or not. An Englishman, needless to say. He took a shine to me, God knows why. One morning after his lecture – on blood clotting, as I recall – he took me down to Kirwan's and ordered a couple of doubles. It wasn't noon yet. "I'm sorry, professor," I said, "but I don't like to drink in the morning." He goggled at me, from under his famously bushy eyebrows, and said, "For God's sake, man, what are you talking about? None of us *likes* it." And he knocked back the double and ordered another.' He paused, and smiled bleakly. 'Thus began a long and troubled love affair between me and the bottle.'

Strafford nodded. He could think of nothing to say.

Quirke walked to the window and stood looking across to the canal. The daylight was fading.

'I used to love this hour,' he said. 'Even the word sounded lovely: twilight. Now it gives me the shivers.'

Strafford thought he should try to get his visitor to eat something. He could make him a sandwich, say. Yes, but what would he put in it? Strafford's pantry was a spartan place. Maybe offer him a slice of that cake he had bought on a whim in the Kylemore bakery last week and which he could neither bring himself to unwrap nor throw away? But the idea of Quirke eating stale plum cake, even plum cake washed down with whiskey, was hard to sustain.

Despite the hollowing effect, Quirke, since Strafford had seen him last, in April, in Spain, seemed to have expanded. He hadn't grown fat, but larger, somehow. Yes, bereavement had enlarged him, enlarged him even as it hollowed him out. He was pumped full of grief and a kind of pent-up, seething rage against the world in general and his immediate surroundings in particular. His presence in it made the room seem small, small and confined.

It was as if a wounded animal had blundered into the

house, baffled and lost and in search of shelter, and perhaps of prey, too.

Strafford thought of the polar bear he had seen in the zoo in the Phoenix Park one day when he was a little boy. He had been taken to Dublin on the train – was it his birthday? – and the visit to the zoo was the main treat of the day.

He hadn't liked the place, hadn't liked it at all. It smelled to him of raw meat and dung, and the animals all seemed wretched and half demented. As he remembered it, he had looked down on the polar bear's enclosure from above – he and his parents must have been walking on a terrace higher up. There was a pool of foul-looking water, and below a high wall of rock a concrete pathway where the bear paced back and forth, its front paws pressed together and its flabby haunches swaying and shaking.

This poor beast must have gone entirely mad, after years of captivity. The fur at one side of its neck was rusty with old blood, where it had been chafing itself on something, a piece of sharp metal, or an edge of the rock face.

Strange, that the memory should have stayed with him so vividly and for so long – thirty-five years or more. That day, he had told his father that if he could he would open the cages and let all the animals escape and then blow the whole place up with a bomb. His father got angry and told him he was an ungrateful little brute, which made him cry.

Quirke just now had said something to him – had asked him a question, was it? – but he had been away in the past and had not been listening.

But why was Quirke here in the first place? He still hadn't said. It was worrying.

There was little love lost between these two. Strafford knew well that Quirke resented him for his Big House origins, while Quirke wondered if this languid fellow with his waistcoat and watch chain and drooping lock of hair could be the same person whom he had witnessed shooting an assassin to death on the floor of a restaurant in Spain not half a year ago, seemingly without turning a hair of that drooping lock.

If he had fired a few seconds sooner, Evelyn might still be alive. Strafford wasn't to blame, Quirke knew, but he blamed him anyway.

He turned from the window now and glanced about, vaguely frowning.

'The wife not here?' he asked.

'Visiting her mother,' Strafford said tonelessly.

Quirke lifted an eyebrow.

'You're a grass widower, then.'

'Yes. I'm living away from home, as you see.'

'Oh?'

'Temporarily.'

'Right, yes,' Quirke said, losing interest. He looked into his glass and swished the whiskey around in it. 'That young one that died,' he said, 'what was her name? The one Perry Otway found smothered in his lock-up.'

'Jacobs,' Strafford said. 'Rosa Jacobs.'

'That's it. Rosa Jacobs.'

Quirke was still peering absently into the whiskey glass.

Time passed.

Strafford put up a hand and brushed the strands of hair away from his forehead with a flick of four stiff fingers. He wished this large, afflicted and alarming man would go away and let him get back to *Der Rosenkavalier*, where matters of love and loss, however intricate and troubled, were so much simpler than in real life. Quirke lifted his head.

'I had a look at her,' he said.

'At Rosa Jacobs? You did a post-mortem?'

Quirke shrugged.

'Yes, I had a look. Straightforward. Cause of death was carbon monoxide poisoning, as you'd imagine.' He turned back to the window, still twirling the quarter-inch of whiskey in the Woolworths cut-glass tumbler. 'Nice view you have,' he said. 'The water, the trees. Very restful.'

'Straightforward, you say?' Strafford prompted.

Quirke nodded slowly. He had become distracted again. Perhaps, Strafford thought, perhaps grief was like the weather, always changeable, but always there.

'Yes,' Quirke said, 'carbon monoxide. Classic case, all the signs. The cherry-pink skin, the bright-red lips, the fingernails. The carbon binds to the haemoglobin, you see, that's what causes the pigmentation.'

'Otway mentioned it. The garage fellow. How pink she was.'

Quirke wasn't listening.

'The thing is—' he began, and stopped.

He moved closer to the window, looking down to where something in the road had caught his attention. Strafford had the urge to go and see for himself what it was the other man was seeing, but he held back.

Oh, Lord, would the fellow never leave?

The fact that in Spain that day Strafford had shot to death – had executed, one might say – the little runt who, a moment

50

previously, had fired at Quirke's wife and wounded her fatally had set up between him and the bereaved man, so it seemed to Strafford, an unwilled and unwelcome flesh-warm, awful intimacy. He wondered if Quirke felt it too. It was indecent, somehow, somehow shameful, and oddly discomfiting.

Quirke was humming to himself.

'Thing is, I don't think she took her own life,' he said. He was standing so close up to the window that his nose was almost touching the glass. 'There's a man beating a dog down there,' he said. 'I should go and have a word with him. No, wait, he's stopped.' He took a sip of whiskey, making a small sucking sound. 'The way dogs cringe, it would break your heart. People shouldn't keep pets. If that fellow's spirit wasn't broken, he'd have gone for that bastard's throat in a flash.'

Strafford shook his head as if to ward off a tiny but persistent flying creature. He had a sense of deep foreboding.

'You say you don't think it was suicide? You think she—?'

'I don't know,' Quirke said, as if irritated by the question, and he turned from the window with a suddenness that made Strafford start. 'There were marks around her mouth. You didn't notice?'

'I didn't see her. Inspector Hackett was the first on the scene. Perry Otway called Pearse Street and—'

'Well, there were,' Quirke said, 'there were marks. She had been gagged, I'd guess, or something had been stuffed in her mouth and then taken out later. There was some bruising, and some small contusions.'

'You're saying she didn't kill herself? You're saying she was murdered?'

*

Strafford so far had not touched his drink, but now he did. He disliked the taste of whiskey, and the bitter scald of it. How could people, Quirke, for instance, go on drinking glass after glass of it, hour after hour, until they were too drunk to drink any more, and collapsed in a stupor, and had to be carried home and put to bed? How their mouths must burn, how their innards must shrink. Awful stuff, yet it looked so seductive, with that shade of old gold, and the spiked lights flickering in the depths of the glass. He supposed there was a kind of romance to it, a kind of magic. And comfort, too, no doubt. The fellowship of the copper coil.

Quirke had come away from the window, and the two of them were sitting at the table now, on the uncomfortable mismatched straight-backed chairs that Mrs Claridge must have bought in a jumble sale.

'I believe she was related to the biscuit people,' Quirke said. Strafford frowned, not understanding. Quirke did his lopsided smile, that had no warmth in it, and wasn't really a smile. 'Jacob's Cream Crackers? Come on, don't say you've never eaten a Jacob's Cream Cracker. Or a Kimberley biscuit? A Coconut Cream? Surely Mummy would have set out a plate of assorted bickies when it was time for tiffin?'

There it was, the blood resentment, masquerading as humour. This was not the first time Quirke had picked at Strafford about his privileged background, which he supposed, or pretended to suppose, to have been stupendously grand. Strafford couldn't be bothered to set him straight. And anyway, his shabby-genteel upbringing probably had been replete with grace and favour in comparison to Quirke's early days. Quirke had been a foundling, and had spent the better part, or the worse, of his childhood in an orphanage.

'Marietta, that was my biscuit of choice,' Strafford said, with a bland smile. 'Rather dry, I'm afraid.'

Quirke's own non-smile had abruptly died. There was no telling when his teasing might turn into something more ugly, no telling how far he would go, though the set of his jaw and the glitter in his eye suggested it could be very far indeed. He was a doctor, a pathologist, he knew the body intimately, he would know where the flesh was most vulnerable, where the nerves were closest to the surface and therefore most sensitive.

Strafford studied him, the seamed forehead, that jutting jaw, the blunt, thick-veined hand encircling the whiskey glass. Violence had been done to him. He still had a trace of a limp after a beating he had got from a couple of toughs one dark night years before. It was a warning to him to give up meddling in the affairs of powerful people. Now, years later, he still carried something inside him from that night, a hard knot of anger and pain and blind resentment. And now there was his grief to draw the knot tighter still.

'Let me make sure I understand you,' Strafford said. 'You're certain she was murdered?'

Quirke shrugged, tilting his head to one side.

'I can't be certain,' he said, 'of course I can't. But I have a strong suspicion, more than a suspicion, that she didn't rig up that pipe herself and wedge it in the window of her car and turn on the engine.'

'Then what do you think did happen?'

'I think she was gagged, and an anaesthetic was poured on the gag to knock her out. Ether, maybe, chloroform, or one of the newer, stronger ones. Chloroform doesn't keep you

53

under for long, except in gangster films. Then, I assume she
was put into the car with the engine already going, the gag
was removed, the door was shut, and she was left to die. Even
if she came round, she would be too groggy and disorientated
to save herself. If the engine was going full blast and the seals
on the windows were tight, she could have been dead within
minutes.'

Strafford thought about this. He looked doubtful.

'It seems a very elaborate way to go about getting rid of
her,' he said. 'Why couldn't they have forged a suicide note
and pushed her off a cliff?'

'You tell me,' Quirke said. 'You're the detective.' Strafford
did not miss the scorn in the words. 'Anyway,' Quirke went
on, 'before you tackle the who, shouldn't you be trying to find
out the why?'

'Was she pregnant?'

'No.'

'Was she a virgin?'

'No.'

Strafford looked towards the window, gnawing at the flesh
at the side of his left thumb. Foreboding had given way to
something like fear. It was not fear for himself, or for anything
in particular. It was a general dread. The world had a way of
opening its hand and showing slyly the fatal ace of spades.

Quirke's look had turned sour, as if something with a vile
taste had welled up in his throat. His anger came in wafts,
Strafford noted. It rose suddenly and swept through him like a
wind in a cornfield, then subsided, but remained there, ready
to rage up again at the next provocation, imagined or otherwise. Grief, again, grief the ever-changing.

'So: she wasn't pregnant, and she wasn't a virgin.' His tone had switched to rasping sarcasm. 'That's all the possible motives exhausted, is it? Done in by a jealous boyfriend, or by the same or some other fellow because she got inconveniently knocked up.'

'Have another drink,' Strafford said.

Quirke set down the empty glass and propelled it across the table with the tip of an index finger.

'No thanks, I've had enough.'

He cast about the room again distractedly, then took out a packet of Senior Service, lit one, and expelled a cone of smoke at an angle upwards. Strafford didn't smoke, and so he had no ashtrays. He fetched a saucer from the kitchen alcove and put it on the table in front of Quirke, who looked at it and snickered.

'Tell me, Strafford, have you any vices at all?'

'I bite my nails, sometimes.'

Quirke lowered his head and looked at him in silence, the irises of his eyes seeming to contract. Strafford blenched. Oh, God, surely the man wasn't going to start a fight? Quirke's mere presence in a room had an incendiary effect. He was like phosphorus, that burns in air. But the moment passed, and Quirke leaned back, scowling.

'Did I ever tell you,' he said, 'about the first post-mortem I did? I was an intern, knew next to nothing, scared of my own shadow. There was a bastard of a consultant I was put to work under. Rossiter was his name. Paediatrician, well respected, people swore by him. I knew he was useless. One day I was with him on his rounds, in Temple Street. There was this child, this four-year-old boy, had a tumour on the brain. His skull was swollen to twice its size. No question but that he was going to die. Even the parents had given up. They stood side by side by the bed, not touching each other, not saying anything, just looking down at the child, unable to believe what was happening to them. The poor little brute was in agony. Rossiter told me to give him a shot. I did, and then, I don't know why, I sat down on the side of the bed and picked him up and held him in my arms. He weighed next to nothing. He clung on to me, grabbing the sleeve of my white coat. I thought of a baby monkey I had seen in some wildlife film, wrapped in its mother's arms and clutching on to her like that with one tiny claw. He was so hot, he was burning up. Then he died, just breathed out a long, shaky breath, and was gone.' He paused, gazing blank-eyed into the past. 'I think I will take that drink,' he said.

Strafford took up the empty tumbler and went again to the alcove behind the curtain and poured another measure of whiskey. He drew a glass of water from the tap for himself. When he came back to the table, Quirke was lighting a new cigarette from the butt of the old one.

'Then of course Rossiter was all bustle,' he said. '"There must be a PM," he says in that plummy accent he affected. "It must be done right away – right away!" I don't know what he was afraid of, but he had the jitters. God knows what he'd done to the poor little thing, or hadn't done. The parents were still just standing there, numb. I took the child down to the lab, laid him out, got the scalpel and made an incision round the skull, as I'd been taught to do.'

He paused, then went on.

'You start here,' he said, drawing a finger across his forehead just above the eyebrows, 'and you get your nails under the flap of skin and peel it back, all the way to the back of the skull. That's what I did. It was like pulling off a big, resistant plaster. Then I cut open the skull and the fluid gushed out. The child hadn't even begun to cool yet, there was steam coming off the brain. I scooped it out, the whole thing, a grey lump of dough, and there was the tumour sitting in the middle of it, the size of a golf ball. "Good man," Rossiter said, "good man," and he clapped me on the shoulder. I wanted to punch him in the face. I could tell he was relieved. I'm sure he'd been negligent in some way, and was afraid he might be found out. That's why he left the job to me, so it would be my name on the PM report. They were always doing that, the consultants, leaving the junior doctors in the shit.'

He stopped, and sat in silence, smoking.

'I'm sorry,' Strafford said.

Quirke gave him a look.

'For what?'

'I don't know.'

From the not quite extinguished cigarette end in the saucer, a narrow line of blue-grey smoke flowed straight up, swift and shivering. Quirke held the whiskey glass against the light from the window and squinted through it.

'What was your first death?' he asked.

'I shot an IRA man,' Strafford said. 'During the war. He had a tommy gun pointing at my midriff. It would have cut me in half, if I hadn't got him first.'

Unspoken words moved in the silence. *Why couldn't you have done the same with the bastard that shot my wife?*

'Do you dream about him, the IRA man?' Quirke asked.

'No. Do you? Dream about the child?'

'I remember him, that's all. Him, and Rossiter fussing, and the parents standing by the bed, looking helpless and – I don't know, embarrassed, almost, as if they felt they were imposing. All that, and the wisp of steam coming off the child's brain.'

Outside, below the window, someone gave a harsh, ululating shout, like a battle cry. It was unusual to hear a voice raised in public in this tranquil reach of the canal. The drunks rarely strayed above Baggot Street bridge, and anyway they didn't come out before closing time.

'This girl, this Rosa Jacobs,' Quirke said, and he ran a hand across his face, in front of his eyes. 'Will you talk to Hackett about her?'

'Yes. Yes, of course. I'll tell him what you've told me.'

'He won't thank you. He likes a quiet life, these days.'

Strafford lifted the glass and drank a mouthful of water. It tasted of iron, and some chemical. The city's water supply was getting worse all the time.

Quirke finished his drink and crushed his cigarette on the edge of the saucer. This one didn't go out fully either, and in its turn sent up a new thin spiral of smoke. He put a fist to the table and pushed himself to his feet. He seemed exhausted suddenly. Strafford handed him his overcoat and hat.

'Thanks,' he muttered. 'I'll see myself out.'

Passing by the gramophone, he paused a moment to look at it, gave a cold chuckle, and went on.

When he had gone, Strafford stood by the window, looking down. There was the sound of the front door shutting, and a moment later Quirke appeared below, a bulky, foreshortened figure. He crossed the road to the canal side, and there turned right towards Leeson Street. Strafford watched him go, the dark, behatted figure, walking in a sort of huddle, seeming to bear himself along, clasped in his own pained embrace.

5

Quirke was right, of course. Hackett was not at all happy to hear what Strafford had to tell him on the morning after Quirke's visit. Though he didn't admit it, the Chief Inspector was not entirely surprised. There had been something not right about the young woman's death, he had felt it, but hadn't followed up on the feeling. Trust Quirke to spot the awkward details and start asking questions.

Rosa Jacobs's father had come up from Cork on the first train that morning to identify his daughter and take her body back with him for burial in the Jewish cemetery down there.

He was a fleshy, moon-faced man with greyish jowls and heavy-lidded, soft brown eyes. He spoke quietly, so much so that at times he might not be speaking but sighing. He ran a successful drapery shop on Patrick Street in the centre of Cork city. Things had gone well for him in his life, but that had changed in recent times. His wife was in a nursing home, dying of cancer, and now he had lost his daughter. He gave off sorrow like a smell.

Chief Inspector Hackett hadn't known what to say to him, what to do with him or for him. He might have taken him to the pub, but he wasn't sure if Jews were permitted to take alcohol. Anyway, in the circumstances he could hardly have suggested a stroll across to Mooney's for a couple of pints of stout and a chat about Cork's performance in this year's All-Ireland football final.

'Have you other children?' he had asked.

They were in Hackett's office high up in the Garda station in Pearse Street. Alfred Jacobs turned on him his pained, humid gaze, and the policeman frowned and lowered his eyes and shuffled the papers on his desk.

'I'm sorry,' he mumbled, 'I only meant—'

He let his voice trail off.

'I have another daughter,' Jacobs said. 'She's older.'

'Does she live in Cork too?'

'No. She's in London. She will come home tomorrow, for the funeral.'

'That will be' – Hackett searched for a suitable word – 'that will be a comfort.'

At this, the grieving man had produced a brief, sad laugh, and said no more.

'How,' Hackett now demanded of Strafford, 'how in the name of the Lord God am I going to break this to him, on top of everything else?' They were in Hackett's stuffy top-floor office. The first gale of autumn was blowing outside; they could hear the chimney pots rocking in the wind. 'As if the unfortunate man hadn't enough on his plate. First he's told his daughter did away with herself, now he has to hear that it looks like she was murdered.'

Hackett had put on weight, and his hair was greying at the temples. His teeth had been giving him trouble for years, and at last he had decided to have them out, all of them, and be fitted with dentures. Something had gone wrong with the procedure, however, and he had been left with a crooked, sagging jaw. He had more than ever the aspect of a pale, flat-headed, sharp-eyed frog.

'Are you going to release the body to him?' Strafford asked.

'Tomorrow, I told him.' Hackett was rubbing his hands together vigorously, producing a rasping sound. It was a habit he had developed after the dental debacle and the nagging pain it had left him with. 'Now I suppose Quirke will tell me I can't let her go yet.'

'I don't see why. There's not much more it can tell us.'

Hackett scowled at that 'it'.

'The father was on about her car, too, wanting to know when he could have it. Kept on at it, as if it was the most important thing in the whole sad business.' He swivelled in his chair to look out at the storm-tossed day. 'God, that's a fierce wind.'

'I suppose he was trying to take his mind off things,' Strafford said.

Hackett turned back and stared at him.

'What?'

'Talking about the car, you know, rather than thinking about his daughter.'

'Oh. I see. I suppose that was it, right enough.' He paused, and ran a hand over his face from forehead to chin, squashing the rubbery features and letting them fall back into place. 'He thinks she was drugged, you say?'

'Quirke?'

'Yes, Quirke – who else, man!'

Strafford ran the tips of the fingers of his right hand along the edge of Hackett's desk. The old boy's sudden flashes of annoyance had become more frequent of late. For the most part, Strafford paid them no heed. The years he had been obliged to spend with his ageing father had taught him, not tolerance, perhaps, but patience, at least.

'She was drugged, yes, that's what he thinks, and then put into the car with the pipe fed in through the window and the engine running.'

'Jesus.'

Hackett's blue suit was as baggy as ever, and as shiny at the elbows and the knees, and especially so in the seat. This suit was a matter of ongoing speculation among his colleagues here at Pearse Street. Could it be the same one he had been wearing since time immemorial? Surely not, surely it would have been worn to shreds by now, yet no one could remember ever seeing him in a new one.

'How sure is he of all this?' he asked. 'I mean, could he be mistaken?'

'Quirke doesn't make that kind of mistake, as a rule,' Strafford said.

Hackett, sunk in gloom, nodded. He knew he shouldn't, yet he couldn't but wish that on this occasion Quirke had gone about his job with less than his accustomed thoroughness.

People were quietly done in more often than was generally realised. Aged spouses were pushed off ladders or down flights of stairs. Electric fires fell into baths and electrocuted a rich uncle or an inconvenient aunt. Newborn babies died mysteriously, suffocated in their cots. There were always suspicions but no one acted on them, and Hackett couldn't but think that in some cases it was for the best.

'What about the car?' Strafford asked. 'Anything there?'

'You mean a Lascar's thumbprint, or the butt of a Turkish cigarette?'

Strafford didn't smile.

'What about the hosepipe, and the rags packed around it?'

'The gentlemen of our forensics department inform me, in their wisdom, that, as their head man said, "we found fuck all". Hardly a surprise to you and me, eh, Detective Inspector?'

If Rosa Jacobs had been murdered, it was going to cause not only further heartache for her father – it would also put an extra burden of work on Hackett's already work-worn shoulders. He knew he shouldn't be thinking such a thought. But he wasn't far off from retirement. He could do with a few easy years before he got the gold watch and a handshake from the Commissioner.

'I put in a call to Trinity,' Strafford said. 'Spoke to the head of her department.'

'How did he take it?'

'I didn't tell him.'

Hackett stared.

'What *did* you tell him?'

'Just that we needed to speak to him about one of his colleagues.'

'Did you say which one?'

'Yes.'

Hackett nodded again.

'Right, you go and talk to him.'

Strafford stared.

'Me?'

'Yes, you. You're a Trinity man, aren't you? You'll know the ropes over there.'

And Hackett did his crooked, froggy grin, his false teeth glistening.

Strafford passed under the stone archway, went through the vaulted porch and walked across Front Square. The wind was still blowing hard, and dead leaves skittered over the cobbles, making a scraping sound. The leaves were fire-red, dark gold, umber. Strafford felt a twinge of bittersweet nostalgia for a time in his life he had not particularly enjoyed.

He had spent three terms here at Trinity College, studying law, but had lost heart and left to join the Garda force. Now, nearly a quarter of a century later, he still found it surprising that he had opted to become a policeman. It had never been his ambition as a young man. He had just drifted into it, as he drifted into so many things, marriage included. He was like the autumn leaves, subject to whatever breeze might chance to blow.

Anyway, what else would he have done? He wasn't cut out to be a lawyer, obviously. He might have settled for being a gentleman farmer, if his father hadn't sold off the land piecemeal over the years. By now, all that remained were the few acres occupied by the house and gardens. What his father had spent the money on was a mystery. Not women, surely. Perhaps he was a secret gambler.

Professor Armitage was waiting on the steps of the History building. He was tall and thin, with a narrow face and oiled black hair brushed straight back from his forehead, which gave him a look of vague but permanent surprise. His eyes were set too close together, his mouth was too thin and wide. Also, he sported an unfortunate moustache, small and bristly. He wore a three-piece tweed suit and a dark blue tie with white stripes. He offered a hand as if he would rather not. The hand was limp and cool and dry.

He was English, and spoke in a refined drawl.

'What did you say your name was? Stafford, is it?'

'Strafford. With an "r".'

'Ah. Knew a Strafford when I was in the forces. Have you relatives on the mainland?'

Strafford suppressed a smile. In the Republic of Ireland, only an Englishman would refer to England as the mainland.

'Not that I know of. I believe the first of our lot came over with the Anglo-Normans.'

'Indeed?' The man examined him with a speculative eye. 'You won't mind my saying, but you're not what I would have expected an Irish detective to be.'

'I'm often told that,' Strafford replied mildly.

He mounted the three steps to Armitage's level. He didn't care to be looked down on, and certainly not by this man.

They entered the building and climbed a flight of bare wooden stairs that turned halfway up and gave onto a carpeted landing. There was a strong smell of boiled cabbage.

'Through here,' Armitage said, and led the way into a communal dining room. 'I could offer you lunch, though I don't recommend it. Anyway, it's a bit early. Glass of sherry, perhaps?'

He led the way to a corner table beside a tall window that looked out onto a mass of trees, the turning leaves of which filled the panes with a gilded radiance. It was not yet noon but already a number of the other tables were occupied, and there was a buzz of talk interspersed with the clatter of cutlery and the clinking of glasses. Trinity used to be known to keep quite a good table. However, the reek of cabbage reinforced Armitage's words of caution. Times had changed, obviously.

'You wanted to speak to me about Miss Jacobs,' Armitage said, fingering his bow tie. 'Don't tell me she's got herself into trouble again.'

'Again?'

'Oh, she's something of a tearaway, you know. Organises protests, gets up petitions, that kind of thing. We indulge her, here in the department, though perhaps we shouldn't. She's rather brilliant, in her bolshie way.'

'What does she do?'

'She's my assistant, you could say – one of my assistants – while she's completing her doctorate.'

'A doctorate on what, may I ask?'

Armitage smiled with one eyebrow arched.

'The Jewish diaspora in Ireland, would you believe. A rather limited topic, as I tell her, but she's making the best of it. I have high hopes for her. It's not easy for a woman to get ahead in academe, and especially a woman of her – well, of her background.'

'You mean because she's a Jew?'

Armitage's reply was another lifted eyebrow and a small, pursed smile.

Their sherry was brought, in tulip-shaped glasses. It was dark brown, and of an oleaginous consistency. Strafford lifted the glass and sniffed the wine, but didn't taste it. He supposed it must be good, though it smelled to him like molasses.

'I have bad news,' he said, putting down the glass and rotating it slowly on its base.

'Oh?'

Armitage's look had turned wary. Those close-set eyes and the twitchy little moustache put Strafford in mind of some cartoon creature, though he couldn't think which one. It added to the man's general air of shiftiness.

He brought out a metal cigarette case, flipped it open and offered it across the table.

'No, thanks,' Strafford said.

'You don't mind if I—?'

'Please, go ahead.'

The professor selected a cigarette, tapped one end of it and then the other smartly on the lid of the case, and lit it with a slim gold lighter. Through a billow of smoke he watched Strafford narrowly. It came to Strafford that Rosa Jacobs might have been more to the professor than an academic assistant.

'I have to tell you, professor, that Miss Jacobs is – well, that she's dead.'

Armitage blinked and inclined his head to one side, as if he thought he must not have heard correctly.

'Dead? But she was – I saw her—'

'She was found last evening in a car, her own car, in a lock-up garage in Herbert Lane, off Upper Mount Street. She had been dead for some time, I mean for some hours. She died from carbon monoxide poisoning.'

Armitage was shaking his head.

'No no,' he said, 'no, I don't understand. Are you saying—? What are you saying?'

'It seemed that she committed suicide.' He touched the sherry glass again. 'I'm sorry.'

Armitage sat very still for some moments, the cigarette smoking in his fingers. Suddenly then he snatched up the glass of sherry and drained it in one draught. Strafford watched him. Ratty! That was it – Ratty, in *The Wind in the Willows*. Strafford had been given an illustrated edition of it one Christmas when he was a little boy. It had been his favourite book for years and years. He wondered what had become of it, that copy. Maybe it was still on the shelf in his old room, at home.

Home. The word fell with a soundless thud.

The professor crushed the butt of his cigarette into an ashtray and pressed his hands flat against his cheeks so that his mouth opened. For a second, he looked like the figure on the bridge in *The Scream*.

'Christ,' he said, in a low, hard voice, 'how I loathe this godforsaken country.'

'Oh?'

'Well, don't you?'

'Not really. I am Irish, you know. I was born in Ireland. How long have you been here?'

'A couple of bloody centuries, it feels like,' Armitage muttered savagely. He took up his empty glass and looked around for the waiter. 'I need another drink.'

'Here, have mine,' Strafford said, pushing the glass across the table to him. 'Alcohol in the middle of the day doesn't agree with me.' *None of us likes it!* A voice said in his head.

Armitage took up the glass and drank off half its contents and set it down again on the table. It did not occur to him to say thanks.

'Have you a family?' Strafford asked.

'What?'

'Are you married?'

Armitage gave a snort.

'Am I married? I'll say I am. No children, though, thank God. Or not yet, at any rate. I sometimes think I detect a gleam in Mrs Armitage's eye.' He glared unseeing across the room. 'It can't be true,' he said, quietly but with an almost savage force. 'Rosa wouldn't take her own life.' His previously plummy accent had slipped a few notches, Strafford noted. It was less Oxford and Tom Quad now than the purlieus of Manchester or Birmingham.

'Why do you stay here,' Strafford asked, 'if you hate it so much?'

'I'd be gone in the morning if I could. Mrs A. likes it here, or professes to, for reasons that remain unknown to Mr A.' He took another sip of sherry, and grimaced. 'Filthy stuff, sherry, don't know why I drink it.' He blinked. 'What was I saying?'

'You were saying you'd leave Ireland in the morning.'

'Yes, yes.' He glanced about the room with a hunted look. 'I went for a job at Peterhouse,' he said, 'as good as had it, and then – poof! That was in 'forty-five. I was just out of the army. Signals Corps. I'd picked up a couple of languages, French, German. Did a doctorate, Metternich and the Congress of Vienna. I was a bright fellow, how could they refuse me? Well, they could. Not Eton and Oxford, you see, but grammar school and a red-brick college up north.' He assumed his former accent, but in mockery now. *'Not our sort of chap at all, don't you agree, Fotheringay-Williams?'* He set his elbows on the table and hunched his shoulders and sighed. 'What about you?'

'What about me?'

'How did you end up in Paddy's pretend police force?'

Strafford smiled.

'Well, as I say, I am a Paddy, for a start.'

'Well, let me say, you don't sound like a Paddy. Oh, wait – you're one of the beleaguered five per cent, I suppose.'

'If you mean am I a Protestant, then yes.'

'I thought your crowd had given up after 'twenty-two and left them to it. What did old Yeats write? *Weasels fighting in a hole.*'

'Many of us thought we should go. Maybe it was lack of will that kept the Straffords here.'

'They burned down enough of your big houses.'

'Yes. All the same, some of us wanted to do our bit, after all the years of doing nothing much.'

'Very noble, I'm sure,' Armitage said with a crooked sort of leer. He put up a hand and caught the attention of a passing waiter. 'Bring me a Bushmills, will you?'

'Certainly, sir,' the waiter said, with the faintest hint of disapproval – gentlemen usually didn't switch from sherry to whiskey in the middle of the day. He was a stooped old body with a bald, pitted skull and lines etched deep at either side of his weary mouth. He turned to Strafford.

'For you, sir?'

'Nothing, thank you,' Strafford said.

He remembered the waiter from his student days. He seemed hardly to have aged at all. What was his name? Something odd. Giddings, was it? No: Gatling, like the gun. Strange, he thought, how details, of so little consequence, snag in the memory.

'Tell me,' he said to Armitage, 'you and Miss Jacobs, were you close?'

Armitage made a rueful face.

72

'It depends what you mean by "close". She's – she was, a grand girl. Tough as old boots, mind you, despite the pretty face and the shy and retiring manner.'

He leaned back on the chair and flexed his shoulders, as if they ached. His mouth was small and naturally pursed. Ratty's mouth, to the life.

'She was in thick with a family of Krauts.'

Strafford raised his eyebrows.

'Germans?'

'Yes. You wouldn't expect it, would you, her being a Jewess.'

'What sort of Germans? Here at the college?'

'No, no. Big place in Wicklow, horses, house parties, weekend hunts. I don't know how she managed to fit into that sort of world. The old boy, Herr What's-it, runs a factory somewhere in the Fatherland, churning out widgets.'

'His name?'

'I can't remember, for the moment. Horst Wessel, something like that.'

The bald waiter came with the glass of whiskey.

'Will you be paying, sir, or will you sign a chit?'

Armitage signed a chit. He laughed.

'Makes you think you're getting it for free,' he said to Strafford, and winked.

The old man shuffled away, folding the slip of paper into his waistcoat pocket.

Armitage sipped his whiskey. His wetted lips had a purplish shine.

'Surely not,' Strafford said.

'Surely not what?'

'Horst Wessel. That's the title of that song the Nazis used to sing.'

Armitage shrugged.

'Must be something else, then.' He put a hand to his forehead, striving to remember. 'Kessler,' he said after a moment, lowering the hand. 'Wolfgang Kessler. They call him Wolf, with a soft "w" as in English. He's a count, I believe, or used to be. Graf von Kessler. For some reason he dropped the title, and the "von". There's a son, too, Franz, though they call him Frank.' He gave a bitter laugh. 'He's the one Rosa was "close to", if she was close to anyone.'

'They were going out together?'

'If you want to put it that way.' He puffed up his cheeks and blew out a breath. 'She always had this little secret smile when she mentioned him. A liberated girl, our Rosa.'

He clicked open the cigarette case again and brought out his gold lighter. He blew smoke at the ceiling. He was pretending to be bored, but the pretence was obvious. Behind it lay the bitterness and jealousy of a spurned lover.

'The Kessler place,' Strafford said, 'where is it?

'Up in the mountains, just this side of – what's it called – Roundwood. Near the reservoir. Big old house on lots of grassland. I forget the name. Makes you wonder who really won the war.' He took an angry drag at his cigarette. 'Ask in the village, someone will tell you, though you'll probably need an interpreter. Don't give them my regards.'

'In the village?'

'Them, too. But I meant the Kesslers.'

'So you know them?'

'I know *of* them. I met the son, Frank. He was with Rosa. A smooth character. One of the "good" Germans – quote unquote.'

Strafford pushed himself to his feet, and took up his coat from where he had draped it on the back of his chair. His hat had a dent in the crown. He reshaped the grey felt with the side of his hand.

'I'm sorry,' he said. 'About Rosa.'

'Yes,' Armitage responded, making his shiny damp lips into a snarling shape, 'so am I.' He sounded less sad than angry. He sounded like a man who had been let down. 'Grand girl, as I say,' he said sourly.

Strafford tarried a moment, wondering how much to disclose.

'You should know,' he said slowly, 'that there's a possibility it wasn't suicide.'

Armitage stared at him, wrinkling his forehead.

'An accident?'

'No, not an accident.'

'You mean she was—? You mean someone did for her?'

'It seems likely.'

Armitage let himself fall back limply against the chair, his lower lip hanging slack.

'Who'd want to murder Rosa Jacobs?' he said, in a tone of shocked incredulity.

Who indeed.

As he walked back across the windy square, Strafford found himself juggling a number of questions, the main one of which was, why had Armitage made a point of mentioning the Kesslers in the first place?

75

6

Quirke used to like the smell of vanilla, or at least he used not to dislike it. It reminded him of the first time he had tasted ice cream. He must have been, what, eight, nine? He and a few other boys of his age in the orphanage were taken one Sunday afternoon up to Sligo to attend a hurling match. The outing was a hitherto unheard of treat. It was never repeated, so there must have been some special reason for it.

Brother Barry was in charge of them. He was young and not as brutal as the others, or not yet, at any rate. He stopped at a sweet shop in the town and bought ice cream cones for all of them, himself included. Quirke had heard of ice cream, of course, but he had never had it before that day. He was delighted by the chilly, luxurious texture and the creamy taste. He ate his too quickly, gulping it down, and a searing pain started up at a spot behind his forehead, just above the bridge of his nose.

The pain frightened him, and he turned pale and started to cry. The others laughed at him and called him a softie. It was a day never to be forgotten, because of the ice cream, and the pain in his forehead, and the mocking laughter, but also because Brother Barry, though he said nothing, had put a hand on his shoulder and given it a squeeze while the others were jeering at him.

Now he was assailed every day by the smell of the stuff, at

morning before he went out and well into the evening after his return, and he had come to detest it. Rich and cloying, it rose in great warm wafts from the pastry shop on the ground floor below Phoebe's flat. It prevailed against the clouds of cigarette smoke that Quirke surrounded himself with, and even against the evil-smelling little black cigars that he took to smoking instead of cigarettes, and against which Phoebe had raised so strong an objection that he had to give them up and go back on the fags.

Phoebe told him he was being ridiculous, about the vanilla smell. She said she had got used to it and didn't notice it any more, and he could do the same, if he would just stop going on about it, which only made it worse.

'You're obsessed,' she said, 'you smell it even when it's not there.'

She was right. Often he woke in the middle of the night and was convinced he could smell it, even though the pastry shop had been shut since six o'clock. And anyway, a smell so delicate would not have penetrated to the far back bedroom where he lay on his back with his eyes wide open and his fists clenched on his chest.

His nights were bad enough already, and some were worse than bad.

The flat consisted of the first and second floors of a house at the Holles Street Hospital end of a long, red-brick Georgian terrace. In fact, the bricks weren't red, but a warm deep brown, with splashes of yellow and grey, and chips of something black that gleamed like coal when it rained.

It was owned by an Englishman, who lived in exile, and in unspecified disgrace, in the South of France. There were five bedrooms, or six, if a box room behind the kitchen were to be included, but it was locked and the man at the shady property company that collected the rent had told her the key was lost and couldn't be found.

The Locked Room was the source of much speculation between father and daughter. Quirke said there was probably a mummified corpse in there, the remains of a previous owner who had got locked in by mistake and starved to death. Or maybe the Englishman had murdered his wife and shut her up in there before fleeing to Menton. Phoebe went along with the joke, as best she could. Privately she thought it odd, even a little shocking, that Quirke should think it funny to talk so skittishly about death, and corpses, when his own wife was hardly six months in her grave. There was often a savage edge to Quirke's sense of humour.

He had been living at the flat since they had returned in April from that fatal trip to Spain. It was intended that he would stay in Mount Street only for a couple of weeks, or a month at most, while he was getting over the initial shock of the appalling and violent death of his wife. Time had gone on, however, and somehow the question of his moving out had ceased to be a question.

The room he occupied overlooked an untended and overgrown garden that stretched all the way down to the backs of the houses on Verschoyle Place. He always had a fondness for the back view of things, houses especially. Drainpipes in particular fascinated him, in their crazed and comic ugliness. How was it that no one had ever thought to straighten them, or for that matter to sink them inside the walls when the houses were being built?

He lived out of a suitcase, the same one he had packed for Spain and which he kept now under his bed. It contained underwear and socks, half a dozen folded shirts, a linen jacket, a couple of old pairs of slacks that he didn't wear any more but didn't want to throw away, along with a few other odds and ends.

When he needed something from the mews house in the lane behind Northumberland Road, where he and Evelyn had lived for their brief time together, he would ask Phoebe to fetch it for him. He couldn't bring himself to go into the house, couldn't bear even to see it from outside.

It had belonged originally to Evelyn; she had lived there in the years before they were married. Every corner of it, he knew, would hold stark remembrances of her. Would he ever go back there to live? For now, at least, it was impossible.

It was ordinary things that pierced him most sorely. A tiny silver spoon Evelyn always carried with her, to what purpose he never knew. A cheap detective novel she had been reading in her last days, with a strand of green wool for a bookmark. A shopping list he had found in her purse:

Bread
Oranges
Bottle of ink
Notizpapier

She had underlined the last word, to indicate that it was German. But for whose benefit?

Perhaps, he thought, he should put his and Evelyn's things into storage and sell the place. It would never be quite lost to him. Something of him, something of him and of her, some pained remnant of what they had been together, would always be there, even if strangers were to move in and impress their own mark on it.

It was a small comfort to think of these things, but still, he couldn't step across that threshold. If he did, he might not be able to step back again. He recalled reading somewhere of someone coming upon a steel trap containing a fox's bloodied paw, which the fox must have gnawed through in order to free itself.

This evening he had intended to take his dinner at the Stephen's Green Club, but Phoebe had insisted that he stay in and eat with her.

'You're never here,' she said, 'I never see you.'

He gave in, trying to disguise his reluctance. Phoebe had many wonderful and endearing qualities, but she was no cook. Still, he was pleased that she wanted his company.

She left to him the task of setting out wine glasses and opening a bottle of Beaujolais, while she served up the meal. She had fried two lamb chops, and made a salad of lettuce and sliced tomatoes and chopped shallots.

The tomatoes were Dutch and had no flavour, and the chops were overcooked, and badly charred on one side.

Phoebe apologised, making a clown's face with lifted eyebrows and downturned mouth. Quirke said it didn't matter, that the food was fine, that everything was fine. And he meant it. Phoebe was good to him, and for him. He wished he could show how much he appreciated her care and protectiveness, but he had always been shy of her, and always would be. The thought of the years when he had kept up the charade of being her uncle stood ever between them, unmentioned, but as unavoidable as a tree trunk fallen across a path.

They ate in silence. A slanted ray of sunlight retreated in the window as the September dusk came on. Phoebe switched on a standing lamp by the fireplace. It shed a pallid glow on the faded carpet and the legs of the chairs. In the depths of each of their wine glasses an identical tiny red spark hung suspended, radiating spikes of light in all directions.

When they had finished eating, Quirke looked to the window, while he got out his cigarettes.

'Do you ever hear from David Sinclair?' he asked, trying to sound casual.

Phoebe kept her gaze fixed on her plate. David Sinclair had been Quirke's former assistant in the Pathology Department at the Holy Family hospital. He and Phoebe had gone out together for some months, until David decided to move to Israel and work there, as a surgeon in a hospital in one of the cities – Haifa, was it? She couldn't remember. There had been no question of her accompanying him, even if she had wanted to.

'No,' she said, without looking up. 'He wrote a couple of times. I didn't reply.'

'Why not?'

'There seemed no point. He was full of the idea of Israel, of its future, the challenges it faces, all that – the threats to its very existence. He sounded like a different person to the one I knew – the one I thought I knew.' Now she looked up. 'Why do you ask?'

Quirke paused before replying. He must go carefully. There were so many ways in which he could upset her, so many of her demons he could inadvertently summon from the past.

'Did you see the paper this morning?' he asked. 'The story about the girl, about the young woman, who died in Perry Otway's lock-up garage?'

'What happened to her? I didn't see the story.'

'She was in her car. Carbon monoxide poisoning.'

'Was it suicide?'

'That's how it looked.'

'The poor thing. Was that the same garage where you used to keep the Alvis?'

'Yes.'

'Oh.'

Quirke poured more wine for them both. The lamplight was growing stronger as the last of the day faded in the window and the dark of the approaching night asserted itself. All round there was a general sense of lapsing, of everything silently settling, as of leaves falling asway through the dimmed air.

'I thought Sinclair might have known her, or her people,' Quirke said. 'She was from Cork, originally, like him.'

The tip of his cigarette flared briefly in the gloaming, then faded to grey again.

'I never heard him mention anyone from Cork,' Phoebe answered, and laughed. 'He didn't have many fond memories of the place.'

She sipped her wine. It was thin, and had a bitter edge. She knew nothing about wine. She should have left it to Quirke to choose it. He sometimes bought a bottle in Mitchell's on his way home in the evening. All the years of drinking spirits had not destroyed his palate entirely.

'Why did she do it, do you know?'

'Well, that's the point, you see,' Quirke said. 'I don't think she did do it. In fact, I'm sure she didn't.'

'Then—?'

'She had been gagged and knocked unconscious.'

'Knocked unconscious how? Was she hit?'

'No. She was drugged. Chloroform, or something like it.'

'So someone drugged her and put her in her own car and locked the car in the garage with the engine going?'

'Yes. To make it look like she had taken her own life.'

She gazed at him.

'Do you know who did it?'

'I have no idea. I don't know anything about her, except that she was from Cork, that she was Jewish, and that she was doing a doctorate on the Jews in Ireland.'

'So that's why you thought David might have known her.'

'It can't be a very big community, down there in Cork.'

'Maybe he did know her. There would have been no reason for him to mention her to me.'

'Of course not,' Quirke said quickly. 'Of course not.' He had caught the hard, sharp note that had come into her voice. Did she think he was hinting that the dead woman had been romantically involved with Sinclair, and he hadn't told her about it? 'No, it was just a thought,' he said. 'With the Cork connection, and – and so on.' She drank her wine, and said nothing. 'I'm sorry,' he said.

'What for?'

She gazed at him steadily, trying to keep the annoyance out of her voice. She would not be pitied. She hadn't thought of David Sinclair in a long time, and Quirke didn't need to apologise to her just for mentioning his name. She folded her napkin and put it aside.

'By the way,' she said, 'what was her name?'

'Jacobs,' Quirke said, and cleared his throat. 'Rosa Jacobs.'

Phoebe leaned back on her chair.

'Rosa Jacobs who was at Trinity?'

'Yes,' Quirke said. 'She was in the history department. Did you know her?'

Phoebe, frowning, looked first to the right and then to the left and then at him again.

'Yes,' she said. 'Yes, I knew her. Rosa Jacobs. My God.'

7

The plane had been circling above the airport for what had seemed to her a very long twenty minutes. The captain had come on to say he couldn't land because of poor visibility, and that there was a possibility the flight would be diverted to Shannon, or maybe Liverpool, but he hoped not. Since then, he had been silent. He had come through the cabin earlier, smiling and murmuring politenesses, grasping the tops of the seat backs alternately, which made it seem as though he were clambering effortlessly up an incline. In his braided cap and black uniform, he looked like a South American dictator – all he needed was a few rows of medals and a shiny holster on his hip.

Her seat was beside the window, and when she looked down she could see only a smooth grey expanse resembling a huge wad of soiled cotton wool. It wasn't cloud, it was fog. Cloud didn't look like that.

She leaned back and closed her eyes. She clasped her hands tightly together in her lap, and set her feet firmly side by side on the throbbing floor. She always kept her feet like that when she was in an aeroplane, grounding herself, otherwise she would become dizzy, and dizziness would lead to nausea. She had an incurable fear of flying. Even as a child she had no head for heights. That was what she really feared, being up here, so far above the ground, speeding along on empty air.

If planes were to fly at the level of the treetops, she probably wouldn't be half so nervous.

She opened her eyes and put her forehead against the curved glass and looked down again at the fog. She knew she shouldn't, but it was somehow irresistible, that frightening bland impenetrable greyness stretching away to the horizon. She supposed there must be other planes in the – what did they call it? – in the holding pattern, all circling, following each other, round and round. It would take only one tiny miscalculation and – smash! She shut her eyes again.

Adrian would laugh at her, and call her a silly goose, in that arch, languid English way he had of showing her how superior he was. The fact that he would be right, that her fear was silly – she wasn't afraid in motor cars, which everyone said were far more dangerous than aeroplanes – would only make his mockery all the more infuriating.

In general, she wasn't the nervous type. The things she was afraid of were few. This, this being in the sky, was her chief, unignorable terror. She knew it was irrational, everyone told her it was, but so what? That it was irrational didn't make the panic fright abate. That was what she couldn't make Adrian understand. As he often told her, he was a firm believer in the power of reason to resolve life's challenges. Yes, well.

He had insisted on giving her a lift to the airport, although she would rather have taken the bus from the terminal on the Cromwell Road. She preferred to be alone with her dread.

She shut her eyes more tightly still. She wouldn't think of Adrian now. She would have more than enough to deal with today, and in the coming days. How was she to face her father, what would she find to say to him?

She put up a hand and caught the attention of one of the two air hostesses on the flight, a brittle blonde with scarlet lipstick and a long, straight back. She asked for a brandy, and the man beside her in the aisle seat, fat, bald and wearing a shiny mohair suit, glanced at her with seeming disapproval. It was still only mid-morning.

The hostess didn't smile, and pointed to the illuminated seat-belt sign and said that the bar was closed. She was wearing too much make-up, and specks of face powder clung to the tips of the tiny, colourless hairs on her upper lip.

Now the address system crackled, making her jump. The co-pilot, or the first officer, or whatever he was called, came on and said they would be landing in ten minutes. There was a general murmur of relief.

She looked out of the window again. The fog seemed to her just as dense as it was before. Had the captain decided to take the risk and go ahead and land anyway? She unclasped her sweating hands and clenched them into fists, pressing her nails into the palms. The sound of the thrumming propellors altered.

If the thing were to crash, her father would have lost two daughters in the same week.

But they didn't crash. The plane dipped its nose and dived into the fog bank, and for some minutes seemed to hang suspended in an eerie, faintly glowing void. Then suddenly the ground became visible, with buildings, and runways, and traffic crawling along a road far over on the right. In the greyish light everything had a soiled look, as if submerged in dishwater.

Where was the sea? The fog must have been below them already when they crossed the coast. She relaxed her hands.

Her fear began to abate. Landings she didn't mind, indeed she welcomed them, even though she supposed this was when the risk of disaster was greatest. Her mind, her rational mind, as if released from a steel trap, flexed itself, reasserting its authority. Adrian would be impressed. And would make a point of telling her so.

At once, of course, she began to think again about her sister.

In the baggage hall, while she was waiting for her suitcase to be delivered, the fat man in the shiny suit came and stood beside her. Suddenly he spoke.

'I could have done with a brandy myself, up there in that ruddy pea-souper,' he said ruefully, in a broad Yorkshire accent.

So the glance he had given her had not been one of disapproval, but of fellow feeling. She felt guilty for having made the wrong assumption about him.

She walked through the arrivals hall carrying her bag, and stopped at the bureau de change to trade twenty pounds sterling for Irish money. The look of the notes, at once known and unfamiliar, caused her a pang of something, homesickness, she supposed, even though she was home, in theory anyway. She wasn't sure if Ireland was her native place any more. But if not here, where could she claim to belong?

The green airport bus was waiting at the stop. She climbed aboard. The man with the Yorkshire accent smiled and took her bag from her and stowed it on the overhead rack. She was afraid he would sit in the seat beside her, but instead he sat across the aisle, at the window seat. Another relief. She was in no mood for small talk.

Outside, the sunlight was striking through the fog and giving to the air a peculiar, sallow radiance.

When the bus was full, it set off. Maybe it will break down, she thought, and the moment when she would have to face her father would be put off for another little while.

She felt only sorrow for him, in his great sorrow. Still, she had no idea of what she could find to say to him. They had not spoken since the previous Christmas. She had phoned him on Christmas Eve and before they had exchanged a dozen sentences, they had stumbled into a squabble.

The cause of the argument, as always, was Rosa.

Recently, her sister had got into serious trouble at Trinity College for distributing pamphlets demanding that the state set up abortion clinics throughout the country. Abortion, in Ireland! The campaign was typical of Rosa, rash, hopeless and slightly dotty as it was. Admirable too, all the same. Rosa had her principles, and no one could persuade her she was wrong. About anything.

Not long ago, she had been agitating for the introduction of contraception, defiantly ignoring the fact that there was not the faintest hope of such a thing coming about, as she well knew.

Her sister.

She looked out at the spectral landscape gliding past, and was suddenly made breathless by a surge of grief.

What had happened, what terrible calamity had led her sister to take her own life? She had always been highly strung, and could behave almost insanely on occasion. But to destroy herself, at the age of – what was it, twenty-seven? – that made no sense.

She would not say it to her father, she would not say it to anyone, but she would have thought Rosa's lofty estimation of herself and her place and value in the world would never have allowed her even to contemplate something so drastic and final as suicide.

Had she made a mistake and got pregnant, maybe by one of her fellow agitators? It wouldn't be the first time a young man had joined a radical crusade in the expectation of some unencumbered sex.

In Ireland, pregnancy was still the worst misfortune that could befall an unmarried female. It didn't matter that Rosa was a Jew. To have a child outside wedlock was a disgrace that no campaign, no weeks of pamphleteering, no marching in protest and shouting slogans in the street could deflect or meliorate.

The bus had reached the outskirts of the city. She watched the drab streets passing by, as she had watched the fog under the aeroplane, and her spirit quailed. This was the country she had fled ten years previously, the country to which she returned only with the greatest reluctance and with feelings of the deepest despondency.

She had made her life in London. That was where she lived now. If she had a home, that was where it was. And yet.

Home. Again, that plangent word. To be a woman, Irish and a Jew was not easy in London, but in Cork it had been nigh on impossible. The sense of alienation had intensified with each day that passed with nothing changing. Rosa had stayed, to fight, as she so often declared, for liberty and the rights of women, for the freedom for her and others like her to lead the fullest life possible. And now she had killed herself. What torments had driven her to it, what unbearable pressures had worn her down, until there was only one possible escape route left to her?

Oh, Papli, she thought, what shall I say to you, who have lost your daughter, and soon will lose your wife? What shall I *say*?

It was yet another guilty relief to discover, when she arrived at Buswells Hotel, that there were people with her father. She would not have to face him alone quite yet. He was in the dining room, sitting at a table by a window that looked out on Kildare Street and the gates of Government Buildings. When she saw him there in the misty light with his shoulders slumped and his hands resting slackly before him on the table, the word that came unbidden to her mind was *sodden*: he was sodden with grief.

There was a touch of the feminine to his thickset, soft-looking body. Oddly, this was something she had always cherished in him. It provoked in her feelings of tenderness and what she thought must be love. She and her mother had never been close. Papli was mother and father to her, always had been, from earliest days. And then she had gone off to London and abandoned him.

Strange to think this was the trip she had expected to have to make when the time came and her terminally ill mother had died at last. Papli had not told his wife of Rosa's death. He was right. Why heap more misery on the barely living woman?

Opposite Papli at the table sat a man of about his own age, wearing a shabby blue suit under a gaberdine raincoat.

She knew at once, without having to be told, that he was a detective. She was a journalist. She had an eye for these things.

There was another man seated in an armchair in a corner of the room, wearing a bulky black overcoat. Who or what he might be she couldn't tell. She noticed his well-tailored suit, his expensive shoes. He had a large head and attractive if somewhat ravaged features. As she entered the room, with her suitcase in her hand, all three men turned their heads to look at her, and for a second she was paralysed by the thought of all the awfulness and misery that lay ahead of her in the coming days.

'Ah, here you are,' her father said, rising to his feet.

He came from behind the table and folded her in his arms. She caught his familiar smell, sweetish and slightly musty. At first, she stood stiffly – they didn't often embrace – but then she let go of her suitcase and clung to him. His breathing was shallow and rapid. In the course of her work she had dealt with many people in shock, and this, she knew, was how those in that state breathed, as if they had been running headlong and had stopped only for a moment before lumbering off again in desperate flight from themselves and their loss.

'Darling Papli,' she said. They were both weeping, a little, and smiling, too. 'I won't ask how you are.'

She glanced past him at the other men. They were watching her, out of expressionless eyes.

'Come,' her father said, taking her by the elbow and drawing her forward, 'I'll introduce you. This is Mr Hackett – Chief Inspector Hackett – and – and Doctor Quirke.'

Hackett rose awkwardly, nodding. His hat was on the

94

table. There was something wrong with his mouth, it sagged peculiarly at one side.

The one named Quirke had stood up from the chair but had not come forward. He too nodded, unsmiling.

'This is my daughter, Molly,' Jacobs said.

Hackett pulled out a chair for her and the three of them sat down at the table. Quirke made no move to join them. He had crossed to the window and was lighting a cigarette.

'How's Mam?' she asked her father quietly. He shrugged, turning up the palms of his hands. 'I'll go and visit her later,' she said.

'I haven't—' her father began, broke off, then shrugged again. 'I haven't told her, about Rosa.'

'Yes, you said, on the phone.'

'And I probably won't tell her.' He wasn't listening to her. He gestured vaguely. 'She's very bad, you know – sometimes when I visit her now, she doesn't know me.' He looked down at his hands. 'She'll wonder why you're here.'

'Maybe I should stay away, then.'

She had heard the eagerness in her voice, and blushed.

'Maybe so,' her father said gently. His glance kept flickering about the room, as if he were in search of some stable object on which to fix his agitated attention.

Quirke came to the table.

'Will I order something?' he said. 'Tea? Coffee?' He looked to Molly. 'Something stronger?'

'No, thank you,' Molly said, smiling. 'But coffee would be nice.'

He went on looking at her, and she turned her eyes away, feeling self-conscious suddenly. There was something about this large, looming man, a quality of stillness, that filled her with an odd disquiet, that was not unpleasant. She wondered again who he was, and why he was here.

He went away to order the coffee. Between the three people at the table, a silence fell. Chief Inspector Hackett coughed softly into a fist.

'A terrible business,' he said. 'Tragic.'

He had a strong midlands accent.

'What happened?' Molly asked, looking from the policeman to her father and back again.

'She was found in her car,' Hackett said, 'in a lock-up garage not far from here. A rubber hose was connected to the exhaust pipe, and the other end of it was fed in at the window on the driver's side and wedged with rags. The engine had stopped, it had run out of petrol, but your poor sister had died long before.'

Molly was frowning, and now she gave her head a small quick shake.

'Rosa did all that?' she said. 'Rigged up the pipe and put it in through the window and all the rest of it? Doesn't sound like her.'

Again, there was a silence. Quirke returned. He was lighting another cigarette.

'They're bringing the coffee,' he said. He turned to Hackett. 'I ordered tea as well.'

'Ah, good man, good man.'

Molly looked at them both. Her father had turned his eyes to the window again to look out at the misty street. The sun, higher now, was shining more intensely; soon the day would clear.

'Well?' she said. 'Tell me.'

'Tell you what, miss?' Hackett asked.

That blandly innocent look of his, she didn't believe it for a second.

'Why are you here, with my father? What's going on?'

Quirke and Hackett exchanged a glance, and Quirke went and stood at the window as before, this time with his back turned to the room. Her father stirred himself, and gave a fluttery sigh.

'The doctor' – he gestured towards the man at the window – 'he thinks it mightn't have been – he thinks your sister may not have—'

He stopped. He was gazing at his hands again, in perplexity, as if he didn't recognise them, as if he wasn't quite sure what they were. Molly turned in her chair to look at Quirke.

'You're a doctor?' she said.

'Yes,' he said hesitantly, giving her a sideways glance.

'You think she may not what?'

Her voice gone hard, her tone was peremptory. She might have been in her office, addressing a copy boy.

Quirke did not stir, and turned his face to the window again, as if he had not heard her. She saw the defensiveness in the set of his shoulders. What was happening? What had happened?

'It seems, miss,' Hackett said, 'that someone else might have been involved in your poor sister's death.'

She stared at him incredulously. For a moment, it seemed she might laugh.

'You mean, she didn't kill herself?'

Quirke left the window now and came across to the table,

cigarette smoke trailing in his wake. He stood a moment with lips pursed.

'There were indications,' he said, 'that she may have been drugged and put into the car—'

'*May* have been?' Molly Jacobs said. 'What do you mean? Was she, or wasn't she?'

Quirke tilted his head from side to side, his eyebrows lifted.

'It seems fairly certain to me,' he said evenly, 'that she was murdered.'

Molly shook her head again.

'"May not have." "Fairly certain." Could somebody please say something definite? This is my sister's death we're talking about.'

Her father lifted his hand from the table in a hushing gesture. She glared at him.

'Your sister was murdered, Miss Jacobs,' Quirke said. 'I'm sorry.'

At that, as if on cue, a young waitress entered, in black and white and wearing a little lace cap, bearing before her a silver tray with elaborate handles on which were set a coffee pot and cup, a teapot, tea things, cruets, and a plate of sandwiches cut into tiny triangles. She set the tray on the table and unloaded it. She smiled at Molly, and asked if there was anything else she could bring. No one replied, and she stepped back uncertainly, then quickly withdrew.

'Who did it?' Molly asked of Hackett. 'Do you know?'

Hackett looked embarrassed.

'No, miss,' he said, and for a moment he might have been a misbehaving schoolboy caught red-handed.

Molly turned to her father.

'Papli? You hear what they're saying?'

'I hear,' he said, not looking at her. 'They told me this already.'

She leaned back on her chair, her eyes wide and her mouth a little way open. Her look was one of indignation and amazement. It was as if she felt she had been brought here under false pretences. She *had* been brought here under false pretences. Her father lifted his hand again.

'Please, Molly, don't make a fuss.'

'A fuss? A *fuss*? Jesus Christ.'

'Molly,' her father said softly. 'Molly.'

All were silent.

The coffee pot and the tea things stood untouched on the table. They looked smaller than they were, somehow, and faintly silly, like toys brought in for children to play with.

At last, Hackett spoke.

'Have you heard lately from your sister?' he asked. 'I mean, did you keep in touch, the two of you?'

Molly made a brusque, dismissive gesture.

'I saw her at Christmas, when I was here. Since then, no, I haven't heard from her.'

Hackett considered this. He hadn't known that Jews celebrated Christmas. Maybe they had some feast of their own on the same day. The early Christians adopted a lot of the old Jewish stuff, took from the pagans, too. As a schoolboy he had been surprised, indeed shocked, to learn that on what is now Christmas Day the old Romans celebrated Mithra, their sun god. He drummed his fingers on the table, watching Molly as she tried to absorb what Quirke had just told her. He couldn't remember ever having met a Jew before, not to talk to, anyway.

Now here he was in the middle of a family of them, and a stricken family at that, with one of them murdered. He should have sent Strafford to deal with this. Strafford knew how to handle things that were out of the ordinary, being out of the ordinary himself.

'Would you know who her friends were?' Quirke asked of Molly. 'The people she knew, people she went around with?'

Molly glanced at him sharply and then away. He wasn't a policeman. Why was he asking her these questions? That was the detective's job, surely?

'I knew very little about her life,' she said, looking down now, with her chin lowered. 'We didn't' – she lifted her shoulders and let them drop again – 'we were never very close, she and I.'

Her father turned his head and let his large dark eyes rest on her for a moment. She shifted in her chair, turning away from his gaze. Abruptly, she stood up.

'I haven't checked into my room yet,' she said, and looked about her distractedly.

She reached for her suitcase, but Quirke got to it first.

'Let me,' he said.

She hesitated, then glanced at her father. For a second she was an uncertain daughter, asking a parent what to do next.

Quirke took up the bag and led the way to the door. Molly stood, biting her lip. Her father gave her a small nod, slowly letting fall his heavy eyelids and lifting them again.

At the reception desk Quirke waited patiently, standing behind her, holding her suitcase. From the way she stood, her back straight, putting up a hand to touch her hair, he knew she could feel his eyes on her.

She was tall, nearly as tall as he was, and her figure, narrow at the shoulders and heavy around the hips, carried echoes of her father's soft pliancy. He guessed she was in her middle thirties. Her face would be beautiful if it were less interesting. She turned at last from the desk, with the room key in her hand, seeming a little flustered and somewhat cross. She reached again for the suitcase, which he was holding by its handle. He took a step back.

'I'll carry it up,' he said.

They climbed the stairs in a tense silence.

Her room was on the first floor, at the end of a narrow, carpeted corridor. The air was stuffy, and there were the usual lurking hotel smells, the sources of which it was better not to speculate on.

She went ahead of him. She wore a long, oatmeal-coloured wool coat over what to his eye seemed an impressively expensive-looking two-piece suit of petrol-blue silk. She did not wear a hat, and carried in her left hand a pair of doeskin gloves that had not come cheap. Hackett had told him she was a journalist. She must be a successful one. Her hair was pinned up at the back in a heavy, heart-shaped loop.

As they approached the door to her room, one of the floor-boards sagged under the carpet when Quirke stepped on it. For the rest of his life he was to remember that moment, the small but curiously vertiginous sensation he had when his foot pressed down into the soggy hollow, and then the pleasant lightening when he lifted his heel and felt the board rise up again, as if there were a spring underneath it.

The room was small, with an oppressively low ceiling. A single, square window looked out on a yard with dustbins and a heating-oil tank.

'Will I put this on the bed?' Quirke asked.

The pigskin suitcase was old but good. The handle was worn smooth. She must travel a lot.

She dropped the gloves on to a small, rickety-looking table wedged into a corner at the head of the bed. She wore no wedding ring. Why had he looked? What business was it of his? In not very many years' time, he would be old enough to be her father. He had left the door open, to reassure her, but all the same she had gone to stand opposite him at the other side of the bed. He turned to leave, but she stopped him.

'That man,' she said, 'that detective – what's his name?'

'Hackett.'

'Is he – I mean, is he competent?'

'Yes, he is.'

'He doesn't look it.'

'I'm sorry,' he said.

Neither of them knew what he was apologising for.

She leaned forward and snapped open the clasps of the suitcase where it lay on the bed.

'It's all very confusing,' she said testily. 'I can't take it in.'

He brought out his cigarette case and looked at her enquiringly.

'Go ahead, smoke,' she said.

Her manner now was at once haughty and uncertain. He applied a flame to a cigarette. There was a heavy glass ashtray on the bed table, beside her gloves. He put a knee on the bed and leaned across and picked it up, straightened again.

'So you and your sister didn't get on?' he asked, and immediately wished he hadn't. 'You said, downstairs, that you – that you weren't close, you and she.'

She had been standing motionless, gazing down emptily at the open suitcase. There was something faintly suggestive in the way the squat thing lay there, the lid agape and lolling on its hinges, and her tightly packed things bulging upwards slightly, as if they were taking in a deep, much needed breath. He caught a glimpse of salmon-pink silk, and looked away. She had taken off her coat. The light from the window glittered all down one side of her tight silk skirt.

'You're a doctor, you say?'

'That's right.'

'A police doctor?'

'No.'

She frowned. Her upper lip was the shape of a Greek archer's bow.

'Then forgive my asking, but why are you here? Why are you with the policeman?'

He stood before her with one hand in a pocket of his jacket, holding the cigarette in the other.

'I'm a pathologist,' he said.

She waited.

'Yes?

'I give Inspector Hackett a hand, now and then,' he said. 'It's a kind of – kind of a private arrangement.' He tried a smile. 'We've known each other a long time.'

Suddenly, she laughed.

'You're Doctor Watson!' she said, and gave another, brittle

laugh. 'I must say I can't see that man down there as Sherlock Holmes.'

'He's sharper than he looks.'

'He'd want to be.'

She glanced again at the things in the suitcase.

'Did you do a post-mortem on my sister? Did you cut her up?'

'I did an examination, yes, but no, I didn't' – he had decided to lie – 'I didn't dissect her corpse. The cause of death was beyond doubt.'

'I see.' She paused, thinking. 'Could I have one of your cigarettes?'

'Of course, sorry, I thought you didn't—'

'I don't.'

She took the cigarette with an unsteady hand and fitted it inexpertly between her lips. He held out the flame of his lighter and she bent to it, touching the back of his hand lightly with the tip of a middle finger. All this had to be done by them leaning towards each other across the bed. She wore no lipstick. The smell of her perfume was thin and sharp and unignorable. He imagined it was expensive too, like her silk suit and the pigskin case and her smooth grey gloves. She turned to the window and stood there looking out, with the cigarette held aloft, her right elbow cupped in the palm of her left hand.

'My daughter knew your sister,' Quirke said to her back.

'Oh?' She didn't turn, didn't seem interested. 'You have a daughter?'

'Yes.'

'How did she know Rosa?'

Quirke had finished his cigarette. He stubbed it out and

leaned across the bed again and set the ashtray back on the little table.

'It was some years ago,' he said, straightening. He smoothed the buttoned-up front of his double-breasted suit. 'They were both part of a – a set, I suppose you'd call it. My daughter was going out with a friend of your sister's. David Sinclair – do you know him?'

She had turned from the window. She shook her head.

'He was my assistant in the Holy Family hospital,' Quirke said.' He made a wry face. 'Dublin is small, as you'll remember.'

'So he's a doctor too?'

'Yes. He left here, and moved to Israel.'

'Oh,' she said flatly. 'Israel.'

He was struck by the coolness of her tone. No Zionist she, it seemed.

'He got a job there,' Quirke said, 'in a hospital somewhere – not Tel Aviv, some other city. The country was something of a cause for him. I was surprised.'

'Why?'

'He didn't seem the type to commit himself, not to something as vague as a country.'

'They don't think of it as vague,' she said briskly, setting him straight. 'The Israelis.'

She too had finished her cigarette, and had stubbed it out in the ashtray. Now she seemed not to know what to do with her hands.

'I'm sure you're right,' he said, feeling wrong-footed. 'I don't know anything about it, except what I read in the papers.'

'Most of which is lies.'

He was silent, not knowing how to respond. Perhaps he had

been wrong, perhaps she was a bearer of the flame after all. Dangerous ground. He decided on a strategic retreat.

'I don't think Phoebe – that's my daughter – I don't think she knew your sister well. Phoebe is not' – he smiled – 'she's not very forthcoming on the subject, which makes me suspect there might have been some romantic rivalry there. David Sinclair was popular with the girls, so I'm told.'

'And Rosa was a man-eater.'

She said it so flatly that a second or two passed before Quirke registered it fully. He was startled. She was her sister, after all, her dead sister – her murdered sister. She smiled into his face, smoothing down the front of her jacket with both hands, as he had smoothed his. She had, he noticed, just the hint of a belly, pressing against the waistband of her skirt. Her hair was of a shade he had not encountered before, light brown mostly, with steely streaks that were silvery at the tips. Was it dyed? She had her father's eyes, large and darkly shining, with lids that drooped slightly at the outer corners.

He was taking another cigarette from his case.

'I've shocked you,' she said.

'No,' he said.

Another lie.

'Yes, I have. I can see it.'

'Well, a little, I admit. It's not what sisters usually say of each other.'

'Oh, is it not?

'Well,' he said, stumbling on the words, 'well, not in my experience, no. But then, I have no experience, in that area.'

'No sister?'

'No. No brothers, either.'

She folded her arms across her chest, as if she felt cold suddenly.

'I shouldn't have said it,' she said. 'She wasn't a man-eater. Only—'

She broke off, and turned to the window again. After a moment, he saw that her shoulders were shaking.

'I'm sorry,' he said again, extending a hand in a futile gesture, one she couldn't even see. 'I didn't mean to upset you.'

At that, she turned on him, angry suddenly, despite the tears.

'Upset me?' she cried. 'Who do you think you are? My sister is dead – *that* upsets me.'

He felt his forehead redden.

'Look,' he said, 'it's one o'clock. Let me take you and your father to lunch.' She opened her mouth and her eyes grew round with indignant disbelief. He didn't want her to shout at him again. He lifted both hands, showing her his palms. 'You've come a long way, both of you,' he said cajolingly. 'You have to eat. There's a nice place just down the street.'

She went on glaring at him for a moment, then let her shoulders go slack.

'All right,' she said, and gave a hiccupy sigh. 'All right.'

She came from behind the bed, with a slow and weary gait, weighed down, he could see, by the weight of all the morning's awfulness.

He took them to Jammet's on Nassau Street. It was busy, but not full. Molly seemed not to notice how grand it was, with its opulent decor and obviously moneyed customers. Her father, however, was plainly intimidated. They were being shown to their table when he balked, and stopped, and shook his head. Molly asked him what the matter was and he gave her a panicked look, and said he had changed his mind, that he felt unwell. He would go back to the hotel and lie down for a little while.

Quirke saw the flicker of annoyance passing over the woman's face. She made herself smile, however, and touched her father on the shoulder and said that it was all right, that yes, he should rest – they could have an early dinner together. He was about to go, but paused, and turned to Quirke.

'When will Rosa's car be returned to us?' he asked.

Quirke gave an apologetic shrug.

'I'm sorry, I – I have no control over that.'

Jacobs was not listening. He shook his head rapidly, as if he felt he had been misunderstood.

'But I must have it,' he said.

'Why do you want it, Papli?' Molly asked.

He turned on her a look of desolation, baffled and defence-less. Quirke thought of Goya's painting of the little dog in the corrida. He had seen it years before in the Prado and had never forgotten it.

'I don't know,' Alfred Jacobs said. 'I just want to have it. It was her last – her last place.'

He said no more then, but turned and went off quickly, making his way stumblingly between the tables, his shoulders sloped and his head bowed.

'I'm worried about him,' Molly said to Quirke as they were being shown to their table. 'His heart is not strong. He had a serious scare a couple of years ago. We thought we might lose him.'

The waiter, a no longer young Lothario with narrow Mediterranean features and oiled black hair, flourished the menu at Molly, but she waved it away.

'I'll have a plain omelette and a glass of Perrier,' she said.

'The usual for me, Anton,' Quirke said, trying not to smile at the waiter's indignantly pursed mouth and flared nostrils.

'And the claret, as usual, Doctor Quirke?'

'Yes, the claret.'

Anton nodded, gathered up the menus, flared that darkly aquiline nose again, and went off. Molly sniffed.

'You seem well known in these parts,' she said, somewhat sourly. 'Is this your regular watering hole?'

'I bring my daughter here sometimes, for a treat.'

'Oh, yes? What age is she?'

Quirke hesitated. In fact, he wasn't sure of Phoebe's age.

'Twenty-seven,' he said gruffly.

It sounded right. Anyway, Molly had lost interest in the topic.

A woman seated at a table at the far side of the room had been watching Quirke steadily, and now he caught her eye. He experienced a faint shock.

It was Isabel Galloway. She had been his lover, years ago.

Should he smile? Should he look away? He still felt guilty about Isabel. She didn't seem to have changed much since he had last seen her, at least so far as he could make out, at this distance.

The man she was with, a brawny fellow with rust-red hair, looked faintly familiar. Someone in the theatre, probably. Isabel was an actress.

Quirke couldn't make out her expression. Was she glowering, or just staring? She certainly wasn't smiling.

He had been heartless, at the end of the affair, had dropped her without a word of explanation or apology.

At last, she turned her eyes away and said something to the red-haired man, and they both laughed. The red-haired man turned in his chair and looked at Quirke with candid interest.

Haughty Anton brought their plates and glided them onto the tablecloth in front of them. Molly looked at Quirke's lamb chop and salad and asked if he was on a diet.

How strange life is, Quirke thought. Yesterday, this woman's sister was murdered in a laneway, and today here he was with her, lunching at the city's fanciest restaurant and making small talk, while across the room an old girlfriend sat and smirked at what was most likely her newest lover. Isabel had a reputation.

'Did your sister ever mention to you a family by the name of Kessler?' Quirke asked.

'Kessler?'

'Yes. Germans. Big house in Wicklow. The father breeds horses. Rosa and the son, Franz – Frank – were an item, it seems.'

Molly sliced off a narrow wedge of omelette.

'Rosie and I didn't talk about things like that,' she said. 'In fact, as I told you, we didn't talk much about anything. She was Papli's favourite, I was the black sheep.'

'Why do you call him Papli?'

'I don't know. It's what we've always called him.'

Quirke nodded. Papli. It suited him, somehow, the poor fellow, with his sloped back and his cow eyes.

'Seems odd sort of company for your sister,' he said. 'The Kesslers.'

She stopped chewing for a moment and looked at him.

'Why? Because they're Germans?'

'Well, yes.'

'Not all Germans were Nazis.'

'True.'

'Besides, she liked breaking taboos. She always went against the grain.' Tears welled up in her eyes again and sat trembling on the lower lids. 'Oh, for Christ's sake,' she muttered, and squeezed her eyes shut. Then she opened them again and glared at her plate, blinking rapidly. 'What am I doing, eating a fucking omelette and weeping in front of a stranger.' She threw Quirke a pleading look. 'Distract me, will you? It's embarrassing, crying in a restaurant. They'll all think you're dumping me.' He stopped himself from glancing in Isabel's direction. 'Tell me something,' Molly said. 'Ask me something. Anything.'

'You're a reporter, yes? What paper do you work for?'

'The *Express*. And I'm not a reporter, I'm a journalist.'

'What's the difference?'

'I write background stuff, news features, that kind of thing. Reporters are grubby little men in raincoats, who spend every free moment they have in the pub, and get sent out to interview murderers and harass brand-new widows.'

Quirke's appetite had deserted him. It was because of Isabel, he supposed. He pushed his plate aside and lit a cigarette.

'You like living in London?' he asked.

'I don't dislike it. Though it's not always easy. They laugh at an Irish accent.'

'You've lost yours.'

'Not to their ears, I haven't. Also, they're anti-kike.' Quirke choked on a mouthful of smoke and coughed until his eyes watered. Molly regarded him with a sardonic half smile. 'You're easily shocked, I see.'

He drank off the wine in his glass and signalled to Anton to come and refill it. Had he attempted to pour it himself, Anton would have been there at a run to snatch the bottle out of his hand.

'I'm sorry,' he said to Molly.

'You keep saying that.'

'I know.'

'I wish you'd stop. Everybody is sorry, today.'

They were awkward with each other suddenly. Some moments passed. Molly leaned her elbows on the table and looked about the room.

'Those people over there are talking about you,' she said.

Quirke didn't look where she was looking.

'How do you know?'

'I just do. They keep glancing over at you and saying things.'

'I used to know her – the woman. She's an actress.'

'Yes, I can see that.'

'How?'

'I don't know. She has an actressy look. Something in the eyes.'

'How can you see, at this distance?'

'I'm a journalist,' she said.

He didn't quite grasp the logic of this, but let it go.

Anton collected their plates. Would they care to see the dessert menu? Molly shook her head.

'I'll take a coffee,' Quirke said. 'And a brandy.'

He knew he shouldn't drink like this in the middle of the day – the bottle of claret was half empty. But the wine had begun to cloy, he needed something sharper. He took another cigarette from his case. Was his hand shaking? This was ridiculous. How Evelyn would laugh. And at that thought, something seemed to clutch his heart, and he thought again of the baby monkey and its mother.

'You think these Krauts killed her, then, killed our Rosa?' Molly asked, in a conversational tone.

'I have no idea who killed her,' Quirke said.

She had meant to shock. Now she looked aside.

'This is unreal,' she muttered. Then she fixed on Quirke again. 'You really think she was murdered?'

'Yes, I do,' he said. 'The evidence all points that way.'

She gave him a quizzical look.

'You sure you're not a detective?'

'I've been around detectives all my working life. I suppose it rubs off—'

He stopped, sensing a presence beside him. He looked up. Isabel, of course. He knew she wouldn't be able to forgo an opportunity of embarrassing him. She wore a black dress and a short midnight-blue cape. A little hat was perched on the side of her head, like a dainty little bird that had alighted there.

'Hello, Quirke,' she said, bright and brittle, pointedly ignoring Molly Jacobs. 'Haven't seen you about in a while.'

'Hello, Isabel,' Quirke replied, looking up at her with a weary smile. 'How are you?'

'Tickety-boo, as always.'

'I like your hat.'

'Why, thank you. I got it in that shop where Phoebe used to work.'

'The Maison des Chapeaux?'

'The very place.'

A silence fell.

Molly Jacobs was studying Isabel with a neutral eye. Quirke glanced across the room, to where the red-haired man was counting out banknotes as Anton stood by with a bored expression.

'I see you have a new beau.'

Molly laughed.

'Not a beau,' she said, 'no fear. That's Matt Mallon. He's trying to get me to be in something he's producing.'

'Ah.'

Molly stirred.

'I must go,' she said.

'Oh, don't let me drive you away,' Isabel drawled, still not looking at her.

Quirke stubbed out his cigarette and rose to his feet.

'Nice to see you, Isabel,' he said.

'Right,' Isabel said. 'Pip-pip, then.'

And she turned on her heel with a swish of her cape and stalked away, swaying her hips.

'I take it you and she didn't part amicably,' Molly said.

'How do you mean?'

'Come on, don't act the innocent.' Again she studied Quirke, her eyebrows lifted. 'I suspect you're something of a cad.'

Quirke laughed.

'I suspect you're right,' he said, and after a pause he heard himself adding, 'My wife died.'

'Oh,' Molly said flatly. 'I'm sorry.'

He nodded. There was something slightly odd about this woman, he had registered it from the start, and now he realised what it was. She had no handbag. He had never known a woman before now who didn't carry a handbag. All she had was a man's bulging, worn leather wallet held shut with a strap and a clasp.

He took a sip of coffee, then lifted the brandy, folding his hand around the fat little bulb of the glass.

'In fact,' he said, 'she was murdered.'

'Your wife?'

'Yes. By mistake.'

'By—?'

'In Spain. A man was hired, a professional, to go down there and get rid of someone. He got my wife instead.'

'Jesus. Really?'

'Then he was shot, and died. It was a shambles.'

Quirke drank off the brandy and set the glass down on the table and sat gazing at it. The seconds ticked past. He couldn't hear the sounds of the people around him. Then he stirred himself.

'I'll get the bill,' he said.

But just then Isabel Galloway came back, appearing at his side without a sound. She had always had that knack of seeming to materialise out of nowhere. Perhaps it was something actors learned to do.

'I forgot to say,' she said, 'how sorry I was to hear about your wife.'

She made no attempt to soften the brittleness of her voice. He had told her once she sounded like a fishwife. It was towards the end, during one of their increasingly frequent quarrels.

'Thank you,' Quirke said.

'It must have been terrible.'

'Yes, it was.'

Isabel wavered. It was suddenly plain that she was sorry she had crossed the room again, and wished to go but didn't quite know how to do it. Quirke felt no sympathy for her – indeed, he took a small sadistic pleasure in her dilemma. The red-haired man had finished paying, and was approaching between the tables. Isabel sensed him coming and, without turning, extended her left arm behind her and put up her hand in a traffic-halting gesture. The man stopped, smiling uncertainly.

'I'm sorry,' Isabel said to Quirke. 'Of course, you're right, your loss is none of my business.'

People at nearby tables had caught the tension in the atmosphere, and some of them had turned to look at Quirke and the mildly famous Isabel Galloway.

'I appreciate your sympathy,' Quirke said, looking down steadily at the table.

'Yes, well,' Isabel said, and, frowning, turned away with a flounce.

When she came level with the red-haired man, she didn't stop but went on, and soon was through the door and gone. The man gave Quirke a scornful glance and followed her.

'That was good,' Molly said. 'I enjoyed that.'

Quirke sat for some moments in silence, looking down at the table. Then he signalled to Anton for the bill. He paid, and rose, still not speaking, and Molly stood up too. Anton had brought their coats with the bill, and Molly put hers on and slipped her wallet into a side pocket.

'How was the omelette?' Quirke asked as they moved towards the door.

'Scrumptious.'

The last of the fog had cleared, and they walked along Nassau Street in tawny autumn sunshine. Quirke's heart was in riot. Bad enough to be condescended to by a spurned lover, now there was this handbagless woman to be dealt with. He had a feeling – more than a feeling, a conviction – that Molly Jacobs was set to play a part in his future. He thought of Evelyn, and saw her face for a second, so clearly and with such immediacy that his breath caught in his chest and he thought he might fall down.

8

Strafford rarely gave way to anger, and when he did, he made sure not to show it. This equanimity, if such it was, he knew to be due less to a tranquil spirit than to simple indifference. It was another of the things he had inherited. Like his father, the son declined to engage to any large degree with the majority of the people he encountered in the course of his life. The contrast between the two Straffords was that Strafford senior was almost passionate in his disdain, while his son was merely detached. Or so it seemed to him. He supposed that was why Marguerite had left him, that lack of affect.

Today, however, he was annoyed, extremely so, and was finding it hard to hide the fact. Chief Inspector Hackett had ordered him to go down and interview Wolfgang Kessler, at Kessler's house in Wicklow. Hackett should have gone himself, but claimed to have a problem with foreigners.

'I'm so busy trying to cope with their accents,' he had said, 'that I only hear the half of what they're saying.'

This was not the real reason, Strafford knew. Hackett had a keen sense of social status, and was afraid of being looked down on by the German grandee. Kessler was a count, no less, even if he had renounced the title – a fact he took care to make as widely known as possible.

None of this mattered to Strafford. He didn't at all mind going to Wicklow, and was curious to meet a German aristocrat, even one who liked to pretend he wasn't. The true source of his annoyance was that Hackett had insisted that he take Quirke along with him.

'But Quirke is not a policeman,' Strafford had objected.

'Yes, but that's the thing,' the Chief responded, screwing up one eye and doing his gleaming enamel grin. 'He's as sharp as a tack, though you wouldn't think it to look at him. He often sees things a professional might miss.'

Strafford felt a hotness behind his ears. *He's sending Quirke to keep an eye on me!* he thought. He was as close to being outraged as he ever got. He said no more, though, for fear of saying things he would afterwards regret.

Matters worsened as the day went on. The more he saw of Quirke, the less he cared for him. What was he but a boor in a Savile Row suit? Look at him now, sitting here silent in the back of the police car, with his fingers laced together in his lap and twiddling his thumbs as he watched out of a brooding eye the bleakly lovely moorland rolling past. Did he really find it nothing odd that he should be accompanying a detective on an official investigation?

The Chief had spoiled him over the years, letting him tag along to crime scenes, and indulging his opinions and supposed insights.

Strafford turned away and looked out of his own window. They had passed Djouce Woods and were crossing the high flat moors in thin autumn sunshine. The heather was still a rich deep shade of purple against the turf-brown bog.

The driver, whose name was Dolan, a Brylcreemed young Garda sergeant with a faintly insolent air, was driving too fast along the narrow winding road, and the tyres squealed on the numerous sharp bends. More than once Strafford had been thrown to the side, almost on top of Quirke, though Quirke seemed not to notice.

He resents me, as I resent him, Strafford thought. He feels I bungled it that day in Spain, firing too late at the little runt with the gun and letting him shoot Quirke's wife dead before dying himself. But Strafford had done his best. He wasn't accustomed to handling weapons. God knows how many more the killer would have shot if Strafford's bullet hadn't stopped him. Quirke himself might have been felled by the next fusillade. Did he ever think of that?

They rounded a bend and the reservoir came in sight.

Sergeant Dolan, it turned out, knew the whereabouts of the Kessler estate, though he hadn't bothered to say so until now. Presently, he slowed the car, and turned in at a pillared gateway. Two yew trees stood one on each side of the entrance, their polished dark green foliage aquiver. In the limpid mountain light, they struck a sombre note. Strafford wondered idly if there were any other species of tree the limbs of which point upwards.

He rarely thought about the man he had shot. What was his name? Terry something – Terry Tice, yes, that was it. Turned out he had been in the same orphanage in the west of Ireland where Quirke had spent his earliest years. It must be some place, Strafford reflected, to have produced men of the stamp of Quirke and Terry Tice.

The drive swept in a long curve between two sets of iron railings. Beyond the railings on the left, a wide swathe of grass was bordered by a stand of old timber, oak and beech, tall pines, holly. Half a dozen thoroughbreds were cropping the grass in the shade of the trees. They stopped grazing and lifted their long heads to watch the car as it went past.

A many-chimneyed roof appeared above the trees. There was a weathervane in the shape of a rearing Pegasus.

'What's it called, this place?' Quirke asked of the window.

'St Fiachra House,' Dolan said over his shoulder, and for some reason snickered. 'They changed it, it used to be something else. Brookwood, I think. Brook something, anyway.'

And there was the house itself.

It was a handsome stone mansion, with numerous tall windows and a broad front doorway within a frame of striated yellow marble. A set of shallow, moss-flecked steps led down fanwise to a gravelled semicircular turning space.

The door was open, and on the threshold a man stood framed against the darkness of the hallway behind him. He was a slight figure, slim, not tall, compactly made. He had a high forehead and a narrow skull, balding, steeply sloped, the skin polished like leather. He wore a green loden jacket, brown jodhpurs and high brown boots so narrow in the leg they might be puttees. Checked shirt, black velvet waistcoat, a scarlet cravat stuck with a pearl pin.

Dolan stopped the car side-on to the house. Strafford was the first to alight. The man moved out of the doorway and descended the steps, smiling.

He was in his late fifties, Strafford judged. His face continued the lines of his skull, and was long and narrow and burnished brown by long hours spent in the sun. The cheeks were concave, and the mouth was hardly more than a line marking the upper limit of a sharply sculpted chin.

'Welcome to Wicklow,' he said, as if the county were his

private domain, his thin smile broadening. 'You are Chief Inspector Hackett?'

He had hardly a trace of an accent. So much for Hackett's excuse for not coming, Strafford thought.

'Sorry,' he said, 'Inspector Hackett had a number of things to see to. He sent me instead. Strafford is the name. Detective Inspector Strafford.'

'Ah, forgive my mistake!' the man said, lifting a hand. 'I am Wolfgang Kessler.'

Quirke had got out of the car and stopped to look all round, at the house, the trees, the winged weathervane. Now he came forward.

'This is Doctor Quirke,' Strafford said shortly, with calculated ill grace.

No one shook hands, which brought a momentary chill. The occasion seemed not to allow of social niceties. It came to Strafford as quite possible that sooner or later, and as a matter of course, an arrest would be made. Kessler seemed to see him thinking it, and his colourless lips twitched in an ironic smile.

An Alsatian dog appeared around the side of the house, loping along at a trotting pace and making not a sound. It stopped beside its master and calmly scrutinised the strangers. It had a very long muzzle, and its haunches were low. Its coat was coarse yet looked silky, too.

'Come in, gentlemen,' Kessler said, turning sideways and taking a step back, a hand extended towards the door.

Quirke had not spoken yet, and had replied to Kessler's greeting only with a nod. He followed Strafford up the steps, with Kessler a little way behind him. Strafford had told

Dolan to stay in the car, and in return had got a resentful glare.

The hallway was paved with black and white chequerboard tiles. A long, highly polished antique table stood against the wall on the left, with a tall mirror above it. Further along the wall, on a wooden plaque, was the magnificently antlered head of a stag, with eyes of black glass and an expression of supercilious amusement. On the gleaming table, a copper bowl of chrysanthemums stood base to base on its shadowy, upside-down reflection. The chrysanthemums were dry and of a bleached shade of blue, though in their image in the polished wood they were ebony black.

Kessler's boot heels clicked on the stone tiles. Strafford, who came of a long line of soldiers, knew a military step when he heard it.

Halfway along the hall, Kessler stopped outside a tall white door.

'Let's go in here,' he said, as if offering a treat. 'There is the best view in the house.'

They followed him into the room.

Here was another, larger, mahogany table, circular in shape, polished to the same deep shine as the one in the hall. Ranged beyond it, in front of the window, were a sofa and two deep armchairs. The fireplace was carved from the same yellowish marble as the front doorway. The brass fender and brass fire irons had a high shine. Strafford pictured a bevy of housemaids moving through the house each morning at first light, buffing and polishing. A log fire burned in the grate, giving off the pleasant, smoky aroma of beech and oak.

At the end of the room, the long window with many small

panes gave onto another sweep of greensward. In the middle distance there was a small, irregularly shaped lake overhung by willows. The lake water was unnaturally still, and so dark it was almost black. The surface gleamed with an odd, menacing intensity.

'Sit, gentlemen, please sit,' Kessler said. Again the faint, cool glint of amusement, half suppressed. It was as if he knew something about his two visitors that they didn't know. 'You must forgive me, but I'm not sure of the correct etiquette when the police come to call. I would offer you something to drink, but in the movies, the detectives always refuse because they are on duty.'

The dog settled down, sphinx-like, on the rug in front of the fireplace, head high and front paws extended, alert and watchful.

'I'm not a policeman,' Quirke said, with an edge almost of truculence.

Kessler's smile widened and turned bland.

'Then I'll offer you something, at least.' He went to an ornately carved sideboard under the window where many bottles were ranged in strict order of height. Those housemaids again. 'There is whiskey, gin, vodka. Or sherry?' He glanced over his shoulder at Quirke. 'Perhaps a sherry?'

'I'll take a whiskey,' Quirke said.

Of course you will, Strafford thought. At least he remembered to smile when he said it. Although it was a question as to which was preferable, Quirke smiling, or otherwise.

Kessler poured the whiskey into an ornate tumbler and carried it across the room. Quirke thanked him. The German turned to Strafford.

'And for you, Mr—?'

'Strafford. With an "r".'

'Of course. You said already. Mr – Detective Strafford. Forgive me. Will you—?'

'Nothing for me, thank you.'

'Please, sit,' he said again. 'Unless' – another wisp of a smile – 'you cannot because you are on duty?'

Strafford perched himself on the front edge of one of the deep-seated armchairs. It was upholstered in a heavy creamy-white fabric with a design of red roses and dark green leaves. He held his hat between his knees. Quirke sat down in the other chair. He had not taken off his overcoat. Neither had Strafford.

Kessler poured a glass of water for himself from a crystal jug. He settled himself on the sofa and regarded them both with an air of bright enquiry. Quirke noticed his eyes, the irises pale translucent grey with black flecks, the lids pale too, and papery.

The moment had somehow a touch of the archaic. It was as if, Strafford thought, a pair of rough-hewn villeins had come to the manor house in their Sunday-best rags to petition their gracious feudal lord for an extra ration of corn, or an easing of taxes.

The cuffs of Kessler's immaculate jacket of woodland green had strips of leather sewn on to their edges, and there were leather patches on the elbows. Strafford thought of the Tyrol, and wondered where it was, exactly. Was it a country, or just a region? And do they yodel there, or is that just in Switzerland?

'So, gentlemen,' the German said, 'do please take me out

of my suspense. Has Klara' – he indicated the dog – 'been chasing after sheep? Or has my son been caught speeding, yet again?'

'Your son is Franz, yes? – Frank Kessler?' Strafford asked.

'That's right.' Kessler lifted his hands in a theatrical gesture. '*Ach*, what has he been up to now?'

He still sounded amused. Strafford gazed at him in silence. For a moment, he couldn't think quite how to proceed. None of this was as he had expected. Wolfgang Kessler, formerly Wolfgang Graf von Kessler, was as smooth and pliant as the leather patches on his jacket.

'Do you read the papers, Mr Kessler?' Quirke asked.

Kessler turned to him with eyebrows raised.

'The newspapers, you mean? Sometimes, yes. Why?'

Strafford cut in.

'I believe you know a young woman by the name of Jacobs. Rosa Jacobs.'

Now Kessler frowned.

'Yes, of course, we know Rosa. Is it about her that you have come?'

'It is.' Strafford paused, and coughed slightly, watching the man before him. 'She was particularly friendly with your son, is that so?'

A silence fell. Kessler looked from one of them to the other.

'Please say what you have come to say, gentlemen.' He spoke softly, in a tone that made the dog turn its long muzzle towards him and prick up its ears. 'Has something happened? My son is not here, by the way. Is it him you have come to talk to?'

'I'm afraid I have bad news, Mr Kessler,' Strafford said. 'Miss Jacobs is dead. She was found in her car in a lock-up garage in the city. She died of carbon monoxide poisoning.'

Kessler was as alert now as the Alsatian. Strafford noted the resemblance between them, the man and the dog. They both had long narrow faces and the same glossy grey eyes.

'She killed herself?' Kessler said. '*Ach, nein!*'

Quirke looked out of the window at the lake and its un-ruffled, strangely glowing surface. He was thinking, as he had so often thought in recent months, how strange it was to be still here, his heart beating, his mind working, while Evelyn was nowhere, and nothing. She existed, if it could be called existing, only in his memories of her, and in the memories of a few others. It didn't seem real, that she had been erased from the world, and yet it was. He heard again her singing to herself in her cracked, Dietrich voice:

Am Brunnen vor dem Tore
Da steht ein Lindenbaum

Kessler rose from the sofa and walked to the window and stood with his back to the room, his arms at his sides, looking out at the sunlit greenery.

'Such a fine day,' he murmured. 'September in Ireland—'

His voice trailed off. The dog was still watching him. Each time he spoke it wagged its tail, delivering three soft thumps to the rug on which it lay.

'You say your son is not here,' Strafford said. 'Where is he, may I ask?'

Kessler let fall a heavy sigh and turned from the window

and went back and sat down on the sofa. He seemed to have become weary suddenly.

'Frank is in Israel,' he said.

Strafford and Quirke exchanged a glance, then Strafford turned back to Kessler.

'Israel?'

Kessler nodded.

'We have business interests there.' He paused. 'You are surprised, I can see. People are always surprised. What dealings can a German have in the land of the Jews? Oh, yes, I can see it in your faces.'

'What kind of business?' Quirke asked.

'Machinery. Tools. Spare parts. I have a factory in south Germany.' He paused, and his face clouded. 'Rosa,' he murmured. '*Das arme Mädchen.*' He looked at Strafford. 'Why did she do it? Was she—?'

'Pregnant? No.'

'Then why? She was such a – such a lively girl.'

Strafford was silent. He looked at the dog, the dog looked at him. It was as if there were a fourth person in the room, one who did not speak but was a tireless monitor.

'When did you come to Ireland, Mr Kessler?' Quirke asked.

For a moment Kessler didn't understand, then he shrugged. 'Not long after.'

Quirke waited, then said: 'Not long after what?'

'The war,' Kessler answered softly, not so much speaking the words as breathing them. 'What else, doctor?'

He has forgotten my name, Quirke thought, but isn't troubled about it. He had the air of a man who would not trouble himself about many things.

'Just you and your son?'

'My wife died three years ago.'

He crossed himself and kissed his thumb as if it were the crucifix on a rosary.

'I'm sorry,' Quirke said.

Kessler turned sideways and laid an arm along the back of the sofa and looked out of the window again. A mare and her foal had come into view, walking slowly along, over the grass. The mare's dark flanks shone in the sun. The foal's legs were so long and frail-looking it seemed a wonder they did not buckle under even so slight a weight.

'This is what brought me here,' Kessler said. 'The horses. Ireland has the finest horses in the world, and the finest land to graze them on. I was urged to settle in Kildare, everyone told me I should, that was where the best grass grows, so they said. But Wicklow grass is better, to my mind. And the county is beautiful. Kildare is very flat, for a man from the mountains.'

'Forgive me,' Quirke said, 'but are you German, or Austrian?'

Kessler turned from the window.

'Your glass is empty, doctor,' he said. 'Would you like another?'

For answer, Quirke offered up his glass. Kessler rose and took it from him and crossed to the sideboard again.

'I was born in Munich,' he said, lifting the stopper from the whiskey decanter. 'But my family had a house in the Bavarian Alps. I spent a lot of time there. It was, I suppose' – he smiled – 'my spiritual home.' He looked back over his shoulder. 'Do you know the Alps?' Quirke shook his head. Kessler carried the glass to him, then went back and sat down on the sofa. 'I say a house, but it was not much more than a *Hütte*, you know – a hut.'

'Like the one the philosopher has.'

Kessler smiled his faint, cold smile.

'Ah yes, you know of Heidegger.' Quirke could see himself being reassessed. 'He has his hut – architect-designed, mind you – in Todtnauberg, in the Schwarzwald, the Black Forest.' He paused. 'An interesting case, the Herr Professor.'

'Yes,' Quirke said, 'he hasn't recanted. In fact, I'm told he never resigned from the party.'

'A man of principle. But the wrong principles, of course. Whatever Plato may say, philosophers should stay away from politics, don't you think, doctor?'

Quirke made no reply. Strafford shifted on his perch on the edge of the armchair. His hat was still in his hands.

'When did your son travel to Israel?' he asked.

'Yesterday, as it happens,' Kessler said. 'He flew to London early in the morning, then took an El Al flight to Tel Aviv.'

Strafford nodded, thinking.

'Is it the case that he and Rosa Jacobs – that they were romantically involved?'

'I'm not sure what you mean, detective.'

Quirke was lighting a cigarette. It was the fifth one he had smoked since his arrival – Strafford had been counting.

'He means were they going out together,' Quirke said. 'Were they in love.'

Kessler gave him a long look, his colourless lips pursed.

'We are Germans, my son and I,' he said. 'We do not discuss such things, between a father and his son.'

Oh, yes? Quirke said to himself. *You wouldn't ask your blue-eyed boy if he was sleeping with the daughter of a Jew?*

Strafford stirred again, turning the brim of his hat in his fingers.

'But they were close, would you say?' he urged.

The dog made a peculiar sound, a kind of low whimper. Kessler leaned back and extended his arms at either side along the top of the sofa.

'Gentlemen,' he said, 'I confess you are making me nervous with these questions. What, I ask myself, is behind them? What exactly is it you wish to know?'

Quirke, sipping his whiskey, looked at Strafford over the rim of the glass.

'The thing is, Mr Kessler,' Strafford said, and paused, and looked at his hat. Then he raised his head again. 'The thing is, it appears Miss Jacobs didn't take her own life.'

'Ah, yes?' Kessler asked, bringing his arms forward and clasping his fingers together and lifting two questioning thumbs. 'Then what?'

'Doctor Quirke here believes she was murdered.'

Kessler turned to Quirke, frowning.

'You are – what?'

'I'm a pathologist.'

Now it was Strafford that the German turned to, with an exaggeratedly puzzled look.

'Is this the way, here,' he asked, 'that the coroner accompanies the detective in his investigations?'

'Not a coroner,' Quirke corrected him, without emphasis. 'Pathologist.'

Kessler did not take his eyes off Strafford.

'No, it's not the way, usually,' Strafford said, making sure not to look in Quirke's direction. 'But these circumstances are not usual. They are not usual at all.'

In the silence, they heard a horse whinny outside. Quirke's head was buzzing a little – Kessler had poured a generous measure of whiskey. Once more, he looked out at that lake. It was a pool of darkness at the heart of the smokily golden day. Yet the water was not wholly dark, it had its own sombre radiance, as if a glimmer of light were burning in its depths. Quirke felt a tremor along his spine. *There is a willow grows aslant a brook.*

Kessler seemed to have been holding his breath, and now he released it in a wordless exclamation.

'Who would take the life of such a person, a young woman who was so much alive?'

The dog whimpered again, not in distress, it seemed, but perhaps as a comment, an echoing of what its master had just said. Animals sense the mood of a room, Strafford knew that. He had a sheepdog for a pet, when he was a boy. Patch, he called it. It had been the runt of the litter, and highly strung and lacking in stamina. It wouldn't have survived, if he hadn't rescued it. His father mocked what he considered his son's sentimental attachment to the poor, shivering creature. The boy had been determined, though – where had it gone to, the grown-up Strafford wondered, all that boyhood resolution? – and Patch had lived a long and, so far as his young master could tell, happy life.

Patch loved to run on the beach at Tramore, and never wanted the day to end. One Sunday evening when Strafford had turned for home, Patch had hung back on the sand, scanning the holiday crowd. A young woman in a skirted swimsuit and a rubber bathing cap had stopped on her way up from the sea to talk to a boy. Patch fixed on her, sized her up, then went and stood beside her, giving Strafford a look as if to say, *You can go now, I'm staying with her.*

In the end the dog had to be dragged away, and looked at Strafford with mournfully accusing eyes all the way home.

Kessler slapped his palms on his knees and stood up.

'Come, gentlemen, I want to show you something.'

Quirke finished his drink and set down the glass. His colour was a little high, Strafford noted. The two whiskeys Kessler had poured for him had filled half the glass. All the same, the alcohol hadn't done anything to cheer him up, if his scowling look was anything to go by.

Kessler led the way out to the hall, the sleek dog padding at his heels.

What he had to show them, as Strafford had guessed, were the horses.

At the side of the house, they boarded a vehicle resembling a golf buggy – perhaps it was a golf buggy, Strafford thought – and bumped along a rutted track towards the distant stables. Green grass flourished between the parallel ruts.

Their driver was Kessler's groom. His name was Venables. He was a short, wiry Wicklow-man with prominent red ears and a twitch in his left jaw.

'How much land have you got here?' Quirke asked of Kessler, being polite.

The German thought for a moment, and laughed.

'I do not know!' He addressed the groom. 'Jimmy, the size of the estate – can you say?'

'A shade over three hundred acres, sir,' Venables answered, keeping his eye on the track ahead. 'And fine rich land it is too, every acre of it.'

'Jimmy is very proud of the place, you know,' Kessler said in an undertone, smiling. 'His father was head gardener here, in the time before us, his grandfather also, long ago. So there is a family tradition, you see.'

They arrived at the stables. Single-storey granite sheds surrounded a flagstoned yard on four sides. They entered the main shed and walked along the row of stalls. There was a mingled smell of horse feed, horse dung and dust. Quirke sneezed, startling the others.

'Sorry,' he said.

'You are allergic to the horses, perhaps?' Kessler said. 'Some people are.'

'No,' Quirke said, rubbing his nose, 'it's just the dust.'

There must have been a score or more of animals. They put their heads out over the half doors of the stalls, nodding and snorting and rolling their round, dark eyeballs, big glass marbles in which the incomprehensible world was convexly reflected.

Strafford regarded them warily. There were always horses about when he was young, but he had never got used to them. They seemed to him prehistoric creatures, or aliens from another, far-off planet, misplaced here. Thoroughbreds, which all of these were, always seemed to him terror-struck, or mad, or both. And they were so tall, standing on all fours. He thought of Swift's equine philosophers – what did he call them? Houyhnhnms. He still wasn't sure how to pronounce it.

Venables, he could see, was attached to the animals in his

care. Indeed, there was a touch of the equine about him, short and scrawny though he was. He reminded Strafford of the lone donkey so often to be seen grazing placidly among a herd of horses.

Kessler had stopped at one of the stalls. The horse inside it was smaller than the rest, with a coat of shiny deep black and an arched neck.

'This is Sinbad,' Kessler said, 'my special one. Pure Arab. He talks to me, when we are alone.' He stroked the horse's jaw, a gleaming flange. '*Wir erzählen einander unsere Geheimnisse, nicht wahr?*'

Geheimnisse, Quirke thought: their secrets? He wondered what they might be.

'Some coffee, gentlemen? A little schnapps, to warm the blood?'

There was an internal phone that connected to the house. Kessler spoke into it briefly. Then he invited Quirke and Strafford to sit with him on a hay bale. He enquired solicitously of Quirke's susceptibility to the dusty air. Quirke lit a cigarette.

'Take care with that flame,' Venables said sharply, but at a glance from Kessler he rushed to soften his tone. 'It's only,' he said, 'the place is packed with combustibles.'

Another glance from his boss sent him on his way, muttering something about a vet's impending visit, and touching a finger obsequiously to the peak of his cap.

An elderly maid came with a bottle and glasses on a tray. She and Kessler spoke to each other in German, in a soft undertone. He turned to his guests.

'You'll take a small glass with me? It is an excellent vintage – do you say vintage when it is distilled?'

Strafford declined the drink.

'I'll try a glass,' Quirke said gamely.

Kessler poured two tiny measures into the shot glasses.

'*Prost!*' he said.

He looked back at Sinbad's compact, handsome head poking out of the stall. The horse was watching with interest the three men seated on the bale. Strafford thought: *Probably I seem as alien to him as he does to me.*

'I have two more warm-bloods – Arabs, that is – a mare and another stallion, like that fellow there. The other two are being exercised. I intend to experiment with them, mixing them into my thoroughbred line.' He nodded, still watching the horse watching them. 'The results will be interesting, no?'

'I'm sorry,' Strafford said, 'I know very little about horses.'

Quirke reared back where he sat and stared at him in large-eyed, mock amazement.

'What, and you a horse Protestant?' he said.

Kessler put on a smiling frown.

'A horse Protestant? What is that?'

'Brendan Behan defined an Anglo-Irishman as a Protestant on a horse. He had a little rhyme he used to recite at the top of his voice in McDaid's when he had got enough porter inside him:

> *Don't speak of your Protestant minister,*
> *Nor of his Church without meaning or faith.*
> *For the foundation stone of his temple*
> *Was the bollocks of Henry the Eighth.*

Mind you, Behan was a thundering bollocks himself.'

'That is funny, yes, the poem,' Kessler said, nodding, though he didn't laugh.

He exchanged a glance with Strafford. The whiskey Quirke had drunk in the house had worked its bilious magic after all, and his eyes had taken on an unsteady gleam. Now he smiled in that way Strafford was coming to know all too well.

'Don't mind him,' he said to Kessler, jerking a thumb in Strafford's direction. 'There hasn't been a Prod born yet that doesn't know his horseflesh.'

'Oh, now,' Kessler, tut-tutting, said lightly, 'surely you would not compare our friend here to the fat King Henry?'

Quirke seemed not to hear. He made a sideways cutting gesture with his left hand.

'Son of the Ascendancy,' he said loudly, 'a relic of oul' decency.'

'Ah, so you too are a poet, eh, doctor?' Kessler said. 'You make the rhymes.'

Quirke looked away. He should shut up, he knew, but there was in Strafford something that always sparked his ire. And it wasn't just his class, or his religion, neither of which mattered a damn, as far as he was concerned.

'I'm no poet,' Quirke muttered.

Who was he to sneer at Brendan Behan? He recalled, with a shiver of shame, how in the old days, when he was out on one of his protracted benders, he would silence the pub by declaiming Yeats – '*We had fed the heart on fantasies!*' – over the heads of the drinkers in roiling, smoke-filled pubs, making a fool of himself and a travesty of Yeats. He laid a contrite hand on Strafford's arm.

'Sorry,' he said. 'I was out of line.'

He took his hand away. He had felt how Strafford stiffened at his touch. Kessler, sensing the tension between the two men, refilled Quirke's glass, but not his own, and said:

'My son is fond of poetry. Goethe, Schiller. Heine, too.'

'When does he come back?' Strafford asked.

'From Israel? He will stay there only for some days. We are building facilities to reclaim large areas of desert. It is a big project.'

There was a silence, then Quirke spoke.

'Do you mind my asking—'

He hesitated. Kessler smiled.

'You mean, how is it the Jews would make such a contract with a German firm? I understand why you ask.' He thought for a moment, looking along the stalls. 'Israel, you know, is a strange – how do you say? – a strange phenomenon. It's not unlike Ireland, I think. Yours too is a young country, and your people too have a history of oppression and suffering. I have read about this. Oliver Cromwell was your Adolf Hitler, I think?'

He looked from one to the other of the two men, but neither spoke. He went on smoothly:

'The Israelis, I would say, are a new kind of Jew. They are tough, up here, yes?' – he touched a finger to his forehead – 'and always, always – *ach*, what is the word? – pragmatic. Always they are pragmatic. They still value scholarship, the Talmud, the Old Testament, all this. But they are a people not only of the Book, but of the world, too, and they will become increasingly so. They have left the shtetl far behind.' He broke off then, laughing. '"Ah," you are saying to yourself, "what does this German know about the people his country tried to annihilate?"' He nodded. 'I understand. But you too must understand that if there is a new kind of Jew, there is also a new kind of German. My son and I, we wish to offer something back, a little, a very little reparation, for all that happened in those terrible years.'

He was silent. Quirke and Strafford were avoiding each other's eye. At length, it was Quirke who broke the silence.

'How did you set up this business, in Israel, you and your son?'

'Ah, Franz – Frank, had no part in establishing Kessler GbmH' – he pronounced the letters in the German way – 'he was too young then, when I set out.' He paused again, nodded again. 'I have a friend, you see, in Israel, an old friend and partner. Teddy Katz. He's a very successful businessman, a great entrepreneur. Teddy brought my company to Israel, found the contacts for us there.' He made a twisting motion with his right hand, as if turning a doorknob. 'Yes, he opened many doors for me. I owe much to Teddy, *mein guter Freund.*'

Quirke rose, and dropped the butt of his cigarette on the clay floor and ground it out with his heel. Strafford too stood up. Kessler sat on, gazing before him.

'Can you tell me how to get in touch with your son, in Israel?' Strafford asked. 'An address, a telephone number?'

Kessler stirred himself and rose to his feet, brushing at the front of his jodhpurs.

'Of course,' he said. 'Let us go back to the house.'

As they walked by the stalls again, the Arab reared its head and whinnied. Sinbad the Sailor, Quirke thought. Was he the one who got into the cave of the Forty Thieves? No, that was Ali Baba. Open sesame. What was that name again? Teddy Katz.

In the car on the way back to the city, no one spoke for some miles. Quirke smoked cigarette after cigarette, grimly, as if it were a penance imposed on him for his uncouth behaviour at the stables. Strafford opened his window a little way and gulped at the fresh air streaming in.

'Well,' he said, 'what did you make of Herr Kessler?'

Quirke tapped his cigarette on the edge of the ashtray in the armrest beside him.

'A Nazi, I'd say, though a smooth one. It would be interesting to know how he made his money in the first place.'

Strafford thought about this.

'They weren't all Nazis,' he said, 'surely? What about Rommel?'

'What about him?'

'He seemed an honourable fellow. Committed suicide after the plot against Hitler failed.'

'He was given no choice.'

'All the same, he took the honourable way out.'

Quirke shrugged. He didn't care whether Rommel was a good man or a villain. Nor was he much concerned as to what Kessler had or hadn't been. It seemed clear to him the man was a fraud, down to the patches on his expensive Tyrolean jacket and the shine on his handmade riding boots. Why couldn't Strafford see that? But then, Strafford too was a pretence, a son of the Big House masquerading as a Dublin flatfoot. He was a conceited ass, too, for all his got-up diffidence. To hell with him. He lit another cigarette.

They were crossing the moorland again. After a time, Strafford spoke.

'Didn't know you read Heidegger,' he said.

'I don't.'

'Well, you impressed the old boy.'

'That was the intention. I was showing off.'

The miles wound past. Dolan, at the wheel, glanced at them now and then in the driving mirror, seeming amused. At what? He was driving faster even than on the way down, taking the bends at fifty or sixty miles an hour. Strafford felt dizzy, but he was reluctant to tell Dolan to slow down. Quirke would take Dolan's side, he knew, in any dispute.

'How is your daughter?' Strafford asked.

'My daughter?' Quirke growled, surprised and wary.

'Yes. Phoebe. How is she?'

'She's all right, as far as I know. Why?'

'I just wondered how she is, after – after Spain.'

Quirke said nothing, and smoked his cigarette with increased violence. It wasn't just Strafford he was angry at. He was thinking of Evelyn. At times, the loss of his wife struck him anew with the force of a heavy steel door blowing open in a storm, leaving him breathless and inwardly tottering in the darkness and the rushing, relentless air.

Strafford was speaking again.

'What?' Quirke snapped.

'I said, can you give me her phone number?'

'Why?' Quirke again demanded.

'Because I'd thought I might call her,' Strafford said. 'Just to say hello.'

Quirke turned back to the window.

'I haven't got her number on me,' he muttered.

As the car sped along, the heathland seemed to keep

opening on both sides like a giant dun-and-purple fan.

'Perhaps I'll call round,' Strafford said.

Quirke shifted on the leather seat. Was this fellow out to provoke him?

'Call round?'

'Yes,' Strafford said. 'I could drop in one evening. To her flat, I mean.'

Quirke snorted. In his world, you didn't drop in on people of an evening, for a chat and a glass of tonic wine – didn't this fellow understand that?

'I'm not in very often,' he said shortly.

'But perhaps Phoebe is?'

Strafford realised, to his surprise, that he was rather enjoying himself, sinking his picador's blades into the bull's rough, heaving hide. Why shouldn't he visit Phoebe? She was a grown-up woman, wasn't she? And he had liked her, from what little he had seen of her in Spain. He suspected that behind the demure aspect that she affected, a far livelier spirit was at play. Besides, if by visiting her he annoyed her father, that would be all to the better.

Now Dolan spoke from the front seat.

'By the way,' he said, leaning forward a little to catch Strafford's eye in the mirror, 'I forgot to mention it: the Chief was on the blower.'

'The blower?' Strafford said.

'On the walkie-talkie.'

Dolan pointed to the handset tucked under the dashboard.

'What did he want?'

'To speak to you. He called when you were looking at the horses.'

'What did he want?'

'They searched the girl's room in Trinity. There were letters to her, from' – he leaned to the right, to look in the mirror this time at Quirke – 'from someone who worked with you, doctor. Name of – sorry, it's slipped my mind.'

'Sinclair?' Quirke said.

'That's it. Sinclair. David Sinclair.'

9

Strafford had suggested they meet at the Shelbourne Hotel, or the Hibernian, if she preferred, but somehow they ended up strolling together on the towpath below Baggot Street bridge. It was a Saturday morning, and the sun was shining. Few people were about, which gave a dreamy look to the day. A moorhen swam on the water, delicately unzipping the placid surface as it went, her half-grown chicks strung out in a line behind her, bobbing along.

The tall reeds along the water's edge were sere already. He told her how on winter evenings when he was young, the boys from the village would cut down bulrushes and soak them in paraffin and set them alight and march through the twilit streets with their burning brands held aloft, like a mob of witch-hunters.

'Where was it you were born?' Phoebe asked.

The arch underneath the bridge was dappled with shimmering coins of light reflected from the water.

'Wexford,' Strafford said. 'County Wexford. Not far from New Ross. In the middle of nowhere, you might say.'

He thought she looked very nice, in her neat little coat and sensible shoes. He had never seen her in anything other than black and white. People spoke of spoilt priests: could there be spoilt nuns, too? He found the notion oddly exciting. It offered the vague prospect of tender violation.

Both were aware of a constraint between them, and this too was fraught with possibility. If they weren't constrained, what would they be?

All this was surprising, and pleasurably disconcerting, to both of them. They had not felt any of these things when they were in each other's company in Spain. Or perhaps they had, and hadn't registered the feeling.

'You knew Rosa when she was going out with David Sinclair, yes?' Strafford said.

Phoebe laughed, and touched a hand to her hair.

'I don't know that they *went out* together,' she said. 'In fact, he and I were supposed to be going out, though whatever there might have been between us was coming to an end.'

'Because he was going to Israel?'

'Or because of Rosa Jacobs. Who knows? I certainly didn't – know, I mean.'

They passed by the iron bench where Kavanagh the poet often sat, muttering to himself and glaring at the people going by.

'Sinclair is a Zionist, then?' Strafford asked.

Phoebe looked startled.

'I never thought of it, but I suppose he must be. He was certainly very hot on the idea of Israel, or "the homeland", as he called it.' She stopped to watch another moorhen and her chicks. The tiny creatures looked like moving balls of fluff.

They walked on. The sunlight was hazy. In the calmness of the day, they could hear far-off sounds as if they were near, the ping of the stop-bell in a passing bus, the voices of children playing in a garden somewhere, the plash of water toppling over the edge of the lock at Baggot Street bridge.

146

Strafford glanced at Phoebe out of the corner of his eye. She had a delicate, almost tentative gait, taking short and as it were exploratory steps, as if she were set on a perilous way and not strolling over the packed clay of the towpath. He wondered if she were short-sighted. There was a slight frailness, a slight unsteadiness, in the region of her knees that Strafford found affecting and, again, peculiarly exciting. He knew next to nothing about her. But then, he knew next to nothing about most people. He was confused. It all seemed very strange, suddenly.

'What was Rosa like?' he asked.

'Rosa? Oh, she saw herself as a tearaway, but I always thought that, underneath, she wasn't quite the rebel she liked people to think she was.'

'Her being in with the Kesslers, that was odd, don't you think?'

'Was she "in" with them?'

'Well, she visited their house in Wicklow. She stayed over for weekends, sometimes.'

He told her of his trip to Wicklow with Quirke. He didn't mention how Quirke had been when they were there. He wondered how she could share her flat with such a man, even if he was her father.

They turned and crossed over the narrow footbridge at the Mount Street lock and came out onto Northumberland Road. The leaves of the plane trees were turning, and made faint dry rustling sounds when a breeze passed through them. Strafford found himself longing for the dense, drooping heaviness of summer foliage. What was that little Yeats poem?

Through winter-time we call on spring,
And through the spring on summer call,
And when something something ring,
Declare that winter's best of all.

Despite the day's warmth, he felt himself shiver.

'Isn't it the most evocative name, Northumberland?' Phoebe said, pointing to the green plaque attached to the railings of the first house on the corner. 'Makes me think of – I don't know. Vikings, and mist, and rain on the moors.' She gave a nervous laugh. 'Sorry. I'm not usually like this.'

They walked along in the dappled light. Anyone seeing us, Phoebe thought, would take us for a couple. The thought surprised her. She supposed she must be thinking of David Sinclair. That was something she hadn't done for a long time. David was the past. Had he ever really been the present, or was that something she had imagined?

'It was Frank Kessler that Rosa was supposed to fancy,' she said.

'Yes? Was he part of your set?'

She gave a brief, laughing cry.

'Our set! If we were anything, we were a gang. Or if you want to be fancy, a little band, like in Proust.'

'And Rosa and Frank Kessler were—?'

He was looking at her with his eyebrows raised.

'Everyone considered them an item,' Phoebe said, 'if that's what you're asking. Everyone, that is, except Frank.'

'He wasn't fond of her?'

'Hard to know, with Frank. He's very German, very correct. And very full of himself, though he tries not to show

148

it. Also I think he might be—'

'Yes?'

She blushed.

'Oh, nothing.'

The sun shone benignly on the noble brick fronts of the old houses. Birds flitted in the gardens. Phoebe was thinking that perhaps she should have got a flat out here, instead of in Mount Street. The green of the lawns and the still-green trees gave an aqueous cast to the sunlight. She imagined waking in the morning here, to the quiet, to the faint radiance of the lawns, to the hushing of the trees. *Life is always elsewhere*, she told herself wryly.

Strafford walked along with his head bent, his eyes on the pavement. He was debating something with himself, she could feel him doing it. At length, he spoke.

'Did you know David Sinclair had written to Rosa from Israel?'

She waited a beat before replying.

'No, I didn't. I suspect that where David is concerned, there were many things I didn't know.'

'Is he – secretive?'

'I wouldn't say that. He and Frank Kessler are oddly alike, in some ways. They have that self-assurance that's an inch away from arrogance. Or maybe it is arrogance, only disguised.' She paused, then went on. 'How do you know about David writing to Rosa?'

'Rosa had a room in the Rubrics in Trinity.'

'Yes, I know. It was where she lived.'

'We sent a couple of detectives round there. They found a packet of letters.'

'A packet!' Phoebe exclaimed. 'Well, well.'

What did she feel? Surprise, of course, some pain, and anger, a little. But something else, too, a kind of lightening. Strafford had revealed something hitherto hidden from her. It was like the moment in a gangster film, in the morgue, when the corner of the sheet is lifted for the hero to identify the body underneath. What was it the corpse of, that she was looking down on here? Part of herself, of her life, but changed suddenly, so that she hardly recognised it. She could let it go now, could consign it to a decent burial. *This is the way things end*, she told herself. This is the way things end.

'Are you all right?' Strafford asked.

His voice was soft, his tone concerned. Yes, just like a comforter at a funeral, she thought.

'I'm fine,' she said, 'fine. Only I didn't know, I mean I wasn't aware that David and Rosa—'

She shrugged, and looked away.

'Didn't he write to you?' Strafford asked.

For a moment she said nothing. What right, she asked herself, what right had he to sympathise with her? He knew nothing about her – he was a stranger. But then she thought, no, no he's not. She didn't know what he was.

They came to a crossing, and waited for the traffic lights to change, though there was no traffic. She realised she was clutching her handbag tightly against her midriff. Surely she wasn't going to cry? No, she wouldn't let herself do that, it would be too shameful. This man beside her would think she was weeping for the loss of David Sinclair. But if not for that, then for what? Her mind reeled.

The lights turned to green.

'Come along,' Strafford said, and touched a finger to her elbow. 'There's a pub down here, it should be open by now.'

'I thought you didn't drink?'

He seemed flustered suddenly.

'Well, no, I don't, not really. But we can't keep walking forever.'

They continued in silence down Haddington Road, crossed at the junction and went into Slattery's at the top of Bath Avenue. The pub had its morning smell, of flat porter, stale smoke and soapy water. The barman was a burly fellow in shirtsleeves and a shabby waistcoat.

Phoebe asked for a shandy – 'bit early for a real drink' – and Strafford said he would have the same.

They sat on high stools at the bar. Phoebe opened her handbag and took out a packet of Passing Cloud and lit one. Her hand was quite steady, she was glad to note.

'I don't smoke,' she said, 'the way you don't drink.' She gave him a brittle smile. 'I'm like Mark Twain, I stop smoking ten or twenty times a day.' He laughed politely. 'You don't at all, as I remember.'

'No. Not really by choice. Just, somehow I never got started.'

The barman set their drinks before them. Phoebe eyed the pallid yellow liquid in the glass. It looks like pee, she thought. She took a sip. Sweet and bitter at the same time. Bittersweet. She was thinking of David Sinclair again. She wished she could stop. It was ridiculous. The affair had hardly got started before it was over. And was it even an affair?

She was sorry she had agreed to meet this man, with his pale hands and thin face and that lock of hair that kept falling over his forehead. Her father disliked him. He had never said so, but she knew. Was that why she was here? The notion startled her. She set the glass back on the bar and rotated it slowly with her fingertips. Her father was another thing she didn't want to think about.

When she spoke, she heard herself as if from afar.

'It's funny, I believed part of David's reason for going to Israel was to get away from me, but perhaps it was Rosa he was fleeing from. Though it doesn't seem to have worked, if he wrote her a whole *packet* of letters.'

Strafford hadn't touched his drink. He sat quite still, gazing at the ranks of bottles behind the bar. He seemed a mile away.

'I wonder,' he said slowly, 'if he had any contact with the Kesslers when he was over there.'

She set her mouth in a bitter line. He didn't care a fig about her, or David Sinclair, or what they might or might not have been to each other. He was a detective, and he was working.

'You could ask him,' she said, more coldly than she had intended.

He turned to her, struck by the hardness of her tone.

'Yes,' he said, 'I suppose I could.' It wasn't what he had meant to say. It was only a way of not saying something else. Then, before he knew what he was doing, he had turned to her with a sudden rush of earnestness that surprised them both. 'I wonder—' he began, and stopped and sat a moment silent, and started again. 'I wonder if we might meet.'

She gave him a startled look, wrinkling her nose.

'We are meeting, aren't we?'

'I mean, not to talk about Rosa Jacobs, or – or these other things.'

She wondered how old he was. A lot older than she was, certainly. Twenty years? More? And he was married, so someone had told her – perhaps he had. Strange, though: he didn't seem like a married man. But what did a married man seem like?

'But what would we talk about?' she asked. 'If we were to "meet"?'

He had the impression she was trying not to laugh. He was wrong. She did not feel at all like laughing.

10

On Monday, at mid-morning, Chief Inspector Hackett took Quirke to Mooney's on College Green and bought him a drink and asked him to go down to Cork and talk to David Sinclair.

Quirke had not kept in touch with Sinclair after he went off to Israel, and this was the first he had heard of his return to Ireland. Well then, Hackett said cheerfully, here was the perfect opportunity for Quirke to catch up on all the news with his friend and former colleague.

'He's at the Bon Secours down there. Has a big job, head surgeon, I believe.'

Quirke looked into his drink. He wasn't sure he wanted to catch up with Sinclair. They had worked together amicably enough, but they had never been friends.

In the end he gave in, as he always did. Hackett could always get round him. Why was that? Maybe it was that in his shiny blue suit and cracked shoes, with his bad dentures and Roscommon accent – *was* it Roscommon he was from? – he represented a version of Ireland that Quirke had never quite escaped from, that still had a hold on him. Or maybe he saw in Hackett the father he had yearned for when he was young. Dear God! He pushed the thought away. It was the kind of thing he would have laughed at, if someone had suggested it to him. The things that come into one's mind!

He went to Cork.

By mistake, he got onto a slow train. It was drawn by one of the last of the old steam engines, a squat black monster that chugged and groaned its way south at what couldn't have been more than forty-five miles an hour, fifty at most. The carriages too were old, with windows that wouldn't close properly. They were hardly out of Kingsbridge station before Quirke's eyes had begun to smart from the smoke and the flying cinders.

He was trapped in a compartment with an ancient priest who slept and snored all the way to Limerick Junction, where he got off, sketching a blessing behind him as he departed. At the next station his place was taken by a fat man in a pinstriped suit, who immediately lit up a foul-smelling pipe. Quirke opened his copy of the *Irish Independent* and hid behind it. The fat man wasn't deterred, however, and began to talk about football. Quirke had no choice but to put the paper down. He knew nothing about football.

'The ref shouldn't have given that free kick,' the fat man was saying. 'Up to that, our lads had the run of the field.' He produced a small penknife and began to scrape at the hardened slag inside the bowl of his pipe. 'Amn't I right?'

Quirke said yes, he was right.

The train clattered over a set of points, hooting.

A room had been booked for him at the Imperial Hotel on the South Mall. Years before, he had stayed at the Imperial with Isabel Galloway. Isabel was playing the lead in a production of *The Merry Widow* at the Opera House – she had a nice voice, though it tended to crack on the high notes – which was to run for six performances with a matinee on Saturday. She had bought a Woolworths ring, and Quirke was to stay the week with her. However, the assistant manager, a pulpy-faced fellow with a beer-drinker's paunch, turned out to be one of Isabel's numerous old flames. He saw through the ruse of the cheap ring, and on the morning after their first night Quirke was requested, politely but firmly, to pack his bag and leave.

Yet he was fond of the old Imperial. After he had got the key and put his bag in his room, he settled down in the bar with a book and a glass of whiskey.

Strange, he thought, how Isabel had accosted him, in the flesh, at Jammet's that day, and now here, if only in memory, though brazen as ever. Maybe she was still a bit sweet on him. The thought made him squirm. He hadn't come well out of all that, not well at all.

In the middle of the afternoon, Sinclair arrived. At first, when he appeared in the doorway of the bar, Quirke didn't recognise him – he had grown a thick black rabbinical beard. It suited him, gave him an air of melancholy authority. His eyes were different too, somehow. The expression in them had changed. He seemed calmer than Quirke remembered, calmer and – poised, that was the word. Was it just that he was older? No. Israel had wrought a change in him. He had something of the look of a desert prophet.

However, he greeted Quirke with a familiar smile, cool and guarded.

They shook hands.

'Sit down,' Quirke said. 'Will you take a drink?'

'I have to work later. Just a tomato juice.'

He perched on the stool opposite Quirke. He was wearing a well-cut dark suit, a white shirt and a red tie. There was a pin in the lapel of his jacket, with some emblem on it that

Quirke couldn't make out. Some Jewish club or association, he supposed.

They regarded each other with a certain awkwardness. Things had never been easy between them, in the years they had worked together at the Holy Family. Sinclair was prickly. And there was something about him that brought out the bully in Quirke, though he was well able to defend himself, and even to give as good as he got.

And then there was Phoebe, whom Sinclair had left high and dry when he went off to Israel. Yes, Quirke told himself, the same way that he had left Isabel Galloway when he got tired of her.

Sinclair's glass of tomato juice arrived. He had to ask for ice. 'You're in Cork now,' Quirke reminded him. The barman gave him a sour look.

They drank their drinks.

'I didn't know you were back,' Quirke said.

'Why would you?'

'I thought I would have heard, on the grapevine. Cork city is not exactly Tel Aviv.'

'I was in Haifa,' Sinclair said.

'Sorry, Haifa.'

A silence.

'What's it like at the Bon Secours?' Quirke asked, to be asking something.

'It's all right. Busy. TB is bad in the city. I've made a bit of a specialism of pulmonary cases.'

'Oh, yes? I could never imagine myself cutting open a living body.'

'The smells are not as bad.'

'The smells,' Quirke said. 'Right.'

Sinclair scratched his cheek through the beard, making a small crackling sound. Then he massaged his eyes with a finger and thumb.

'Sorry,' he said, 'I was on an early shift.'

'And now you've to do a late one? They're certainly making you work.'

'I don't mind. I like work.'

Quirke, thinking of Phoebe again, wondered if Sinclair had a woman these days. Maybe that was why he had come back? There might be a wife, children, even. He wouldn't ask. It wasn't the kind of thing one asked Sinclair about. He was private, to the point of secretiveness, always had been.

Was that because he was a Jew in a country run by Catholics?

There had been riots – a pogrom – here in the early years of the century. Or was that Limerick? He couldn't remember. He never understood why the Jews had been persecuted down the ages. It was not only wicked, it was deeply stupid too. Might as well be against people who were left-handed or had red hair. There was no limit to human stupidity.

It occurred to him suddenly, with a jolt, that Sinclair might have thought him an anti-Semite. That would account for the guardedness, the sarcasm, the occasional flashes of resentment and bitterness, over the years.

'Are you here for a reason,' Sinclair asked, 'or just to sample the delights of this fair city on the banks of the lovely Lee?'

Quirke toyed with his whiskey glass.

'Hackett asked me to come,' he said. 'Chief Inspector Hackett, remember him? Pearse Street.'

'I remember. I thought he'd be retired by now.'

'He's counting the days. He has a place in Leitrim, on one of the lakes. He and the missus will transfer up there. Great fishing, he says.'

'What did he ask you to come down for?'

'To talk to you.'

They went into the dining room and sat at a square table among elaborate Victorian splendours. Marble pillars stood about, and there were stone bas-reliefs on the walls, in the shape of carved urns ringed with garlands. The ceiling was a phantasmagoria of floral swirls and stripes.

They ordered ham sandwiches. Quirke switched to beer, and Sinclair asked for another tomato juice.

Did Sinclair eat ham, when he lived in Dublin? Quirke couldn't remember. This was something else he would not ask.

'What are you supposed to talk to me about?' Sinclair asked. 'Rosa Jacobs, I suppose?'

'You heard about her?'

'I read it in the paper. It was a shock.'

'I'm sure.'

Quirke had opened a flap of one of the triangular sandwiches and was peering at the ham. Processed, and far from fresh. He closed the flap and pushed the plate away.

'When you were over there,' he said, 'in Israel, did you ever hear of a Teddy Katz?'

Sinclair leaned far back on the stool in surprise.

'Teddy Katz? Everybody in Israel has heard of Teddy Katz. Why do you ask?'

Quirke signalled to the barman for another drink. The

barman took his time. *The jackeen with the smart mouth could wait.* Quirke didn't mind. He had said it himself: this is Cork. He turned back to Sinclair.

'Some kind of bigwig, then, is he?'

'Yes, he's some kind of bigwig. Owns half the country, if half of what they say about him is true.'

'He's reclaiming the desert, I hear.'

'That's only one of the giant pies he has a finger in. If there's money to be made, Teddy Katz will be there.' He took a sip of his tomato juice and made a face. 'He was in the camps. Belsen, I think, or Dachau, I can't remember which.'

'How did he survive?'

Sinclair chuckled.

'By being Teddy Katz, I imagine – how else?' He put the glass down on the bar and studied it thoughtfully. 'Everybody has a different version of Teddy,' he said, 'none of them the right one, I'm sure. He got to Israel in 'forty-six, God knows how. He had a bag of money – gold bullion, they say – the source of which he has always been vague about. He invested wisely. Started out dealing in pelts, pig bristles, leather, then moved on to fur and women's fashion. In no time he was running the country's garment industry.'

'How did he get into land reclamation?'

'I told you,' Sinclair said, rubbing together a thumb and two fingers. 'Shekels. He had money to invest, he spotted a good thing. I tell you, he's everywhere. He was in on the El Al start-up. He manufactures guns for the army – sorry, the Israeli Defence Force, as we're supposed to call it. The country loves him.'

Quirke was fiddling again with his glass. There was a

marked note of disenchantment in Sinclair's voice. Was that why he had come back, because the promise of the Promised Land had turned out to be false?

'Why are you asking me about him?' Sinclair said, looking at his watch.

Quirke was silent for some moments, then spoke.

'You know these people, don't you, these Germans, name of Kessler? Big place in Wicklow. Horses.'

Sinclair nodded, looking away.

'So it is about Rosa,' he said.

'Yes. It's about Rosa.'

They walked along the Mall together. Sinclair had parked his car over by the river. The day had hazed over, the sun was shrouded in a yellowish mist.

At the corner of Marlborough Street, a tinker woman in a tartan shawl stood with a cupped hand extended. Around her feet a puddle of filthy, barefoot children squatted, staring at nothing out of hollow eye sockets, stupefied by hunger. Quirke passed her by, but to his surprise Sinclair stopped. There was the flash of a ten-shilling note.

'I never heard Kessler mention Teddy Katz,' Sinclair said, when he had caught Quirke up. He stowed his wallet in the inside breast pocket of his sober suit. 'Frank Kessler, that is. I only knew him, and only a little. The father I never met.'

They walked on.

'Wolfgang Kessler is in business with Teddy Katz,' Quirke said. 'Reclaiming the desert.'

Sinclair seemed surprised.

'Not armaments?'

Quirke glanced at him with an eyebrow raised.

'Armaments? Kessler didn't mention armaments.'

'Well, he wouldn't, would he. There are a lot of reasons, all of them obvious, why an old German wouldn't want it known that he's in thick with the Israeli military. Or vice versa, for that matter.'

They arrived at Sinclair's car, which to Quirke was another surprise. A bright-red Triumph Roadster wasn't what he would have expected of Doctor David Sinclair. It had a black canvas roof, which Sinclair now rolled back.

'There's something about the girl's death you should know,' Quirke said.

Sinclair paused, the car key in his hand.

'What?'

'Rosa Jacobs didn't kill herself.'

Sinclair waited, expressionless, still holding the key between a finger and thumb. Quirke told him of his conviction that someone had drugged the young woman and left her in her car to die of gas poisoning.

Sinclair slowly expelled a breath.

'Why did you wait until now to tell me this?'

'I don't know.'

The sun through the mist was producing coppery glints from the steely surface of the river. Quirke looked over to the far bank, where the city climbed the side of a steep hill. Cork was more handsome than he remembered. Or was it just the flattering autumn light?

'And is this why you're asking me about the Kesslers?' Sinclair said tonelessly. A muscle in his jaw was twitching. 'You think—?'

He left the question unfinished.

'Do I think they were involved in her death? The answer is no. Hackett doesn't think so, either. Only—'

'Only what?'

'There are no suspects. No one knows why Rosa Jacobs was murdered, or who murdered her. She was an academic, she was studying the what-do-you-call-it—'

'The Jewish diaspora in Ireland.'

'That's right. Can't imagine any reason there for someone to do away with her.'

Now it was Sinclair's turn to look across to the far hill with its streets and houses, its shops and churches, all made into miniatures by distance.

'Maybe just being Jewish was enough,' he said. He got into the car and started the engine, then paused. 'By the way—' He stopped, and fiddled with the gear stick.

'What?'

It struck Quirke that Sinclair never addressed him directly, didn't say Doctor, Quirke, anything. He might be speaking to the nameless air.

'Rosa had a friend in Tel Aviv.' He revved the engine, making it whine. 'Kind of a pen pal, though Rosa wouldn't thank me for saying so.'

'Man? Woman?'

'Woman.'

'What is she? What does she do?'

'She's a reporter, on *Ha'aretz*. Shula Lieberman. Give her a call, let her know about Rosa.'

How cool he was, about a girl he wrote all those letters to when he was in Israel, the news of which had so upset Phoebe.

'Maybe I could ask you to do that,' Quirke said. 'I'm useless on long-distance calls.'

He knew he must sound like Hackett, getting others to do what he didn't want to do himself.

'I'll phone her this afternoon, from the hospital.'

He drove away at speed, leaving a trail of exhaust smoke that to Quirke's eye seemed a gesture of derision. He recalled the body of Rosa Jacobs on the dissecting table, the chest agape.

11

There was a message waiting for him at the reception desk in the hotel. A person by the name of Molloy had telephoned and asked to speak to him. He knew no one by that name, not that he could think of. Was it a call from Dublin? he asked. No, a local call. He shrugged, and said that if the person called again, he would be in the bar.

He would not have dinner in the hotel, not after his experience with the ham sandwich earlier. He would sit down again with a drink, look through the newspaper, and get the early evening train back to Dublin. He sat at the bar and ordered a whiskey. There was a different barman now, younger, with a thin face and greasy black curls. He was talkative, but his Cork accent was so thick that Quirke had a hard time understanding him. Football, again.

'Are you down for the match?'

No, he wasn't down for the match. Pointedly, he opened his copy of the *Evening Herald*, and the young man went back moodily to polishing glasses.

There wasn't much in the paper he hadn't read on the train coming down – the majority of the stories seemed to be about either horses or priests – and in desperation he turned to the memorials page. This was always good for a few lugubrious but unfeeling laughs.

O mother dear, you went so quick, / We did not know you were so sick.
Dear baby Jesus, meek and mild, / Look after our Jack he was only a child.

The receptionist appeared at his elbow. She was a plump girl
with an affectingly timid manner.

'Sorry, Doctor Quirke,' she said, 'that person is on the
phone for you again.'

He followed her out to the desk, where the receiver lay on
its side at the end of its cord like a landed fish, its mouthpiece
open.

Quirke picked it up. He was surprised to hear a woman's
voice.

'Hello. It's me. I've tracked you down at last.'

Molly Jacobs.

He turned away from the desk, not wanting the receptionist
to see a middle-aged man blushing.

Ten minutes later she arrived in person, coming in at the front
door of the hotel, hurried and flushed, on a gust of the air of
outdoors. She was smiling. He had to make an adjustment to
the image he had of her in his head. Was it because she had
done something to her hair, had got it curled? No, that wasn't
it. Was it the smile, then, the warmth in it?

Quirke looked at her and at the floor. Tracked down,
indeed. How had she found him?

'I hope I'm not too much of a shock,' she said. 'I called
four hotels before I got the right one.' She had rung up the
Holy Family hospital, and had been told he was in Cork, and
would not be back at work until the next day. 'And since I was
in Cork too, I thought, well—'

She faltered, her smile fading into uncertainty.

'I'm glad to see you,' Quirke said awkwardly.

They were both at a loss. It was exciting, in a childish sort of way. Or not childish. *Christ!* he thought, *am I entering on my second adolescence?*

He returned with her to the empty bar and they sat on the stools and ordered gin and tonics. At first they could think of nothing to say, and Quirke felt slightly panicked. He told himself that if she mentioned the weather, he would put down his drink and leave. Maybe he should put down his drink and leave anyway. What was he getting himself into?

A start would have to be made somewhere.

'How have you been?' he asked, sounding wary.

'Not bad,' she said. 'The funeral was a nightmare, as you would imagine. I thought the rabbi would never stop with the platitudes.'

Quirke nodded. This was a let-down. He had thought a Jewish funeral would be an extravaganza of ritual and colour, with banks of candles, and ringletted cantors wailing and grief-stricken women rending their garments.

'Was there a wake?' he asked.

'Yes, if you could call it that. Plates of bread and kosher sausage and tiny glasses of thin wine. Not my father's fault – his sisters were in charge. Minnie and Marge. You can picture them, can't you?'

They sipped their drinks. The thin-faced barman watched them from his post below a big mirror that leaned out over him at what seemed a perilous angle. Quirke produced his cigarette case and lighter.

'Was that your stomach rumbling?' Molly asked.

'Sorry. Haven't had anything to eat.'

'Why not?'

'I tried a ham sandwich.'

'Ah.' She smiled with lips compressed. 'We could have dinner here.'

Quirke shook his head.

'The sandwich, it wasn't – how will I say? – it wasn't encouraging.'

'Right.' She thought for a moment. 'I don't really know Cork any more. I suppose there must be some decent restaurants.'

She looked in the barman's direction.

'I wouldn't bother, if I were you,' Quirke murmured.

'Right,' she said again.

Under the fawn-coloured raincoat she was wearing her blue silk suit with the tight jacket and tighter skirt. Her hair had undergone a radical change. It clustered around her face in shell-shaped curls, and each curl had on its rim its own reflected gleam of light. Her eyes were her most arresting feature, large dark shining pools into which, he thought, a man might sink beyond rescue. Her looks were old-fashioned, in a way that appealed to him. She reminded him, he realised, of Evelyn, a little. Should he be shocked by this? He didn't know. She had none of Evelyn's deliberate and endearing plainness. On the contrary, there was about her something of the rounded, creamy opulence of one of those grand Parisian hostesses of la belle époque.

'We've got to feed that stomach of yours,' she said, after another muffled drum roll had issued from Quirke's innards.

'But what to do? You could' – she hesitated, biting her lower lip – 'you could come home with me and I'll make something for you.'

'Home?'

'My father lives over the shop. That's where I'm staying.'

'Ah.'

'Don't worry, poor Papli is lost in himself. He has a room at the back where he spends all his time, going through old photographs and things. I'm worried about him. Rosa's death has hit him so hard.'

He nodded, frowning. Had she imagined it wouldn't? What could be more terrible than the death of a daughter. He thought of Phoebe. What would he do if—? He didn't finish the question.

'It's very kind of you, but I don't want to impose,' he said.

'You won't. But I warn you' – she laughed – 'I'm a lousy cook, so be prepared. In fact, I may as well tell you, I can't cook.'

'It doesn't matter.'

'Mind you, I can do bacon and eggs. Would that do?'

'With sausages?'

'With sausages. And what about tomatoes, on the pan?'

'Tomatoes, yes. Fried bread?'

'Fried bread, of course. And' – she smacked the edge of the bar with the fingers of both hands – 'Clonakilty black pudding, into the bargain! You are in Cork, after all.'

That was a fact of which, by now, there could be no doubt.

They finished their drinks and went out to the lobby, and Quirke asked the receptionist to call a taxi.

'It will be here in a minute,' she said.

While they waited, they sat in two armchairs on either side of a low mahogany table on which stood a bowl of blowsy saffron-yellow autumn roses.

'A Cork minute can be quite long,' Molly remarked.

Quirke looked at the roses. It seemed to him he had never really noticed roses, before this moment.

He and Molly exchanged complicit smiles. They were embarking on an adventure. They felt childish, and didn't care. It was like mitching from school, Quirke thought. He had mitched only once, from St Aidan's, to meet a girl. One Saturday afternoon he skipped sports and climbed over a fence beyond the dense stand of pines behind the playing pitch and walked along the back road to the arranged meeting place, his heart joggling in its cage.

What was the girl's name? Concepta? Jacinta? She was from the town, and had a bad reputation already, at the age of fifteen. How had he met her? He couldn't remember. They went into town on the bus and had coffee in the lounge at the Hunter's Arms Hotel.

The girl had bought, or pinched, a packet of Player's. Quirke was reluctant, but when she lit up, he had to join her. The waitress came over and asked them what age they were. They said they were eighteen. She didn't believe them, but gave them an arch smile and went away. It was the middle of the afternoon and they were the only ones in the lounge.

On the way back they stopped at a bus shelter and sat on the bench and kissed, and fumbled in each other's clothes.

Assumpta?

She had thin little hands that made him think of a bat, but

her mouth was hot against his, and he could feel her heart beating fast, as fast as his own.

It turned out he had not been missed by the Brother who taught sports, and no one reported him. How grown-up he had felt, with the girl's taste and the taste of cigarette smoke still in his mouth. He never saw her again, Concepta or Jacinta or Assumpta, but he had never forgotten her.

'A penny for them?' Molly said.

'What?'

'You were miles away.' She didn't seem to mind. 'What were you thinking about?'

'Nothing.'

The taxi arrived. Molly was right, it had been a long minute. They climbed into the back seat. The driver was elderly and enormous, too large by far for the little car. He sat hunched over the wheel like an ancient moose, the butt of a cigarette clinging to his moist lower lip.

'Jacobs's Drapery,' Molly said to the driver – she didn't need to give the address – then settled back beside Quirke.

For a moment it seemed she might take his hand. It would have seemed perfectly right, even though as yet they had not touched each other. *The first touch is never easy*, Quirke reflected.

He could see the outline of her legs under her skirt. There was the bulge of a suspender clip. Light shimmered on the taut silk.

They arrived shortly in Patrick Street. Molly got out of the taxi and walked across the wide pavement, while Quirke was fiddling with change. The taxi man looked after her, in her high heels and seamed stockings, with her helmet of lustrous curls, then looked up at Quirke and winked, drooping a crocodile's leathery lid, and leered.

The shop was impressive in its dimensions, occupying nearly half a block. Mannequins stood posed in the windows, showing off the latest styles in frocks and women's hats. There was a men's department, too, Molly said, and in a wood-panelled room at the back a bespoke tailor would run up a suit for you in a day or two.

'He's from Poland, the tailor,' she said. 'Came here after the war.'

She produced a key, and they entered through a narrow doorway to the right of the shop. There was a short hallway and then a carpeted staircase.

'Did Rosa ever speak to you about the Kesslers?' Quirke said.

'You asked me that before.'

'Did I? Sorry.'

They started up the stairs, Molly going first.

'You seem very interested in them,' she said over her shoulder. 'Is there something sinister going on?'

'Sinister? I don't think so. I don't know. I think your sister might have been involved with the younger Kessler, the one they call Frank. Did she ever mention him, Frank Kessler?'

'Not that I remember. But as I told you last time, Rosa and I didn't talk about our – our romances.' She laughed briefly. 'I'm not sure Rosa went in for romance at all. Too busy handing out pamphlets and demanding rights to every-thing for all.'

Quirke caught again the impatient edge in her tone.

They reached the landing, where they paused.

'I'm sorry,' Quirke said, 'I shouldn't be pestering you with questions about her.'

'You're not pestering me. Only I really didn't know much about Rosa, or what she got up to in her private life. She was the younger daughter, and the apple of her father's eye.'

Quirke smiled.

'And you were the black sheep.'

'I was the black sheep. Still am. Baa.'

The apartment extended over two floors and was the same broad width and the same depth as the shop below. Heavy old furniture, things made of brass, framed sepia photographs, the relics of a past, of a lost world.

'I know,' Molly said, looking around her, though Quirke had made no remark, 'it gives me the creeps too.'

Her father's room, the one in which he had shut himself away, was on the next floor up, at the back. They would not be heard, nor, Molly said, would they see him. He had become a recluse. She hoped it would pass, that he would reconcile himself eventually to Rosa's death, but evidently she considered it a faint hope.

She led the way to the kitchen. It was clear from the comfortable look of the room, and from the homely atmosphere, that this was where the real life of the house was lived, or used to be lived. There was a high dresser with plates and jugs and cups, a big black gas stove, a scarred pine table.

'Sit down,' she said, 'while I go and change.'

He sat by the table and drummed his fingers on the wood. He wanted to smoke but felt he should wait until she came back. He was nervous, but of what, he wasn't sure. Or was it nervousness? Anticipation, more like? But what was there for

175

him to anticipate, sitting here in a kitchen smelling of domestic gas and ever so slightly of drains? *Oh, come on, Quirke,* he told himself, *don't pretend you don't know.*

Molly came back, wearing a white blouse and a tartan skirt and flat shoes. She took down an apron from a hook on the back of the door.

'Now you can watch me doing my *Hausfrau* act,' she said.

He took out his cigarette case and asked if he might smoke. For answer, she set a tin ashtray on the table by his elbow.

'Tell me about your work,' he said.

Oh, God. It was the kind of thing people say to each other on a first date. But wasn't this a first date?

He could hardly credit the things that were crowding at the borders of his mind. *Dearest Evelyn, forgive me!* he prayed fervently. In his heart he didn't doubt that she would forgive him now, as she had forgiven him so many times, for so many things, in the past. How keenly he missed her, even here, especially here, in this kitchen, with the elaborately coiffed Princesse de Polignac or the Comtesse de Noailles, changed now into her sensible skirt and shoes.

She had opened the door of the fridge and was peering at the shelves.

'To be honest, my "work", as you call it, is boring. Maybe I need a change. I used to think Fleet Street the most glamorous place in the world.'

'Not any more?'

'Not any more.'

'Would you come back here?'

She stared at him, wide-eyed, over her shoulder.

'To Cork?'

176

'Ireland, I meant. You could work in Dublin. I know people on the newspapers. They'd jump at the chance of hiring someone from Fleet Street. England is still the great mother, though we pretend otherwise.'

'Oh, yes,' she said, 'I've had offers.' She laughed. 'Of a job, that is. There's a chap at the *Irish Times* I know quite well. He comes to London, on some mysterious business or other, and takes me to lunch at the Savoy, no less. You can't beat the Prods for style.'

Quirke thought of Detective Inspector St John Strafford, and frowned.

'The *Times* is a good paper,' he said, 'even if a bit stuffy.'

She turned and stood looking down at him. He caught a waft of her perfume. She must have put it on when she was changing. Violets, was it? It seemed the kind of smell violets would have. There were faint half-moons of greyish-mauve shadow under her eyes. Those eyes, the shining depths of them.

She turned back to the fridge, took out some packages and put them on a wooden worktop beside the stove.

'Here we are,' she said, 'sausages as promised, rashers, black pudding. As you see' – again she glanced back at him provocatively – 'we don't keep kosher in this house.'

She took down a frying pan blackened from use and set it on the stove. She couldn't find matches, and he rose and struck a flame from his lighter and put it to the gas jet. The gas lit up with a soft *whoosh*.

They stood side by side, closer together than they had been even in the taxi.

'Why don't you take off your jacket?' Molly said. 'I've seen a man in shirtsleeves before now, you know.'

Or what is that white flower they sell on the streets in Paris? Lily-of-the-valley? One evening, on the rue Pigalle – ah, one evening on the rue Pigalle. He put the memory out of his head.

'Go and sit down,' Molly said. 'You're making me nervous, hovering there.'

He returned to the table. The thought of Paris had sparked another memory, not of the rue Pigalle, but of one of those ludicrously ornate railway stations, the Gare d'Orsay, was it?

He had stopped even before he saw the girl, the girl in the sheer white summer dress. It was as if he had somehow known she was about to appear.

She was coming out of the station, walking from deep shadow into blazing light, carrying a small suitcase. She had dark hair and enormous dark eyes, eyes like Molly's. There must have been a breeze, or perhaps it was just an effect of her rapid stride, that plastered the lightweight stuff of her dress against her, showing the outline of her figure, down to the shallow, cone-shaped dip of her navel.

She saw him staring, and smiled at him as only, he thought, a French girl could, amused and challenging, and perhaps in a little way inviting too. Nothing happened. He didn't accost her, didn't even try to speak to her. He just stood there, on the wide pavement, watching her walk towards him, with her chin lowered and her eyes lifted, still smiling.

It was the briefest of encounters – it couldn't even be called an encounter, really – yet he had never forgotten her, the girl with the suitcase, and he saw her now in memory as plainly as he had seen her walking past him, with that smile.

'You've drifted off again,' Molly said. She was tossing

178

sausages into the sizzling pan. 'You must have an awful lot on your mind.'

'I was just thinking of something that happened long ago in Paris.'

'Oo, gay Paree, is it?' The sally fell flat, and she made a face. 'Sorry. I say the stupidest things, just blurt them out.'

She sliced three tomatoes and placed the halves face down on the pan, which seethed briefly, spitting droplets of fat. She directed Quirke to fetch plates and knives and forks from the dresser. He set two places opposite each other.

'You're house-trained, I see,' she said. 'That's always a good thing, in a man.'

'I'm living at my daughter's flat. She has a civilising influence.'

'Bullies you, does she? Show me your plate here.' He brought both plates to the stove. 'I should have heated them,' she said. 'It'll all go cold.'

'We can eat quickly.'

'You must be starving.'

Just like a couple, already. He saw Evelyn's face, saw her soft, wry smile.

Molly took off her apron and they sat down to eat.

'Oh, Christ,' she exclaimed, 'we've nothing to drink. Tea – will you have tea?'

'Let's just eat the food.'

'I'm sure there's a bottle of wine somewhere.'

'Eat.'

They ate.

Elsewhere in the house, a telephone began to ring.

'Ignore it,' Molly said. 'It can only be for Papli, he'll answer it if he feels like it.'

The ringing continued. Whoever was calling was determined to be answered. Quirke felt a tremor of unease at this insistent, jangling sound from the outside world. It was as if someone were shaking him, to wake him from a dream. The rich, fatty food seemed gross, suddenly.

'Tell me about your wife,' Molly said, 'about what happened to her. Do you mind?'

'No, I don't mind. I don't think I do. No one ever asked me before.'

'I told you, I'm famous for my want of tact.'

'No, no, it's not – you're not being tactless. It's just – I don't know. People don't ask me outright, like that.'

'I'm sorry—' she began.

'No, no, don't be. I mean, it's a relief to be asked – that you've asked.' He put down his knife and fork and shook his head. 'I'm sorry,' he said, 'you gave me too much food.'

'Yes, I gave myself too much as well. I'll see if I can find that wine.'

She rose from the table and went out of the room. Left alone, he felt the resentment of inanimate things not his own, the stove, the crockery on the dresser, that pan, still faintly smoking after its labours. His lips were greasy; he wiped them with his handkerchief.

I should leave now, he told himself, leave before something happens and it's too late.

He took out his cigarette case. There were two versions of him sitting there, the one urging himself to be gone and the one who had no intention of going.

'It's Spanish, I'm afraid,' Molly said, coming in at the door with the bottle of red wine in her hand. 'Rioja. That name always sounds to me like someone retching.' She set the bottle in front of him on the table. 'You can be the sommelier. There's a corkscrew in the right-hand drawer there.'

He opened the wine. The foil around the neck of the bottle gave him a tiny cut on the tip of his index finger, and a bead of blood welled up. Always a surprise to him, blood, even after all his years in the dissecting room. The dead don't bleed much, that was one of the things he discovered when he first studied pathology.

Molly fetched two glasses, and he poured wine into each of them. *Hic est enim corpus meum.* He had been an altar boy, once. How the old hocus-pocus clings on.

'*L'chaim!*' Molly said, with a sardonic twist of the lips. 'That's "cheers!"'

He smiled, not knowing how to reply. Somehow, she kept managing to wrong-foot him. He didn't mind. More: he liked it.

'My wife was killed, in Spain,' he said. 'She was murdered. It was all a mix-up. We were in San Sebastián, she and I. Her name was Evelyn, did I say that? One night at an outdoor café in the town, I recognised a girl – a young woman, I should say. Everyone thought she had been done away with by her brother, years before. Turned out her family had bundled her off to Spain and told her not to come back under pain of – I don't know what.'

He tapped his cigarette on the edge of the ashtray. The wine had a woody flavour, and was both rich and bitter on his palate. The cut in his fingertip had left a tiny smear of blood on the side of his glass. Blood and wine.

'What had she done, that the family got rid of her?'

'It's too long a story. We'd be here all night.'

He glanced at her quickly, feeling his forehead redden. It was a long time since he had felt this clumsy in the presence of a woman.

'What was her name?'

'Latimer,' he said. 'April Latimer. Her uncle sent a fellow down to Spain to kill her.'

'To *kill* her?'

Quirke nodded.

'A bad business. He was a politician, a family scandal would have destroyed him. He was destroyed anyway, in the end. They never learn, people like him.'

Molly's elbows were on the table and she was leaning forward with the wine glass cupped in both hands before her like a chalice. He looked at her hands and something contracted inside him.

'But your wife,' she said, 'how did she come to—?'

'It was a mess-up. She just strayed into the line of fire.'

'And what happened? What happened to the fellow who shot her?'

'He was shot, too. I asked for a detective to be sent down, an Irish detective. He tried to save the girl, the young woman – April – and he did, he did save her. But Evelyn died.'

In the silence, they heard a hissing sound. Molly had left a gas jet burning. She rose now and turned it off, and sat down again.

'I'm sorry. I don't know what to say.'

'There's nothing to be said. Things happen. The world runs on blind chance, Evelyn would have been the first to tell you that.'

'But you must feel – you must be devastated.'

'Yes, I suppose I am.'

'How long ago did it happen?'

'Six months, more. But it's strange, you know, I don't think of her as dead, not dead dead. I carry her inside me, like one of those corpses of saints you see in Spanish churches, miraculously preserved.'

Molly put down her wine. She looked distressed, not just for him.

'I can't think how you would survive such a thing,' she said, in a kind of wonderment.

'I'm not sure I have survived. I'm certainly not what I was, before. For the past six months I've lived with one foot in the world of the living and the other in the world of the dead. It makes for a ghastly equilibrium. I think if one side weakens, I'll fall over. I don't think I'd mind, much. There are times when I think I'd rather be dead and have done with it. Evelyn wouldn't like to hear me say it, but it's true.'

There was silence above them; it was like a high, dark dome.

'But it will get better, won't it?' Molly said. 'Time the healer, and so on.'

'Yes, that's what people tell me. I suppose it will get less awful. But when, I'd like to know.'

After another passage of silence between them, Molly rose and put on her apron again and began to clear the table. Quirke offered to help but she said it was all right, that she would do it.

'Finish your wine.'

He watched her at the sink. She had a shapely back, long and – what was the word? – sinuous. He had a weakness for women's backs. How alive she was, how vividly here. The land of the dead. No coming back from there.

'You must know something of what it feels like,' he said.

She ran the tap, and did not turn.

'Because of Rosa, you mean? I've told you, Rosa and I hardly knew each other. The little we did know we didn't much like. She thought I was heartless and cold, that I had rejected the family by going to London and selling my soul cheap to cheap journalism. Maybe she was right. I didn't stay as closely in touch with Papli as I should have, these past years. And the *Express* is hardly a crusading paper. Seen from those perspectives, I suppose you could say – she'd certainly say – that she got me just about right.' He said nothing, and she looked back at him over her left shoulder, smiling. 'What do you think?'

'I'm sure she was wrong.'

She had stacked both their plates on the draining board, and now she turned from the sink and began to dry the cutlery with a tea towel. He looked at her profile and tried to read her expression.

'I couldn't be as she was,' she said quietly, as if to herself. 'I suppose I'm essentially frivolous. I love the world too much to be always complaining about it.' She took off the apron, put it back on the hook, and turned to him with her hands on her hips. 'Well, Doctor Quirke, what now?'

He had to search for a reply. He recalled the taxi driver winking at him with that knowing, saurian eye.

'We could go out for a drink, perhaps?' he said.

'Back at the hotel?'

He saw the disappointment in her face, and the uncertainty.

She too was wondering if it was all a mistake, her calling him, coming to the hotel, bringing him here. She was being 'forward', as her mother would say.

'No, we could go to – to a pub.' He heard himself stammering and felt all the more a fool. He should make some excuse and leave. But he didn't, and wouldn't. 'It's early still,' he said.

She leaned back against the sink and gazed at him with candid eyes. Yes, he could see her thinking which she should do, go along with his polite pretences or ask him to go.

The moment teetered.

'The pubs here are so dreary,' she said. 'Besides, most of them won't allow women in.'

She had passed the decision back to him, had dropped it in his lap like some large, shapeless, unhandy thing.

'Well then, maybe we should go back to the hotel,' he said, and added quickly: 'To the bar there, I mean.'

She chuckled.

'Do I frighten you, doc?'

The distant telephone rang again.

'Yes,' Quirke said, making himself smile, 'you do, a little.'

She crossed to where he was sitting and leaned down and kissed him lightly on the lips. The phone stopped ringing. Had her father answered it?

'Dear heart,' she said softly, drawing her head back a little way, 'how like you this?'

It was a quotation; he had to think for a moment to identify it. Wyatt. Sir Thomas Wyatt. *In thin array after a pleasant guise, When her – When she –* but no, he couldn't recall enough of the lines. Something about *her arms long and small*. Oh, what was it?

He rose to his feet, and she stepped closer and put her arms around him, and he put his around her, and so they stood. The strangeness of being other and then suddenly not.

'What are we doing?' he asked.

'Who knows?' she answered.

He looked aside.

'Your father—' He left it unfinished. 'I should go.'

'Yes, you should. But I wish, I really wish you wouldn't.'

Through the window, he could see a slice of sky between two tall buildings. Mare's tails high up, and a single star glimmering. Venus, it must be, he thought, first star of the evening. Yes, Venus.

It was a little room way up at the top of the building, wedged under the eaves. It would have been a maid's room originally, Quirke thought. He could stand fully upright only in the middle of the floor, since the ceiling sloped steeply on either side. Opposite the door, in the end wall, a single, small square window looked across starlit rooftops all the way over to the quays, where a short stretch of river was visible. At first, the September twilight had suffused the room with a dusty glow, rose and gold, then gradually gave way to dusk.

Molly twined her fingers in his. He had told her she had beautiful hands, and she had held them up before her and examined them sceptically. 'Really? Standard issue, I'd have said.' And he had thought: for all we know, the silver swan may think itself the ugliest creature in creation.

The bed was narrow and low. He thought of all the girls who had lain alone here nights out of number, dreaming of love and escape. Another scrap of the Wyatt poem came to him: *I have seen them gentle, tame, and meek.*

He felt the weight of his ageing flesh, and the weight of years. He must not weep, above all he must not weep. And if he were to, whom would it be he was weeping for, his lost wife, or himself?

I have seen them gentle—

He lay on his side and she pressed her body against his and he felt her breath on the side of his neck. He walked a fingertip up the ladder of her spine. She turned over onto her back and trembled, and shuddered.

'O God,' she softly cried, 'O God, O God.'

At one point he went still suddenly and put a hand to her mouth. He thought he had heard a sound, a step, a creaking stair. All old houses do that, she told him, whispering.

What was the word, he asked himself, the one in the poem? *Newfangleness.* Yes. Words were different, then.

He tried to summon Evelyn's face and couldn't. She was out of focus, her image twitching and flickering as if it were reflected in a mirror in a storm. He told himself he was betraying her, but it was a formula, stale words conjured up to save the conventions. He didn't want to lose Evelyn, any more than she was lost to him already. It seemed to him he had never felt more the need of her than now. Yet here was this new woman, shaking in his arms and crying out.

And now they were lying quietly on their sides again, face to face, breast to breast, their feet entangled. He laid a hand against her cheek. He thought he could feel the blood seething in her veins.

'That thing you whispered in my ear,' he said, 'was that Hebrew? Yiddish?'

She sat up, bumping her head against the angle of the ceiling.

'I don't know Hebrew, much less Yiddish. What an idea! Non-Jews think every Jew is a Jew. But look at me. What am I? Look at these arms, look at these nipples – look at this belly button. Do they seem Jewish to you?'

'I'm sorry,' he said, laughing a little, 'I didn't mean to offend you.'

'I'm not offended. Why would I be offended? I'm just saying. Enough with the Hebrew and the Yiddish already.'

He drew her down into his arms.

'I can't remember the last time I laughed,' he said.

She got up from the bed and put on her skirt and a jumper she had found somewhere.

'What are you doing?'

'Shh!' She put a finger to her lips, then touched it to his. 'Shh, my dear.'

She went out and closed the door softly behind her. He got onto his knees and looked out of the window at the night and stars. The air chilled him. He recalled more of the poem, a longer section:

> . . . *once in special,*
> *In thin array after a pleasant guise,*
> *When her loose gown from her shoulders did fall*
> *And she me caught in her arms long and small;*
> *Therewithall sweetly did me kiss*
> *And softly said, 'Dear heart, how like you this?'*

Molly came back, with two glasses and what was left of the wine. They sat cross-legged on the front edge of the bed, facing each other under the slope of the ceiling. They tapped their glasses together, and drank.

'Christ, it's awful stuff, isn't it?' Molly said, with a grimace. 'Papli refuses to buy decent wine.'

Quirke took the toes of her right foot in his left hand and bent them gently back. She moved her leg, and a soft grey shadow fell all the way along the inside of her thigh.

'I was thinking when you went out,' Quirke said, 'that I could stay on, for a few days.'

'In Cork?' She gave a snuffly laugh. 'To wallow in the fleshpots?'

What was it David Sinclair had said, about the delights of the city on the Lee?

'That fellow I mentioned, the one I used to work with who went to Israel. He's here now, he has come back home. If I were to stay, I could see him, say hello, take him for a drink.'

Was it a lie to pretend he hadn't met Sinclair yet? A small deception.

'Oh, sure,' Molly said with heavy sarcasm, 'a lads' get-together, after all these years.' She put on a heavy Cork accent. '"Weren't them the days, boyo, and the nights, too?" Honestly, what kind of an eejit do you think I am? You've no more wish to see your old pals here than I have.'

'Well, I wouldn't—'

He was still holding on to her toes, and now she seized his wrist and shook it.

'Stop pretending to be stupid,' she said. 'What we'll do is, I'll come up to Dublin.'

'How?'

'How? On the train, of course.'

'No, I meant – what about your job?'

'I have holidays owing.'

'But' – he was frowning, looking towards the window again – 'where will you stay?' he enquired faintly.

'Oh, that's easy,' she said, giving her head a toss. 'I'll move in with you and your daughter.' He turned his stupefied eyes to hers. She gave a whoop of laughter and put a hand over her mouth. 'Your face!' she cried. Then she leaned forward and kissed him on the tip of his nose. 'The fleshpots of Cork will come to you, doctor dear. Or one of them, anyway.'

In the morning, he caught the first train to Dublin. There were only half a dozen passengers, all sleepy-eyed, all uncomfortable and cross. He had to turn to the window to hide the inane smile he couldn't suppress. He felt more of a fool than ever. But it didn't matter. When he arrived at Phoebe's flat he felt drunk, but not on wine.

In the hall, he took off his coat and hat and hung them up.

What a feat of memory it had been to remember that Wyatt poem. *They flee from me.* Evelyn had flown, beyond recall. *And she also, to use newfangleness.*

On the hall table there was a small pale green envelope, addressed to him. It was a telegram. His heart thumped. Always bad news, telegrams. He got a finger under the flap and tore it open.

SHULAMITH LIEBERMAN DEAD STOP HIT AND RUN INCIDENT TEL AVIV STOP DRIVER NOT TRACED STOP SINCLAIR

BAVARIA

the last of days

12

He walked across the compound, not hurrying. It was midnight. Beyond the barbed-wire fencing, the sky in the west was ablaze. He could hear the sound of the guns. How much nearer were they since morning?

Strange, how calm he felt. It was not the calm of bravery. In the past days he had discovered that he was not brave, not brave at all. Something inside him had lain down, like an exhausted animal. If they captured him, he would be put in front of a firing squad, or hanged. Better to die by his own hand. Yes, but he didn't want to die.

In his office he switched on the desk lamp, which shed a pallid downward glow. He looked about. His bookcase, his filing cabinet, the high table with the gramophone standing on it, the stack of records in a box on the floor underneath. He took his Luger pistol from its holster high on his right hip and set it on the metal desktop. Otherwise, the desk was bare. He had destroyed everything, armful after armful of documents, into the flames. For some moments, he stood gazing at the weapon. Then he picked it up. That way would be quick. Probably he wouldn't even hear the shot, before everything stopped.

He laid down the gun again and turned away. He didn't have the courage for it. Maybe the point would come when his fear of the firing squad or the noose would be such that he would overcome his terror and put the barrel into his mouth and pull the trigger.

The sound of the artillery was like the rumbling of distant laughter, mocking him.

So tired, too, so tired.

He thought of his wife, of their boy. If he could pray he would pray for them, for their safety, for them not to fear, not to suffer. But who would hear his prayers? The Führer in the sky was gone. Not that he had ever been there. Only the notion of him.

The Franciscan had sent a message, telling him to come. The bishop, over there, had been in touch, offering shelter, a safe haven.

His heart quailed at the thought of the journey ahead of him, back into the mountains of his childhood. What times they were, in the little wooden house, the *Hütte*, on the high lake. In those days, he wasn't afraid of the darkness of the forest; now he was. If they caught him up there, among the pines, they would shoot him on the spot, or string him up from a branch. He had heard how the July plotters died. Piano wire. He shivered.

At least he had his papers. He hoped the Jew had done a convincing forgery. The poor fool thought his life would be spared if he put extra care into the job. When it was done, he had shot him. The look of surprise on the fellow's face!

The bedroom was cold. It had been a cold spring, so far. Many were still dying of it, of the cold. They had no strength to resist it. There was no food either, not for them. Let the invaders feed them, that would keep them busy for a while.

He sat down on the bed and took off his boots, then stood

up again and unbuttoned his uniform. Should he burn it, as he had burnt the files? But it would be difficult, would take a long time. Cloth wasn't as flammable as paper. Anyway, what did it matter if they found it?

In the end, he left the uniform where he had dropped it on the floor. He put on a heavy woollen vest and a pair of woollen long johns. The winds were punishing up there, on the mountain tracks. He hoped he would not have to venture beyond the treeline. He mustn't take his army greatcoat, it would be instantly recognised. Only the loden jacket, the twill trousers, the hiking boots, the old felt hat with the feather in the band that Hilde had given him for a gift one Christmas long ago. He held it in his hands, turning the brim in his fingers.

There was no one left, except him and the ones who hadn't died yet, from hunger and the cold. The others, the officers, the guards, they had all run away. This morning, Stauffel, his second in command, had gone, driving off in a staff car piled high with rations. *Feiger Hund!* There had been no way to stop him. Let them catch him. Maybe they'd put him hanging upside down by the ankles, like the Italian bastard.

Listen! What was that? Someone had come into the office. Who could it be, prowling about at this hour? He reached for his gun and then remembered he had left it on the desk. Could the interloper be a scout sent ahead by the invaders? What if he saw the gun? What if he picked it up?

He was still wondering what to do when he did it, on animal instinct – pulled open the door and stepped boldly into the office.

It was one of the kapos. A tall, gaunt fellow with furtive eyes and a scar on his cheek. He wore a threadbare overcoat that reached to the floor, and a peaked skullcap too small even for his narrow head. He had no boots, had lost them long ago, or had them stolen. Filthy rags were wound around his feet.

'What are you doing here?' the man demanded.

They both glanced at the Luger. The kapo was nearest to the desk. Would he dare to make a grab for it? Unlikely – they were all cowards, every one of them. But still. The man tried to remember if he had left the safety catch on.

'I'm sorry, Herr Kommandant,' the kapo said in a hoarse voice. 'I thought you had gone, along with the rest.'

'You did, did you? What were you going to do – move into my quarters?'

'I thought there might be food.'

For all the fellow's stooping and cowering, there was a touch of insolence in his bearing. Some of the kapos were like that, swaggering about and shouting orders at the prisoners, lording it over them. That was the Jew for you, the man thought: grant him a grain of power and he'll tyrannise even his own people.

'There is no food here.'

'There's no food anywhere.'

The man gave a harsh laugh.

'You people were always greedy,' he said, 'now see where it has got you.'

For a moment, it seemed the kapo might laugh.

He looked somehow familiar. The man would have seen him about the camp, but why should he remember him? There was a weaselly glint in those little dark eyes of his.

For a moment they stood irresolute, the man with his head back and nostrils flared, the kapo with his shoulders hunched, his hands clasped at his chest. Doing the Shylock act. *If you prick me, do I not bleed?*

Then, to the equal astonishment of both of them, he heard himself inviting the fellow to sit down.

Boom thud boom! went the far-off but ever-nearing guns.

There was a straight-backed chair by the wall. The kapo crossed to it and sat down, drawing the overcoat closely around his knees. He too was cold. The scar on his face was an old one. It had been badly sewn, and looked as if it had been painted on. *If you prick me—*

The man walked to the desk, picked up the gun and put it in the holster at his waist and buttoned the flap, then went round the desk and sat down. The noise of the guns was a presence in the room, but one they would conspire together in ignoring.

'Where are you from?' the man asked.

His tone made it clear he didn't care in the least where he was from. Doubtless some steamy city slum in the east, or a tumbledown village in the wastes of the steppes.

'Berlin. I'm from Berlin.' Yes, he had a Berliner accent. 'And you, Herr Kommandant?'

The man stared at him. Either he was a simpleton, or he had nerve. But answer him – why not? Everything was coming to an end, now the cat could laugh at the king.

'Munich.'

'Ah, yes, I thought you were a southerner.'

Indeed, before it was over, an army of cats would get their claws into the king's throat. In the man's mind, the mountains awaiting him seemed a little less high. And there would be no cats up there.

He opened a deep drawer on the right side of the desk and brought out a bottle of schnapps and two small glasses. The kapo stared at these things as if he didn't know what they were.

'Let us have a drink together, my friend, at the gates of the inferno.'

My friend!

He poured a measure into each of the glasses and pushed one to the edge of the desk. The man hesitated, obviously thinking it was all some cruel trick. The man pointed at the glass with his chin – 'Come, take it' – and the Jew stood up and shuffled forward in his foot-rags. He paused a moment, looking into the man's eyes, trying to read what lay hidden there. Then he returned to the chair and sat down again, balancing the glass on his knee.

'*Prost!*' the man said.

They drank. The Jew went immediately into a fit of coughing, a hand clutching at his breast. When would he last have tasted alcohol? He was a long-term inmate, he had the look of it about him. Something in the stance, in the glint of the eye. A survivor, like the rats that swarmed about the floors in the huts, under the bare planks of the beds.

At last the fellow's coughing ceased, and he sat leaning forward, fighting for breath and making a sound like that of a donkey braying. The man drank off what was in his glass and refilled it.

'Come,' he said, 'drink up. The barbarians will soon be here.'

The kapo sipped from his glass cautiously, and this time did not choke.

'This is good,' he murmured, crooned, almost, wistfully.

He took off his cap. There was a bald spot on the crown of his head, neat and round, like a tonsure. He scratched his head vigorously. Lice, the man thought sardonically: they cleave to their own.

'You weren't really looking for food, were you,' he said.

The kapo considered. He took another sip of schnapps.

'I thought there might be money.'

'Money? What would you need money for, here?'

'Not here.' He looked the man in the face with a spark of defiance. Yes, a long-termer, hardened by the years. 'I'm leaving, like the rest.'

'Wise man. Your people here will tear you to pieces, those with any strength left, if you stay.' He paused. 'Where will you go?'

'East.'

'Into the path of the Mongol hordes.'

'Odessa. I have people there. Had. I'll find shelter.'

'I admire your optimism.'

Now they went silent, listening to the guns.

The man thought again of his wife and his son. The farmer, Ullmann, he wouldn't betray them, surely? He was an ox, but not without cunning. He would know where his best interests lay. He had been paid well and had been promised more. Thank God for greed.

Franz would be frightened. The man loved his son but knew him for a weakling. He had tried to toughen him up but nothing had worked, not lectures, not mockery, not beatings, even. The creature was more like a girl than a boy. And yet, he was his child, and he must treasure him, since no one else would. The world is heartless. Not only in this place does cruelty rule over all. *Bellum omnium contra omnes.* It was not a German who said that, but an Englishman. He was right. The war of all against all, the eternal struggle.

'Why?' the kapo said.

Startled, the man stared at him. The bare patch on the fellow's head was grey, the colour of a louse.

'Why what?'

The kapo made a sweeping gesture with his left hand.

'All this – this death machine.'

The man was silent for a moment, then he threw back his head and laughed.

'You have to ask?' he said, wiping tears of merriment from the corners of his eyes. 'Don't play the innocent with me. You people are so proud of your cleverness, and pretend to be stupid to cover your pride. You stabbed us in the back when we were already sorely wounded. Did you think the day of reckoning would never come?'

The Jew had bowed his head and was shaking it slowly from side to side.

'Herr Kommandant,' he said, again in that soft, curiously wistful tone, 'perhaps you will not believe me when I tell you that from the start I admired you. Yes yes, despite myself, despite everything, I thought you were at the least an intelligent man. Now I wonder.'

The man's face tightened, and his lips formed a thin, pale line. He touched the holster on his hip.

'You take many risks, Jewman.'

The kapo leaned back on the chair and lifted the little glass to his lips and tilted it to get the last drop of liquor. He rose to his feet and shambled forward, and put the glass down on a corner of the desk.

'More,' he said. 'Please.'

The man looked up at him for some seconds, then laughed again, but quietly this time, shaking his head. He refilled both glasses. The kapo took his and sat down again.

'You're leaving too?' he said, indicating the man's loden coat, the hat on the desk. 'Where will you go?'

'South.'

'It's arranged?'

The man did not reply. In the window the moon had appeared, a heavy disc with a decayed profile stamped on it. How everything goes on, uncaring.

'You think we'll get away,' he asked, 'before the Americans come?'

'I don't know. There's always a chance.'

Yes, the man thought, for vermin like you, but what about me? I wasn't made to scurry across no man's land with my belly to the ground, to dodge and slither and run along the sewers. I was part of the greatest human project since the Roman Empire. Am I to relinquish everything I ever believed in and flee for my life? The Jew is accustomed to skulking in a hole, I am not.

Yet he felt the weight of the pistol like a hand tugging at his belt. It was urging him to be gone, not out into the night but into that other, final darkness, courtesy of *mein Freund Herr Georg Luger*. It was that, or the piano wire.

But he must not think like this, he told himself. He must not give in. Even if it were to be all up with him, there was Hilde and the boy to be considered. How would they survive if he surrendered? He shivered again, and poured another glass of schnapps. Getting drunk would decide nothing, but he didn't care.

'What will you do,' he asked, 'when you get to Odessa? Will you stay?'

'No. I'll go south, like you.'

'To where?'

'Palestine. Unlike you.'

The man chuckled.

'The Promised Land.'

'Yes. The Promised Land.'

He gestured with the schnapps bottle and the Jew came forward again, sliding along on his rags. He gave off a vile smell. The man poured the drink, for them both.

'You believe in God?' he asked, when the Jew had gone back to his chair. 'You believe in Yahweh?'

'I believe in the land,' the kapo said, impassively.

'Oh ho!' the man crowed, 'the Wandering Jew pledges himself to *Blut und Boden*! That's good, very good. Even though you and all the rest of you haven't an ell of land on which to set your stinking foot.'

'We'll get land. We'll take it. You'll see.'

The man was about to reply with another jibe but instead sat back on his chair and looked at the ragged, lice-infested creature slumped there, and frowned. It will happen, he thought, it will happen as he says. The victors will give them land, out of the goodness of their hearts, supposedly. Their real aim will be to get rid of them. We were going to settle them on Madagascar, island of spices. That was before we understood that no one would lift a finger, much

202

less a weapon, to save them. We could do with them as we wished. Then that fearless genius came up with the most daring solution ever conceived, the final one.

Ashes, now. Ashes everywhere.

'And how will you pay for these grand travels you have planned?' the man asked. 'No money here' – he spread his open hands above the desk – 'and none anywhere, for you.'

'You think not?'

'I think not! That's one thing the forces set against us have granted us. We were right to take back what you stole from us by stealth. We will not permit the people with the dagger in their hands to fill their money bags as they have done for two millennia. We won't be that foolish.'

Now it was the kapo's turn to chuckle.

'My "friend",' he said, putting an ironic emphasis on the word, 'you may not be as intelligent as I thought you were, but surely you're not such a blockhead as to imagine things will change, afterwards. All will revert, and be as it always was. That was the mistake you made, imagining your messiah had come to transform and save you, to lead you in triumph into Valhalla.' He paused, and softened his voice again. 'Listen to the guns, a little nearer by the moment, Herr Kommandant.' Now he let his voice sink to a whisper. '*Götterdämmerung.*'

It should have ended there. The man should have drawn his pistol and put down this insolent pig, but he didn't. Instead, he rose and crossed to the high table on which the gramophone stood. It was a fine machine, the best money could buy. Electric-powered, with a diamond stylus. And such a faithful and clear reproduction! The players might be here in the room.

He picked up a record and unsheathed it.

'Ah, Mendelssohn!' he said, and glanced mockingly at the Jew. 'Just for you. The Octet for Strings.'

He put the record on the turntable and lowered the playing arm. The music swarmed out of the machine, busy and bright.

'Listen,' the man said, lifting a finger. 'The very voice of the Jew, clever, hysterical and terrified. You like it?'

'I prefer Schubert.'

'Ha!'

When the piece ended, the man let the record keep on spinning, the stylus clicking in the empty groove.

They went on drinking the schnapps until the bottle was empty and they were both drunk.

Again, the man challenged the kapo to say how he would get to Palestine. He was genuinely interested to know. One had to give it to the Jews for ingenuity.

'You will have to hand out bribes every step of the way. Have you money?'

The kapo said he had gold in Odessa. It was hidden between the rafters of his Uncle Moishe's house on the seafront in the Suvorovsky District. Poor Uncle Moishe, his mother's brother, he didn't know there was treasure stored under his roof.

'I know it's there still,' the kapo said, with a cunning little grin. 'Bags of it.'

'How did you come by it? You look like a peddler to me. Peddlers don't amass a store of gold.'

'I was not a peddler. My mother's people owned property in the city. Apartment buildings, shops, private houses. When she died, I sold it all and converted the proceeds into bullion.'

It was ironic, the man thought. He too had gold. It wasn't

hidden under some Jewman's roof, though. It was safely resting in a Swiss bank vault. How had he come by it? Another coincidence: from property. His houses and apartments weren't inherited. They had been liberated from the rich Jewish families of Kráków, when he was governor there.

Should he feel guilty? The things he took amounted to a fraction of what that flabby drug addict in his braided white uniform pillaged from the city, and from every other captured city and town across Europe.

The record on the gramophone was still spinning. Clickada clickada clickada clickada. It was a soothing little sound.

He stood up, unbuttoning the holster and taking out the Luger. The Jew sensed danger and woke with a start. He gazed up blearily at the man with the gun.

'Don't.'

The man shook his head.

'I can't let you go free. It's my duty. I took a pledge to carry out this terrible work, here in this place.'

'Did you really think you could kill us all?'

'No, I see that now. The bacillus will survive, despite our efforts to cleanse the world of it.'

The pistol was pointing at the Jew's chest. It was strange: he seemed not to be afraid. Seconds went past. The lamp on the desk dimmed, the light of the bulb flickered, seemed about to die, made a crackling sound and brightened again. Was someone tending the generators, even yet? What a race, the Germans!

'When I said I thought you intelligent, I meant that I saw you weren't a true believer,' he said. 'That you had a doubt – a bacillus of doubt, if you like, working away inside you, and not to be exterminated.' The far-off guns boomed, the moon grinned in the window, the lamplight cast itself downwards into shadow. 'You won't kill me. You haven't the stomach for it any more. I can see it in your eyes. You've grown weary of death.'

The man could feel his eyes turning glassy. He should not have drunk the schnapps. There was a pounding in his head to match the pounding over there in the west, beyond the Ampe. His finger on the trigger was slippery with sweat. How did this *Untermensch* imagine he had the right to make such pronouncements? Yet it was true, what he said. Death had wearied him, had worn him out.

What would happen? How would this end? He had the power to end it, he held that power in his hand. But he knew it wouldn't be the end. The end had happened and yet was still to come. He didn't understand what he meant, but it sounded like the truth.

'What is your name?' he said. 'Tell me your name.'

'Katz. Theodore Katz. I'm called Teddy.'

'Teddy Katz – I will remember it,' the man said. His voice was hollow, and his eyes were haggard. 'I will remember this night. Who knows? Our paths may cross again, one day.'

From somewhere among the huts there came a scream, long drawn-out and fading to a whimper. The two paid it no heed. Then there was silence again, the silence of the vast night.

'I knew your name, Herr Kommandant,' said Teddy Katz. 'You didn't know mine.'

The man lowered the gun. Teddy Katz nodded once, and stood up slowly from the chair, turned, and shuffled out of the room. The man put the gun on the desk and began slowly, almost absent-mindedly, to weep.

DUBLIN

there and then

13

Strafford was in his office, laboriously scaling a mountain of paperwork. He knew he shouldn't have let it build up to this height. It was the part of his job he most disliked. He hadn't become a detective in order to deal with endless reports of petty crimes, complaints from the public, and notifications of outbreaks of rabies and foot-and-mouth disease. But what had he expected? It could not all be guarding princesses and gunning down assassins. He laughed joylessly.

In fact, 'office' was too large a word for the cramped space Chief Inspector Hackett had allotted him. He felt like a dog in a kennel. He was next door to the Chief's room, and through the partition wall he could clearly hear the old boy's mysterious scufflings, his loud yawns and frequent belches, and worse.

He put down his fountain pen, leaned back in his creaky chair and looked to the window. Slate roofs, chimney pots, a wedge of sky that even on sunny days seemed somehow overcast and out of sorts.

It was the middle of a slow and sleepy Tuesday afternoon. The telephone hadn't rung once since before lunch, and when it rang now it made him jump.

There was someone downstairs asking to see him.

'Who is it?'

The desk sergeant put a hand over the mouthpiece, and he heard his muffled voice asking the caller for his name.

'A Mr Kessler, sir.'

He stared out again at the chimney pots. Why would Wolfgang Kessler come all the way up from Wicklow to talk to him?

'Right. Tell him I'll be down in a moment.'

Well, it would get him away from these blasted files for a while.

The man stood in front of the noticeboard with one hand in the pocket of his suit jacket and a cigarette in the other. It was not Wolfgang Kessler. This person was in his early thirties, tall and fair, with high cheekbones and a sharp jawline. Something on the board had amused him, and he was smiling with his head thrown back and his lips compressed. This must be Kessler's son. Strafford could see the resemblance.

He lifted the hinged flap of the counter and went through. The young man turned. His eyes were a remarkably pale shade of blue, so pale they seemed transparent. A lock of fair hair fell across his forehead, and he pushed it back with a quick flick of his fingers.

'Frank Kessler,' he said, coming forward with a hand outstretched. His English had the faintest German burr – no disguising those swallowed 'r's. 'You spoke to my father.'

'Ah, yes. Mr Kessler. I thought you were in Israel.'

'I was. I came back. I heard the news about Rosa. Can it be true?'

'Can what be true?'

'That she was – that someone killed her. This is what my father says.'

'Yes, I'm afraid it is true.'

'My God.' He looked to the side, his brows downdrawn, his eyes fixed on the horror of the thing. 'I can't believe it.'

Strafford had no intention of inviting the young man to climb to his shabby lair on the second floor. He suggested they go for a coffee, to the Hibernian Hotel, which was close by. Frank Kessler shrugged and said that would be fine.

They went out into the drowsily sunlit afternoon. Despite a couple of storms, the season hadn't asserted itself fully yet, summer seeming unwilling to take its leave. The tawny bricks of the Ballast Office glowed, and the gulls wheeling above the river seemed whiter than white.

The two men walked along together in a surprisingly easy silence. For Strafford, this was a novelty. It was not usual for him to be relaxed with people, certainly not on a first encounter. A passer-by would have taken them for relatives – Kessler might be Strafford's younger brother.

In the hotel, the air was heavy with the lingering odours of lunch. The lounge was almost empty. A portly gentleman with silver hair and a waxed moustache, the ends of which were twirled into points, sat in an armchair by a window, discreetly dozing. At a small table by the fireplace, two elderly ladies in flowery frocks were taking afternoon tea. They glanced up at Strafford and smiled demurely, taking in his suit and tie and shoes and recognising one of their own. Why didn't they give Kessler the same smile? His clothes were as good as Strafford's, his demeanour just as reserved. They must have a sharper eye for a foreigner than he had, Strafford thought.

'That table in the corner,' he said, nodding towards it. 'Shall we take that?'

They ordered coffee, and were asked if they would like a plate of cakes as well. Strafford shook his head. From where he sat, he could see out to the lobby. Each time the glass-panelled front door opened, it flashed at him a reflected glimpse of people and traffic moving along Dawson Street.

He turned to Kessler.

'So,' he said, 'you came back because of Rosa Jacobs?'

The younger man gave him a quick, sidelong glance. It was as if he had detected a note of scepticism, even of challenge, in Strafford's tone.

'Yes, I did. When my father telephoned me and told me the awful news, it seemed the thing I must do. I booked a flight immediately.'

'The funeral was held last week.'

'I know. I doubt I would have attended it anyway.'

'Oh?'

Kessler again turned his eyes away.

'It would have seemed a little – a little inappropriate, I think, to the family.'

'Which family?'

Kessler only smiled and shrugged.

The waitress brought their coffee in a silver pot. She set it before them on the table, along with a sugar bowl, a jug of cream, two linen napkins. The dozing gentleman awoke with a start, and blinked, and glanced about the room sheepishly.

'I'm sure Rosa's people would have appreciated the gesture.'

Again, Kessler glanced at him. It wasn't the Jacobses he was thinking of now, that was apparent. He seemed puzzled.

Perhaps he was too polite to say what so many others said, that Strafford was not at all what anyone would have expected an Irish detective to be. The accent was wrong, the tweeds, the watch chain, the oxblood brogues. Well, Strafford reflected, at an essential level they were both, Kessler and himself, outsiders.

They sipped their coffee.

'Let's not pretend, Mr Strafford,' Kessler said, dabbing a napkin daintily to each corner of his mouth. 'I am German. Rosa Jacobs was a Jew. Her family are Jews. And the war was not so long ago.'

'From what I hear of Rosa, she didn't care much about that kind of thing.'

'About the war?' Kessler said, surprised.

'No, I meant – prejudice, and so on.'

The fair-haired young man smiled slowly.

'Ah, but everyone is prejudiced, even if only a little. Don't you think? You must find this yourself.'

The two ladies by the fireplace were giggling about something, pressing fingertips to their mouths, their eyes darting. The silvery gent rose from his chair and made his way creakingly to the door and went out to the lobby. Strafford watched him go. Someone was coming into the hotel, and the panel of light in the glass door flashed its secret signal. It was unsettling, the way the reflection slid like water over the closing door and vanished.

'What happened to Miss Jacobs?' Kessler asked. 'How did she die?'

'Didn't your father tell you?'

'He was vague. What was he sparing me? Was it ugly, her death?'

'I don't know that death is ever pretty.'

'I meant, was it violent. Father only said her body was found in a garage. Why was she in such a place?'

Strafford was wondering why Wolfgang Kessler should have chosen not to tell his son the manner of Rosa Jacobs's death. Was it tact, or squeamishness? Kessler senior had not seemed the faint-hearted type. What, then?

'She was drugged, then put in her car in the lock-up garage, with a hose from the exhaust pipe running in through the window. She died of gas poisoning.'

Kessler was watching him with unblinking attention.

'I take it the identity of the killer is not known.'

'That's right. I have to confess to you, we have no leads at all.' Here was the moment, he judged, to give this determinedly poised young man a bit of a shake. 'In Israel, did you ever come across a young woman called Shulamith Lieberman?'

Kessler stared.

'I don't think so,' he said, with a quizzical frown. 'Who is she?'

'A journalist, on one of the big papers over there. What's it called? Begins with an aitch, and there's an apostrophe.'

'*Ha'aretz?*'

'That's it.'

Kessler waited.

'She's dead,' Strafford said. 'She was killed a couple of days ago by a hit-and-run driver, on a street in Tel Aviv.'

'I'm sorry to hear it. But I still don't see—?'

'She knew Rosa Jacobs. At least, they used to be in correspondence – I'm not sure that they ever met.'

'I see,' Kessler said, toying absently with his empty coffee cup. 'And you think there might be a connection between this person's death – what did you say her name was?'

'Shulamith – Shula – Lieberman.'

'What did she write about? Did she have a speciality?'

'The army, national defence, weaponry, that kind of thing.'

Kessler lifted his eyes to the window and the day outside.

'I may have read something by her. I don't know.'

'You read Hebrew?'

'Why, no, of course not!—' He stopped, and even coloured a little, knowing he had spoken too quickly. 'They publish some articles in English, I think.'

The old fellow with the waxed moustache returned, carrying a copy of the *Irish Times*. He sat down in the armchair and opened the paper, tugging it sharply at both sides so that it made a loud cracking sound. The ladies by the fireplace turned their heads and stared their disapproval.

'You can't remember Rosa ever mentioning her?' Strafford asked.

'No, I can't.' He sat forward a little on his chair and folded his hands before him on the table. 'Listen, detective, I should tell you that I wasn't close to Rosa – to Miss Jacobs.'

'No?'

'No. I mean' – he clasped his fingers together and touched his thumbs together at the tips – 'I knew her, yes. I used to see her around Trinity, when I was there, and then, afterwards, we knew people in common. But she and I, we were not friends.'

'I see,' Strafford said slowly, and ran the tip of his tongue along his lower lip. 'I got that wrong, then.'

'Why, did you think we were—?'

'There was some suggestion that you and she had been –
well, I don't know. She visited your home in Wicklow?'

'Yes, she did, a couple of times, two or three. She was fond
of horses, so she said. I'm not sure that it was true.'

'Why would she lie?'

The young man opened his hands and smiled again.

'She had met my father somewhere, I don't know – at the
RDS Show, perhaps. I think he took – how do you say? –
I think he took something of a shine to her. She may have
reminded him of my mother, who was known for her strong
opinions. And heaven knows' – he laughed again – 'Rosa
Jacobs was a headstrong young woman.'

Strafford picked up on this.

'Headstrong? Do I take it you weren't impressed by her
campaigning spirit?'

This time Kessler laughed outright.

'Her campaigning spirit?' He glanced up at the ceiling
and down again. 'Perhaps, where Miss Jacobs is concerned,
a better word would be wrong-headed. She was full of crazy
ideas, and would listen to no one who tried to talk sense to
her.'

'Did you try to talk sense to her?'

For the first time, Kessler's look became evasive.

'She would have paid no attention. When she got her hold
on to something, nothing would make her let go.'

Strafford allowed some seconds to pass, then quietly asked:

'You and she were not in any way romantically involved,
then?'

'"Romantically involved"?' Kessler stared incredulously.
'Where can you have got such an idea?'

216

'Her sister mentioned something to – to a colleague of mine.'

'The sister, she's – what's her name?'

'Molly. Molly Jacobs.'

'I've never even met the woman. What is she saying about me?'

Now it was Strafford who turned evasive.

'I'm not sure she said anything directly. It was more of a suggestion – no, not even that. A hint.'

Kessler snorted dismissively.

'A hint!' He looked at his hands, where he had clasped them again above the table, and shook his head slowly. 'Why cannot women keep their mouths shut. They must be all the time gossiping and making insinuations. It's too bad. As I told you, I used to see Miss Jacobs about in college, and I met her on one of her visits to the farm, twice at the most.'

'So it was your father who invited her.'

'Yes, of course. I told you – it was he who first met her. Or—'

'Or?'

Kessler looked down at his hands again. 'You must understand, Mr Strafford, my father has a great feeling towards the – towards Miss Jacobs's people, and towards Israel. He feels the great weight of Germany's past, her recent past. He wishes to – atone, in any way that is possible. Miss Jacobs understood that. So my father says, so he believes.'

Strafford watched him as he was saying these things. His tone wasn't right. He sounded as if he were repeating something that had been said to him many times, so that he knew it off by heart.

The waitress came and collected the cups, the jug, the sugar bowl. She asked if there was anything else they required. Kessler consulted his watch.

'I must go,' he said.

He was impatient suddenly, as if he were being unreasonably detained. Strafford was tempted to remind him that no one had summoned him to the Garda station, that he had come of his own volition, and unannounced.

Both rose from their chairs. Strafford was about to brush the hair away from his forehead, but Kessler did it first, to his own drooping lock. Strafford covered up by adjusting the knot of his tie.

They walked across the room, between the tables. The ladies by the fireplace looked up, and one of them, whose eyes were clouded by cataracts, smiled again at Strafford, almost coquettishly, while ignoring Kessler. The man with the moustache glared at them over his newspaper.

As they were passing through the doorway into the lobby, Strafford felt Kessler's shoulder touch his own briefly, and at once he recalled the evening in Dun Laoghaire, years before, when he had been pickpocketed.

He had been on his way to London, and had jumped out of a taxi and was hurrying to catch the mail boat, which had sounded its siren to announce its imminent departure.

It was raining, or misting, rather, and the drops of moisture had deposited a frost-like mantle on the collar and the shoulders of his black serge overcoat.

On the dockside, a noisy band of schoolgirls was advancing towards him, coming back from a holiday abroad. The dock was narrow, and he had no choice but to make his way through them, rather than stepping around them. He was in their midst when someone shouted something behind him, and at that moment he experienced a strange, hardly palpable sensation, a sort of frisson, that rippled quickly down his right side. It was a touch so light, so fleeting, that he thought he must have imagined it. After a few paces, however, something, a subconscious alert, made him reach for his wallet. The wallet was gone. He had dropped it into his overcoat pocket after paying the taxi fare, and now it wasn't there.

On the instant he saw in his mind the schoolgirls, and heard the strange, distracting cry behind him, and felt again that tiny, almost voluptuous shiver along the side of his ribcage.

The loss of his wallet was a great annoyance, of course – he did not get to London that night, and would not for some nights thereafter – yet he couldn't but acknowledge the pickpocket's adroitness and finesse. His touch had been as light as a lover's, lighter. Or perhaps it was not a he. Perhaps it was one of the schoolgirls who had slid a hand into his pocket. That, he supposed, would account for the erotic tremor. But no, it wouldn't. The tremor hadn't been erotic, but something else. As if a melancholy angel had brushed him with its wing.

Now the two men returned in silence to Pearse Street. Outside the Garda station they said their awkward farewells. Kessler's car was parked at the kerb. It was a gleaming, navy-blue model of foreign make, German, or Italian, maybe. Kessler saw Strafford eyeing the low-slung, sleek machine, and had the grace to look self-conscious for a moment. But Strafford's attention had been drawn to it only because it was the kind of car his otherwise unostentatious wife had always longed for. No doubt that was one of the reasons for her having left him. A detective inspector's salary wouldn't begin to stretch to a fancy motor like that one.

Kessler opened the door – he hadn't bothered to lock it – and inserted himself into the bucket seat.

'You will let me know of any developments on Rosa's death, yes?' he said, still with the door open and looking up at Strafford.

'Oh, I'll let you know,' Strafford said, amusing himself by investing the words with deliberate and slightly menacing irony.

The car roared, and Kessler steered it deftly out in front of an oncoming bus. Strafford watched it as it turned into Nassau Street.

14

Quirke's gut was in turmoil. He had lunched modestly in the back room of Neary's on a cheese sandwich and half a pint of Smithwick's ale. That could hardly have been the cause of his nausea. He must have caught a bug. He was rarely sick. At the start of the summer he had come down with what felt like flu, though he suspected it was just another side effect of having lost his wife, and it didn't last long.

Just.

At first, after Evelyn died, there had been only bad days, and worse nights. By now the general gloom had lifted a little, and there were even moments when a weak, watery sun broke through. Then he would stop, like a traveller on a mountain pass, and turn and look back through a break in the mist at the lost land he had come from. It had been a hard climb, and the long path ahead of him was steep.

He was trying not to think of Molly Jacobs, but his thoughts insisted on returning to her. She had left Cork and come up to Dublin, as she said she would. She was staying in a ramshackle little house on one of the narrow streets behind Usher's Quay. The owner was a friend of hers, named Maunsley, an academic who was spending a semester as a visiting professor at Boston College. Quirke judged it wisest not to enquire what kind of friend the professor was, or had been. Molly had a past, that much was clear.

The previous night, he had gone for a drink with her at the Brazen Head. He hadn't drunk much, three or four whiskeys and a couple of small bottles of barley wine. Molly had taken only a single gin and tonic, which she nursed until the ice cubes had all melted and the slice of lemon lay grinning crookedly at the bottom of the glass.

At closing time, she had brought him back to Professor Maunsley's gingerbread house. There, they had made love, not very successfully, in the living room downstairs, on the professor's lumpy sofa. Maybe the bug had already taken up residence in Quirke's gut, and had bided its time before getting to work on him in earnest. If so, he could blame it for his clumsy efforts on the sofa. Afterwards, he had apologised, and Molly had said it was all right.

She was a forgiving soul, was Molly.

What did he expect from her, and what did he think she might expect from him? He had no idea. He didn't care. He wouldn't go so far as to say he was happy, but the mountain mist had parted again, and if what he glimpsed wasn't the sunlit future, it wasn't the wintry past either.

He let himself into the house with the door key Phoebe had lent him.

There was always a curious smell in the hall here. It was partly the smell of vanilla from the shop downstairs, but there was something else as well. It brought him back to remembered schoolrooms, the crevices in the bare wood floors clogged with ancient dust, the tall windows that rattled and seemed always streaked with rain. That was St Aidan's, where he had been sent after he was taken out of the orphanage. Of the orphanage he wished to remember nothing, though he did.

As he mounted the stairs, he thought he heard the faint sound of voices above him. Outside the door of the flat he hesitated, listening intently. Yes, a man's voice, and Phoebe's.

In the time he had been staying here at the flat, he had never known his daughter to entertain a visitor. This he found worrying, a little, though he never had the nerve to mention it. She was solitary, but didn't seem lonely. She had once pointed out to him, with a marked sharpness, the difference between the two conditions.

They went out to dinner together once a week, and sometimes to the pictures. What she did with herself on other nights he didn't know. She seemed not to have many friends, if she had any at all. She used to be friendly with Isabel Galloway, but that had ended when the affair between Quirke and Isabel had limped to a close.

Anyway, what business had he to pry into his daughter's life?

He crunched a key into the lock. He had always found it a problem to go in at a door. Always there seemed to be a hindrance on the threshold, as if something had come forward at a rush from within and wrapped itself around his ankles. His childhood had been mostly a state of unhousedness – he was a snail without a shell. Now, once more, since Evelyn's death, he felt himself nowhere at home.

His insides gave another heave. Molly Jacobs had commented on his rumbling gut. Maybe he had an ulcer. He squeezed the set of keys in his fist, their jagged edges cutting into his palm.

At the kitchen table, under the big window, Phoebe was sitting with, of all people, Detective Inspector St John Strafford. They both turned to look at him as he entered.

'Oh, hello,' Phoebe said. 'You're back early.'

There was no rebuke in her words. All the same, he was daunted. Surprises always had a bad effect on him. He baulked at things when they swerved out of their accustomed way.

'Feeling a bit off,' he said. He felt shy of both of them. 'Thought I'd have an early night.'

Phoebe stood up from the table.

'Would you like something to eat? Can I get you a drink?'

'No, thank you.' He made himself turn to Strafford and meet his annoyingly imperturbable gaze. 'What's Hackett want now?' he asked.

'Hackett?' Strafford said, flexing an eyebrow.

'I assume you're here on "official business"?'

'No,' Phoebe said quickly. 'He came for tea.'

For a moment, Quirke couldn't grasp what she meant. Was she talking about Hackett – surely not – or Strafford? Both possibilities seemed equally unlikely. *He came for tea?*

Phoebe was wearing a black skirt, a white blouse and a dark blue cardigan. She had done something to her hair – he thought of Molly Jacobs and her casque of polished curls – and she was wearing lipstick, which she rarely did. A prospect was trying to present itself to him, but his mind refused it. He felt ridiculous, suddenly, standing there in the kitchen doorway, clutching a pair of keys in his fist.

He went into the living room, taking off his overcoat. Phoebe followed him.

'Are you sick?' she asked.

'I just feel a bit wobbly, that's all,' he said. He wouldn't look at her. 'It will pass.'

'Let me pour you a glass of whiskey.'

She turned towards the sideboard where the bottle stood.

'No, no, I don't want anything. Thanks. I think I'll just—'

His bowels contracted again. He sat down in an armchair by the fireplace. The gas fire was burning. He held out his hands to it – all at once he was cold – and the keys fell into the grate. Phoebe picked them up and gave them back to him.

'You're white as a sheet,' she said.

He caught her by the wrist and drew her towards him.

'What's he doing here?' he demanded in a hoarse whisper.

'I told you,' she whispered in reply, 'I invited him for tea.'

'Christ.'

'Why? Don't you like him? He's very like you, you know.'

In the end, she cajoled him into joining her and Strafford at the table. He was reminded of the Mad Hatter's tea party. He wasn't sure which one he was, the Hatter, the Dormouse or the White Rabbit.

When had Phoebe ever before asked somebody to come round for tea? And why tea, anyway? Wouldn't it have been more natural to ask him in for a drink? He supposed she thought tea would be the thing to offer to Strafford the Prod.

She served it at the big round table in the dining room. She had put out place mats, and her best tea set and her antique silver cutlery, given to her by her step-grandmother, Rose Griffin. Strafford regarded the elaborate spread with a complacent eye. Quirke wanted to punch him in the face.

It was grotesque, the whole thing. He should have gone to the pub, and to hell with his heaving stomach.

He knew he was being childish. This was Phoebe's flat, she had a perfect right to invite whomever she wished to come and drink tea with her and nibble these dainty sandwiches, the little cakes, the scones with raspberry jam. But did it have to be Strafford?

Yet why was he so angry? In his heart, he knew the reason and wished he didn't. It was simple, and awful. He was jealous, jealous of Strafford's easy presence in his daughter's flat. Suddenly, the possibility that he might lose her, might lose his daughter, his only child, was starkly real. And he would lose her, of course he would. Not today, not tomorrow perhaps, yet sooner or later. But please, let it not be Strafford!

When her mother died giving birth to her, he had handed the infant to his half-brother and his wife to raise as their own. For nineteen years – *nineteen years* – he had denied his own daughter. Now he had the gall to expect her to stay by him and look after him – to *love* him – for the rest of his life?

He was ashamed. Yet still he could happily have lashed out at Strafford. That watch chain across his belly – was there even a watch at the end of it? If so, Quirke had never seen him consult it. And then there was that wing-shaped lock of fine, almost colourless hair that kept flopping over his fore-head, and the stiff four-fingered gesture with which he pushed it back into place, only for it to fall down again five minutes later.

Phoebe was talking to her guest about some book she had read. Needless to say, Strafford had read it too, and even knew some scraps of gossip about the author.

Quirke excused himself and left the table.

He stood by the window in his room, clenching his fists in his pockets and swearing under his breath. Outside was the straggling back garden that no one tended any more. It was overgrown with briars and buddleia. Maybe that's what he should do, get himself a spade and a fork and go out there and tame the wilderness, so that his own raging spirit might be tamed too. He laughed a gallows laugh.

She couldn't be serious about that long streak of misery, could she?

Oh, but she could. She had fallen for worse, in her time.

'He's too bloody old for her!' he snarled at the innocent windowpanes, and immediately a small voice inside him said, *Yes, in the same way that you're too old for Molly Jacobs*. The thought of Molly brought on another bout of swearing.

Something slithered along his gut, sudden and quick as an uncoiling snake. Maybe he should just go to bed and leave the two of them out there discussing Graham Greene, or Henry Green, he couldn't remember which it was, and didn't care.

He went out to the lavatory and sat on the bowl. At once, a scalding stream of filth poured out of him. He shut his eyes and bowed his head and softly groaned, smelling his own foulness. This was justice. This was what he deserved.

When he was done, he cleaned himself and opened the window and put his face out into the cool air and took a long, deep breath. Then he went back to the dining room, adjusting his face as best he could, and sat down again in his place at the tea table.

'Are you all right?' Phoebe asked him. 'You look terrible.' She turned to Strafford. 'He was complaining earlier of being unwell.'

'I'm fine,' Quirke muttered, through gritted teeth.

How dare she talk about him like that, as if he weren't sitting there between the two of them.

Phoebe refilled Strafford's cup. She apologised, saying the tea was probably cold by now. Quirke lit a cigarette. His hand was shaking. Strafford watched him. Was that amusement in his eyes, amusement and contempt?

'Frank Kessler called into Pearse Street,' Strafford said.

'Oh?' Quirke tapped ash into his saucer, ignoring Phoebe's disapproving glance. 'I thought he was in Israel.'

'He was. He came back.'

'And what did he want?'

'Well, that's the funny thing,' Strafford said. 'I don't know.' He took a sip of tepid tea. 'He called in and asked to see me. I took him up to the Hibernian and bought him a cup of coffee. We were there for a good forty-five minutes but I was no wiser at the end than at the start as to what he was after.'

'Did he ask about Rosa Jacobs?' Quirke asked.

Talk was calming, he told himself, he must keep it going.

'That was strange too. I thought he and she had been – well, close. But according to him he only met her once or twice, and hardly knew her.'

'That's not what Sinclair said.'

'Sinclair?'

'He used to be my assistant, in the pathology lab. You remember him.'

'I've heard the name.'

'He went to Israel too, but he came back. He's working in Cork now, at the Bon Secours. I went down there and talked to him.'

Phoebe's knife clattered against the edge of her plate. Quirke looked at her. Christ! – how could he have been so clumsy. She hadn't known Sinclair was back.

Strafford touched the rim of his cup with a fingertip. His fingers were long and slim and pale, with pale-pink nails. Inbred, like all his kind, Quirke thought, silently venting his rage.

'Weren't he and Rosa Jacobs—' Strafford began, but stopped when Quirke frowned at him and gave his head a quick shake. Phoebe was making a show of concentrating on her plate. Strafford pressed on. 'Wasn't there something between them, too?'

'Where did you hear that?' Quirke asked.

'I don't know. Someone must have mentioned it – you, maybe?'

'I don't trade in gossip.'

Strafford regarded him quizzically.

'There's an ongoing investigation into a young woman's death. What you call gossip could be material to that investigation.'

Quirke thought something would surely burst inside his skull. He could feel a pulse drumming in his left temple. He rose blunderingly to his feet and went to the sideboard and splashed whiskey into a tumbler and brought it back to the table.

'Cheers,' he snarled, raising the glass in a vengeful toast.

There was a silence. They heard a car pass by in the street below, the tyres fizzing on the tarmac.

'Did you see anything of the other Jacobs woman, the sister, when you were in Cork?' Strafford asked.

Quirke did not reply. He was holding his glass up to the light, as if to admire the way the mellow evening light shone through the whiskey. An ugly little smile was notched at one corner of his mouth. Had the bastard heard something, some whisper about him and Molly Jacobs?

'Fine city, Cork,' he said. 'Along by the river there, the old Georgian houses. Noble. Pity about the Corkonians.'

Phoebe threw him a pleading look. She knew him in this mood. If he went on drinking, there would be trouble.

'And what's wrong with them?' Strafford asked, in his mildest manner.

Phoebe touched his ankle with the tip of her shoe. He didn't look at her. He was watching Quirke.

'I'll say this for them,' Quirke said, 'they're not as bad as the Kerrymen.' He looked slantwise at Strafford, still with that smile, his eyes narrowed. 'Tell me again where you're from?'

'Wexford.'

'That's right. Wexford.' He turned to Phoebe. 'You know what they're called, down there, in Wexford? They're called Yellowbellies. I suppose it's meant to suggest that they're cowardly. Though cowards are supposed to have a yellow streak down their backs, not on their bellies. Isn't that so?' Phoebe did not respond. She kept her eyes on her plate. 'Yellowbellies,' Quirke said again, musingly. 'A queer name. Someone must have known something, way back. Of course' – he sat sideways and threw an arm along the back of his chair – 'it was the Yellowbellies that brought in the English. Dermot MacMurrough was after someone's wife, and hired in Strongbow to back him up. That was where it all started—'

'Please!' Phoebe said suddenly, glaring at him. 'Please stop!'

Quirke drew back with feigned surprise.

'Stop what?'

'*Just stop.*'

Strafford put down his napkin and made to rise.

'I think I had better—' he began.

230

'Stay!' Phoebe commanded, lifting a hand. Then she turned back to Quirke, lowering her head and glaring at him from under her brows. 'Why are you being like this?' she asked, in a quiet, clear voice.

'I'm not being like anything!' he said, puffing out his cheeks in a sort of laugh. 'I'm just making teatime conversation with Mr Strafford here. We don't often have a chance to chat, you know. He's usually so busy, protecting the populace, shielding women and children, and that sort of thing.'

Strafford's pale brow had turned pink. He pushed his fingers through his hair. Phoebe laid a hand on his wrist.

'I'm sorry,' he said brusquely, 'I must go.'

He shook off Phoebe's hand and stood up.

'Oh, you're off, are you?' Quirke said, smiling up at him. 'The Yellowbellies make a strategic retreat.'

Strafford stood and looked at him with smiling disdain.

'Would you like to know the true origin of that nickname?' he asked. 'A Wexford man, Sir Caesar Colclough, was invited by King William the Third to bring a team to England to engage in a hurling match against a team of Cornishmen. To distinguish themselves from their opponents, the Wexford team tied yellows sashes around their midriffs. Hence the term, Yellowbelly.'

In the silence, they heard Quirke swallow.

'Thank you,' he said quietly, 'for enlightening me.'

'You're welcome,' Strafford responded. 'And they won, by the way – the Yellowbellies. They beat the Cornishmen into a cocked hat.'

He turned and touched a hand to Phoebe's shoulder.

'Lovely tea,' he said. 'Thanks.'

Phoebe stood up.

'I'll walk you down.'

She did not look at Quirke, but went with Strafford to the door and out.

Quirke sat, still with his arm on the back of the chair and a fist on the table, looking towards the window. He felt sick again.

Down at the front door, Strafford offered Phoebe his hand, but she laid her own hand against his chest and stood on tiptoe and kissed him lightly on the lips.

'I'm sorry,' she said. 'He's impossible, especially when he drinks.'

'It's all right. I understand. He's in mourning.'

She smiled, and bit her lip.

'Will I see you again?'

'Would you like to?'

There was no need for her to answer.

Strafford put on his hat. For some reason, it made him look impossibly young. He might have been an overgrown, gangling boy wearing his father's trilby on a dare. He was about to speak again when they heard the clatter of feet on the stairs and suddenly Quirke was there, his face flushed and his mouth working.

'Listen, Strafford, listen to me,' he said in a congested voice, 'you stay away from here, stay away from my daughter. You've done enough damage to my family—'

'Doctor Quirke,' Strafford said, holding up both hands, 'this is not the time for—'

Suddenly, Quirke launched himself at the younger man, his right fist drawn back. Phoebe darted forward, stopping him short.

'Don't do this,' she said, calm and commanding, and for a moment she seemed taller than her father. 'You're making a fool of yourself, and you'll regret it.'

He glared at her, his lips moving convulsively. She wondered for a moment if he was going to have a seizure. Then he turned away, as suddenly as he had appeared, and stumped away up the stairs.

Phoebe put a hand to Strafford's cheek. His face was ashen.

'Go now,' she said. 'I'll call you. We'll meet.'

He was looking after Quirke, who had reached the turn of the staircase, pulling himself along with both hands on the banister rail.

'He shouldn't have any more to drink.'

'He won't,' she said. 'I'll hide the bottle. Don't worry.'

'Will you be all right?'

'Of course. He'll calm down, and then he'll be mortified.'

He hesitated, then smiled, and tipped his hat to her and made a little bow.

'Do call me,' he said.

She watched him go, with his raincoat over his arm. He's married, you fool, she told herself. But it was only words, weightless words. She would see him again, and next time she would make sure her father was not there.

He was sitting on the window seat in the living room, weeping, his face in his hands and his shoulders heaving. He had snatched off his tie and thrown it on the floor. She went and stood close to him, and put a hand on his shoulder.

'Oh, Daddy,' she murmured.

15

When Tommy McEvoy phoned him, Hackett's heart sank. It was not that he disliked Tommy. They had been at school together, under the Holy Ghost Fathers. In those days Tommy was a champion footballer, though he had a reputation as a dirty player. If you got tripped up in the tunnel when the teams were going through, you'd look up from where you had fallen and there would be Tommy, trotting on with a big smile on his big red face. He always got away with it, and few of the fellows held a grudge against him. Probably it was because of that smile, his mask of good fellowship.

When Tommy went for the priesthood, no one was more surprised than Hackett. It was always the unlikely ones, of course, but Tommy was the unlikeliest of all. He certainly wasn't handsome – at seventeen he was already fat – but all the same the girls were mad for him. Hackett asked one of them, a redhead named Mary, or Marie, he could see her still, what was attractive about him. 'Because he makes me laugh,' she said, as if it were the most obvious thing in the world, and gave Hackett a pitying look.

But there it was, Tommy decided on the Church and celibacy. He made his announcement to Hackett one fine cold hard autumn afternoon. They were out on the lake in one of the school's clinker-built boats, and had stopped behind a little island to have a smoke. Hackett was shocked, and didn't know what to say. His first thought was, *I'm going to lose a friend.*

At the end of October, Tommy said his goodbyes and set off for the Irish College in Rome, with that big grin on his face and a contraband copy of *Ulysses* in his duffel bag.

Hackett had been fond of Tommy, but a bit wary of him too. Behind the smiles and the jokes there was in him something hard and inflexible. He was a bishop now – Bishop Tom, as the people called him, was one of the best known and most popular churchmen in the country – and the word was that he would be Ireland's next cardinal. Yes, a powerful man, a prince of the Church. And there lay the source of Hackett's foreboding. When you got a call out of the blue from Bishop McEvoy, you would do well to prepare yourself for some sort of trouble.

'I'll meet you for a jar over at the HQ,' Tommy said on the phone.

'The HQ?'

Tommy did one of his belly laughs.

'Wynn's Hotel – don't you know that's where the clergy congregate. On a Saturday night you'd think you were in the penguin house up at the zoo.'

A brief spell of fine weather had ended, and the evening was grey and blustery, with spills of rain that lashed against Hackett's face and made his cheeks sting.

They both arrived together at the steps of the hotel. Tommy had put on weight, and his face was ruddier than ever. He was short and keg-shaped, with a big, flattened nose and a babyish mouth. His heavy lips were always wet and shiny. He wore a tight overcoat and a tartan muffler, and a flat cap with a buttoned peak.

'By God,' he said, 'this is brass monkey weather, what?'

Hackett put out a hand, but Tommy ignored it and put his arms around his old friend and drew him into a bear hug. He smelled of expensive shaving lotion, but behind it there was that mysterious, faint mustiness exuded by all the clergy, even bishops.

They climbed the steps to the ornate doors of mahogany and bevelled glass and pushed their way through. A gush of warm air met them, laced with the lingering smell of generations of bacon-and-cabbage dinners.

The bar was crowded, and sure enough, at least half the customers were priests. A momentary hush fell when Bishop Tom entered, taking off his cap and running a hand over his skull. He was bald except for a fringe of pepper-and-salt curls that gave him the look of a medieval monk.

Hackett noted the almost imperceptible, reverential nods the clusters of priests at the bar and seated round the low tables directed at his friend. Tommy, of course, pretended not to notice these signals of esteem and awe. He liked to present himself as a simple countryman who by inexplicable and hidden mechanisms had been elevated to churchly eminence. Whereas in reality he had shinned up the greasy pole with relentless energy and skill.

'What'll you have, Tommy?' Hackett said.

He was leaning on the bar with a hand in the pocket of his shabby grey overcoat and his felt hat tilted to the back of his head. He might have been a middlingly prosperous cattle dealer relaxing at the close of a fair-day.

'I'll take a brandy and port,' Tommy said, tossing his cap onto the bar. 'It'll keep out the chill on this raw night.'

The barman was tall and thin, with a long neck and a prominent Adam's apple.

'Good evening, Your Grace,' he said, inclining his head solemnly.

'Howya, Mick,' Tommy said. 'The wife and family well, I hope? How many have you now – three, last count, as I recall.'

'There's another on the way,' Mick said, with an embarrassed smirk.

'Good man, good man,' Tommy exclaimed. 'Another welcome soul to swell the flock.'

He rubbed his fat little hands. They were like a baby's hands; they seemed to have been inserted into his chubby wrists and screwed only part way in. Hackett studied his performance with amusement and admiration. No one was more skilled than Tommy at making even the humblest of people imagine themselves among the elect, if only for the time they were in his company.

Mick the barman brought their drinks. Hackett had asked for a small Jameson with a glass of plain water on the side. While he was paying, Tommy leaned towards Mick and lowered his voice.

'Come here to me,' he murmured. 'Do you know the story of Louis Armstrong and his wife when they met the Pope? Louis was on a European tour, and in Rome, Pius the Twelfth received them in audience at the Vatican. The pair weren't long married, and His Holiness enquired if they had children yet. Louis put on his big grin, as usual' – Tommy mimicked the beaming trumpeter – 'and said, "Why, no, Your Reverence, but we sure are having a lot of fun trying."' He laughed, his big belly shaking. He went on, 'There was a shocked silence,

238

as you can imagine – scandalised expressions all round – until Pius, God bless him, suddenly gave a shout of laughter, and clapped Louis on the back and told him what a fine fellow he was.'

The barman smiled uncertainly, not sure that he got the point of the anecdote, and thinking that if he had, it was hardly an appropriate one for a bishop to be recounting. He was rescued from the awkward moment when he saw one of the priests at the other end of the bar signalling to him.

Hackett produced a packet of Gold Flake, proffered it to Tommy, and brought out his lighter.

'God bless,' Tommy said, lifting his glass.

'*Sláinte*,' Hackett responded.

They both drank, and drew on their cigarettes and blew identical cones of smoke ceilingwards.

Tommy was still a keen football follower. They discussed that summer's All-Ireland final between long-standing rivals Wexford and Tipperary. Hackett hadn't much interest in the sport, and had to improvise his side of the exchange. It was all right, though, for Tommy was happy to do the talking, as usual. He had always been fond of the sound of his own voice, even in their days at Rockwell College. He had worked up his Kerry accent too. He rolled the phrases plummily around his tongue, deftly dropping in the odd mild swear word.

Hackett began to think he could relax after all, and that this was what it seemed, a friendly meeting. And at that moment Tommy revealed the real reason for their being here.

He had ordered a second round of drinks, and was lighting one of his own fat cigarettes – an Egyptian brand, strong and darkly perfumed – when he mentioned, casual as you please, the visit Detective Inspector Strafford and Doctor Quirke had paid to Wolfgang Kessler at his house and stables in County Wicklow.

'Do you know him?' Hackett asked.

He was startled, and immediately on his guard. This was the last thing he had expected.

'I do indeed,' Tommy said, busying himself with cigarettes and matches. 'He's a great friend of the Church, you know. A great benefactor.'

'Is he, now,' Hackett murmured, rolling the tip of his cigarette on the edge of an ashtray that bore the legend *Guinness Is Good For You*. He would need to go cautiously here.

What had happened that day down in Wicklow? Strafford's report of the meeting with Kessler had not hinted at any dispute or bad feelings. Had Quirke said or done something to get Kessler's back up, and cause him to appeal to his friends in the Church? Quirke wasn't always the most tactful, especially if he had a hangover, or if, God forbid, he had taken drink.

'Apparently,' Tommy was saying, 'they went down to talk to him about that young one that died in the garage, what was she called?—'

'Rosa Jacobs.'

'That's right. Rosa Jacobs.' The port wine had stained Tommy's wet lips a glistening purple. 'A most unfortunate affair. Is it true there's a suggestion of foul play?'

'So Doctor Quirke says. He did a post-mortem.'

'Terrible, terrible,' Tommy said, and shook his head. 'Have you any idea who did it?'

Hackett thought of lying, of saying that a number of definite leads were being followed up. But before this conversation was over he might be required to tell far bigger lies, so he had better stick to the truth for now.

'No,' he said, 'there are no suspects. We can't even think of a motive.'

'Was she – was she in trouble?' Tommy asked.

By which he meant: was she pregnant?

'No, not in any kind of trouble, that we know of.'

The evening was turning into night, and the air in the bar was heavy with cigarette smoke and the smells of drink. A man came in escorting two women, and all heads turned. Women! In the bar in Wynn's Hotel! It was as if a meeting of a secret society, or a gang of conspirators, had been intruded upon.

'Wolfgang Kessler was acquainted with Rosa Jacobs,' Hackett said. 'So was his son.'

'That's right.' Tommy smiled, his eyes twinkling. 'But I'm sure a lot of other people were acquainted with her too. I hear she was a busy girl, forever holding meetings, and mounting protests.'

'Yes. She seems to have been a great one for causes.'

'Aye. Such as abortion, and free clinics for women. We know what the Archbishop's views are on people who advocate that kind of thing. Not that I agree with everything His Grace says or does.' Tommy was still smiling, but his tone had undergone a subtle shift. There was an edge to it now, an intentional edge. 'All the same, a girl's reputation is her most precious possession, and most easily lost. I've known ones like her. They march around the place, waving their banners, until they crash into the plate-glass wall they didn't know was there, and get their noses broken. And more than noses.'

Hackett made no response. Jokes about the Pope and Louis Armstrong were fine, he was thinking, but a Jewish woman preaching sexual freedom for the women of Catholic Ireland, that was no joke at all. Well, if his old friend Tommy McEvoy was going to come the heavy with him, he had no choice but to defend himself.

'Did Kessler complain to you about Strafford and Doctor Quirke?' he asked, looking straight into the bishop's eyes.

'Man dear!' Tommy almost shouted. 'What would he be complaining about? A young woman was murdered, a young woman who was known to have visited Wolfgang Kessler's farm, and to be acquainted with his son – why wouldn't the Guards pay him a visit? Only—'

He stopped, and took a sip of his brandy and port.

'Only?'

Tommy crossed one fat leg over the other and leaned closer to his friend.

'Only he was a bit puzzled by the whole thing. Why would a detective and a coroner—'

'Pathologist.'

'Sorry. A detective and a pathologist, why would they come down together to question him? You must admit, it's a bit irregular, to say the least.'

Hackett was fiddling with the Gold Flake packet. The Egyptian cigarette Tommy had given him had left a bad taste in his mouth – he had only finished it to be polite.

'And that poor girl's death was highly irregular too, wouldn't you say?'

'No doubt, no doubt. But why send your man down to put Wolfgang Kessler through the third degree? Surely to God you don't suspect him of doing away with the unfortunate girl?'

'Third degree!' Hackett said with a snort. 'If you weren't a man of the cloth, I'd say you'd been going to the pictures too often. We're gathering any scraps of information we can find. I have people over at Trinity College every day talking to people who knew Rosa Jacobs. Her death is a total mystery – no one has the foggiest notion why she was killed, or who it was that killed her.'

Tommy was looking into his glass and nodding slowly to himself, frowning.

'Did you think,' he said under his breath, 'that it might have been some kind of ritual thing?'

The detective, baffled, stared at him. Then he understood. 'Because she's a Jew?'

And this is the man, he thought, who used to read James Joyce, and wrote a famous thesis on some German philosopher no one had ever heard of before.

Tommy kept his eyes on his glass.

'Their ways are different from ours, you know that. They crucified our Saviour, and ever since they've carried the mark of Cain—'

'The mark of Abel, more like. Look what happened to them in the war.'

'There are some,' Tommy said mildly, 'who will tell you they brought it on themselves.'

'Aye – the way we brought the famine on ourselves.'

'Ah, now, there's no comparison.'

'You're right. There's no comparison.'

Tommy sat up straight and slapped Hackett jovially on the knee.

'Well now,' he said, spreading a smile all over his face, 'I'd never have taken you for a Jew-lover. As for myself' – he put his hands quickly over his eyes, then his ears and then his mouth – 'see no, hear no, speak no: that's my motto.'

Now and then, a priest at one of the tables would glance over at the bishop, and turn back and say something to the others. The others too would look, and then they would put their heads together and lower their voices.

A third round was ordered, though Hackett had switched to Guinness. He had noticed lately that he couldn't drink spirits the way he used to. He was getting old, his tolerance for the booze was diminishing.

'How do you know this Kessler fellow, anyway?' he asked.

Tommy was lighting another one of his noxious cigarettes. Hackett had offered him his lighter but he said he only ever used matches. He hated the taste of lighter fluid.

'Ah, we gave him a bit of help at the end of the war.'

'We?'

Tommy almost smirked.

'We have our networks,' he murmured. 'And sure, wasn't everyone in need of help in those terrible days. Anyway, he's in my parish. His place is only up the road from Ferns.' Ferns was where Tommy resided, in the bishop's palace. 'You must come down one day on the train and have your dinner. I'll open a good bottle or two. My esteemed predecessor left a fine cellar behind him when he was called to his reward. The bishop's palace – palace, *marya* – is an awful barn of a place, I'm always looking for company. Will you come down? – bring the missus, if you like.'

'I will,' Hackett said, with deliberate vagueness. 'I'll do that.'

The word was that Tommy had a woman to look after his needs. She ran a hairdressing salon in Gorey. They were often seen drinking together in French's pub. Nobody seemed to mind, and what if they did, anyway? Who would think of revealing Bishop Tommy's open secret?

The storm outside had intensified. Turbulent gusts smacked against the windows, making the panes thrum like drumheads. There was a thrilling sense, even in this cosy room, of the night all round in turmoil, great whorls of wind spinning through the darkness, and the stars shivering.

So the Church had got Wolfgang Kessler out of Germany. Hackett wasn't surprised. There had been rumours for years about Pope Pius, Louis Armstrong's pal, and his connections with Hitler's crowd. Then at this end, no doubt the Knights of Saint Patrick had sprung into action.

Who exactly was this Kessler fellow, then? That question had suddenly become very interesting.

'Strafford says it's a fine spread, down there in Wicklow?'

'Kessler has made a go of it, all right,' Tommy answered. 'He knows his horses. One of them came second in the Gold Cup at Cheltenham last year, and they say he'll win it yet.'

Hackett took a drink of stout. The pint wasn't going down well; there was a touch of sourness to it. Or maybe it was the company. He had the unpleasant conviction that his old friend was going to lean on him about the Kesslers, father and son.

'You must be near retirement, are you?' Tommy said.

'I am – not long now. I'm counting the days.'

'Will you be all right? You'll have things to do? You won't be at a loose end?'

'I have a little cottage up in Leitrim. It's on a lake. Beautiful spot. May and I might move there.'

'Move for good?'

'We've been discussing it.'

'You'll save money then. The living is cheap in Leitrim.'

Money. When a cleric mentions money, you know serious matters are going to be touched on.

'I'll have the pension, and a bit we saved up over the years. We'll live on fish from the lake, and I'll put down a few lazy beds of spuds and a few rows of cabbages.'

Tommy chuckled.

'By the Lord Harry, you have it all figured out.' Then a pause, then thoughtfully: 'It's a great thing, the old age pension. I remember Dev telling me one time that it was one of his big priorities when he took over in 'thirty-seven.'

Hackett was sceptical – hard to believe the old people of Ireland would have been at the forefront of Mr de Valera's calculating mind – but he made no comment.

'I was thinking more of the Garda pension.'

'Oh, sure, sure.' Their glasses were empty. 'Does that come automatically, now? I mean, there's no way it would be stopped, or anything like that.'

Ah, yes. There it was. The first glint on the dagger.

'I'd imagine you'd have to do something fairly world-shaking for your pension to be taken away,' Hackett said, putting on a smile every bit as broad as Tommy's. 'I've made sure to be a good boy, over the years.'

'Well now, I don't know that I'd believe that,' Tommy said merrily, pretending to tease. 'We all have a few skeletons in the cupboard.'

True, Hackett thought – and also in a hairdresser's shop in Gorey.

'I think I'll be all right,' he said drily.

But if he thought that would close down the topic, he was wrong.

'You're a lucky fellow,' Tommy said ruefully. 'No pensions for us crowd.'

For God's sake, was he going to put on the poor mouth? This was the man who lived in a palace, and would live there for life, with no money worries and servants to tend him hand and foot.

'But you're like the amateur footballers,' Hackett said with a sly wink. 'There are perks on the side.'

Tommy looked at him quickly, forgetting to smile.

'The perks are few and far between,' he said, and couldn't keep the steel out of his voice.

Hackett cursed himself. Couldn't he keep his bloody mouth shut? There was no limit to the power of the Church in this country. Of course a pension could be stopped. It would take nothing more than one of the Archbishop's famous late-night phone calls. The Garda Commissioner was an active member of the Knights of Saint Patrick – the Paddy Mafia, as the pub wits had it. Then Hackett and his wife would need all his skill as fisherman and farmer even to subsist, up there on their lake in Leitrim.

Tommy might be bluffing, there was that possibility. But if it was a bluff, it would take a braver or more foolhardy man than Chief Inspector Hackett to call him on it.

The bishop, his work done, his message delivered, was preparing to depart. He got into his overcoat and put on his muffler and picked up his cap.

'Great to see you,' he said, giving Hackett's right arm a squeeze. 'Will you walk out with me?'

'I'll stay a little while,' Hackett said. 'You go on.'

'Right. I'll be off, then.'

Every priest in the place was watching now, not caring if they were seen doing it. Tommy stood there, with that big pumpkin head of his, and that smile. Hackett couldn't understand why he didn't go, then noticed, down at his side, his ring finger flexing. Was the bloody man going to present him with the episcopal ring for him to kiss? He felt the sweat break out on his upper lip. There were only so many things he would consent to do, and kissing Tommy McEvoy's ring was not one of them.

'Good luck, Tommy,' he said, pointedly ignoring the hand twitching down there.

'Good luck yourself, old pal.'

And Tommy turned and waddled away with half the eyes in the room following him. When he was gone, those same eyes switched their gaze to Hackett, the bishop's friend. He felt like a lonely wayfarer faltering at the edge of the wood and feeling himself fixed from between the trees by the wolf pack's smouldering stares.

'Give us a ball of malt there, Mick,' he called to the barman, pushing away the empty Guinness glass. He fetched out his handkerchief and wiped the sweat from his forehead and his upper lip. He didn't want another drink, but he needed one.

16

Surely this was more than a hangover. He felt as if an enormous weight, as heavy as the weight of the world's woes, had been sitting on his chest all night while he slept. His eyelids burned, his joints ached, there was a leaden heaviness in his limbs. He remembered finishing the bottle of whiskey, after which he had gone on to something else. Crème de menthe? Benedictine? Phoebe had tried to get him to stop but he had shouted at her, and she had gone to bed and left him to it. Now his mouth was like the bottom of a beehive, scummed and sweet-tasting.

What had woken him was a shaft of sunlight plunging down from a corner of the window and searing his left cheek and the left side of his forehead. There had been a storm in the night; two or three times it had jolted him out of his drunken stupor. Now all was calm, and here was the sun in the window. He could hear a vacuum cleaner keening somewhere in the building.

The pastry shop was open, and there was the smell of vanilla. Maybe that was what was giving him the sweet taste in his mouth, and not the Benedictine.

When he pushed the heavy eiderdown aside, the slither and crackle of the satin cover made him flinch. He dragged himself out of the steamy bed and stood at the tall window above the unruly garden. He had forgotten to draw the curtains. Just as well – he was so drunk he would probably have pulled them down, rails and all, and ended up entangled in them on the floor.

He went to the door that led into the living room and stood hunched there in his vest and drawers, listening. No sound. Phoebe would have left long ago. She spent her mornings in the library in Trinity College. She was writing something, he couldn't remember what, a thesis, or a paper for a doctorate. He was glad she had gone back to studying. She wasn't working at the moment, and was living on the money she had inherited from her step-grandmother.

Suddenly it came back to him, with a kind of thump. Strafford. The disastrous teatime. His fury. The scuffle at the front door. He gave a moan of anguish and self-loathing. Had he ever been lower than this? Well, yes, but he had thought those days were over. Not many roses, but a lot of wine, and other, stronger things.

But she had called him Daddy. That was the one pinprick of light shining out of the murk. Never before, never once. All she ever called him was Quirke, like everyone else.

Don't mention it to her, don't refer to it, not ever. Probably she regretted it as soon as it was out of her mouth. But she had said it, and what was once said could not be gainsaid.

In the bathroom, the air was warm and dense with the sun shining in. He took a bath, and lay soaking in it until the water had turned grey and gone cold. He held up his fingertips and inspected them. They were wrinkled and waxen. So were his toes. It was as if his body had been drained of all its blood.

The slow thudding in his head was like the sound of a distant machine, a piledriver, ramming itself over and over into resistant ground. The distant vacuum cleaner was still going as well, a mosquito whine.

Blobs of light wobbled on the ceiling. They must be reflections thrown up by the bath water. They were like hieroglyphs, forming and dissolving and forming again, different every time.

At last, when the water was too cold to bear, he rose up like a breaching whale and, shivering, wrapped himself in a towel. He had avoided looking in the mirror, but he would have to shave sooner or later. The razor blade gleamed along its edge with menacing, silvery-blue intent.

He put on a dressing gown and went out to the kitchen. Phoebe had laid the table for his breakfast. Maybe she wasn't as angry at him as she had every right to be. He made a pot of strong tea and put two slices of bread under the grill of the gas stove. The first cigarette of the day tasted like scorched wool. He stood gazing out of the window. He forgot about the toast, and presently smoke began to pour out from under the grill. He swore, and recalled a joke that Phoebe used to tell him, at least once a day for weeks on end, when she was a little girl.

Question: What's bread? Answer: Raw toast.

When he laughed, it sounded as if he were groaning.

He phoned the hospital, and asked the nun at the reception desk to send word down to the pathology lab that he was sick and would not be in today. As he hung up, he pictured the nun shaking her head in silent disapproval. Doctor Death, which was his nickname among the hospital staff, had been on a bender, again.

*

251

He met Molly Jacobs in the café above the little picture house on Grafton Street. He drank three cups of tea – he had an unslakeable thirst – and allowed Molly to persuade him to eat half of an egg sandwich. It was eleven o'clock on a midweek morning. Around them sat women in hats and overcoats and tweed skirts, with shopping bags at their feet. There were only two other men in the place, looking as self-conscious as he felt, or as he would have felt had his head not seemed to be stuffed with damp cotton wool.

He told Molly about the previous evening's debacle at the tea table. Or rather, he gave her a selection of the highlights, and suppressed the worst of the lowlights.

'Oh, Quirke,' Molly said, laughing, 'what's to be done with you?'

'I know. I shouldn't be allowed to associate with other human beings. Or just human beings, since I'm not sure, this morning, if I am one.'

Yet despite everything, he felt strangely cheerful. Over the past six months it had been permanent winter in his head, with occasional brief flashes of exhilarating April weather. There was no accounting for these sunlit moments. He accepted them humbly and with gratitude, as well as a touch of apprehensiveness. Were these moments of lightness granted to him so as to make more terrible his eventual expulsion into a final darkness?

Suddenly, he remembered a dream from last night. In it, he had woken to find himself lying full-length in a shallow pit lined with cold ashes. He knew that he was supposed to be dead, and that this was the shallow grave he had been buried in. Now, quite relaxed, and even a little amused, he scrambled to his feet and brushed at the fine grey ash clinging to his clothes, to his face and to the backs of his hands. Then he sauntered away, into a landscape barren and gleaming like the surface of the moon. However, after a few paces he was brought to a halt by the realisation that the grave he had been lying in was not his own. It was Evelyn's, and the ashes were hers, all that remained of her after she was cremated. He turned and hurried back to where he thought the grave had been, but the ground there was smooth, and smooth all round, as far as the eye could see. His dreaming self saw himself standing there, in the midst of a vast emptiness, turning this way and that, in bafflement and desolation.

Molly was asking him something.

'Hmm?'

'What's the matter?' she said again.

He put a hand to his forehead.

'Nothing,' he muttered. 'I was just remembering something.'

'A pretty bad memory, by the look on your face.'

Should he tell her about the dream? No, he shouldn't.

He lit a cigarette.

'Have you spoken to your father?' he asked. 'How is he?'

'He's all right. Well, no, he's not. But he's managing. He still won't leave the house, but at least he's venturing out of that damned room he had himself cooped up in. But he keeps going on about Rosa's car.'

'Have they not released it yet?'

'They have, but it's in some Garda compound and we don't know how to get it out.'

'I'll see what I can do.'

She was peering into his face.

'You really do look wretched. How much did you drink?'

'It was the Benedictine at the end that did for me. Or the crème de menthe – I can't remember which it was.'

She sat back on her chair and surveyed him evenly.

'Are you an alcoholic?' she asked.

'I used to drink a lot,' he said.

'Used to?'

'You didn't know me then. This is nothing. I once went on a drinking bout that lasted for six weeks. I came to one morning sitting on the edge of the pavement in O'Connell Street. Couldn't remember a thing. I had no wallet, my clothes were in tatters, and someone, me, probably, had taken the laces out of my shoes.' He eyed her wearily. 'Are you shocked? You should be.'

'What happened?'

'How do you mean, what happened? I cleaned myself up and went back to work.'

'I meant, how did you stop drinking – not that you have, but I take it that you don't disappear for weeks on end any more.'

'No, that time is past.'

'When your wife died, were you not tempted to—?'

'Look, Molly,' he said, leaning forward heavily against the table, 'can we talk about something else?'

She gazed at him steadily.

'Like what?'

He sighed, and looked down at the table. It was a little soon to have their first quarrel.

The waitress came to gather up their plates and cups and saucers. Quirke asked for the bill. The girl totted up the numbers on her pad, tore off the slip of paper and put it on the table before him.

'Three and sixpence, sir,' she said.

He counted out the coins, and added a shilling tip. She took up the money and gave him a smile, and to his consternation he felt tears pricking his eyelids.

Daddy.

Later, they went for lunch to the Russell Hotel, and ate black sole on the bone and drank a bottle of Pouilly-Fuissé. The Russell was one of Quirke's favourite haunts. It was here that he used to come with Phoebe for their weekly treat in the old days. That was before he married Evelyn. Phoebe had been working for the termagant Mrs Cuffe-Wilkes at her hat shop on Grafton Street, but had left to become Evelyn's reception-ist in her psychiatric practice on Fitzwilliam Square. It was through Phoebe that Quirke had met Evelyn.

'I didn't think you could get decent food in Dublin,' Molly said appreciatively.

'You need to know the right places, and be with the right person.'

'Which means you, obviously.'

He reached across the table and brushed his fingertips along the back of her hand.

'Do you know how Robert Mitchum proposed to his wife?'

'No – how did Robert Mitchum propose to his wife?'

'He said, "Stick with me, baby, and you'll be farting through silk for the rest of your life."' Molly blushed, but laughed too. 'They've been together for seventeen years, so far,' Quirke added. 'Surely a Hollywood record.'

They ate the fish, they drank the wine. Quirke's hangover was steadily abating. He was granted another glimpse of the sunny uplands.

'There's something I need to tell you,' Molly said.

'Oh, yes?'

They pushed their plates aside. As if to clear the ground for battle, Quirke thought, and groaned inwardly. Molly set her elbows on the table and regarded him with a sombre expression in her big, glossy eyes. Quirke lit a cigarette.

'You know those phone calls the other night?' she said.

'Which phone calls?'

'That we thought must be for my father. Well, they weren't. They were for me.'

'Oh, yes?' he said again, feeling something tighten in his chest. It was altogether possible that this lunch would come to an abrupt end, with him rising ponderously from the table, saying a sad goodbye, and walking out of the hotel. It had happened before, and on that occasion, too, it had started off with a confession. But who was the woman? He couldn't remember. Yet he saw the table as it had been then, with the plates pushed aside, a napkin twisted into a knot, and a cigarette smouldering in a glass ashtray.

As if she too had seen what he saw in his mind, Molly now reached over and took the cigarette from Quirke's fingers, drew in a mouthful of smoke, expelled it, and gave back the cigarette.

'I have a boyfriend, in London.'

'Ah.'

'I don't know how he got the Cork number. I didn't give it to him.'

'What's he called?'

'Does it matter?'

'Yes, it does.'

'He's only sort of a boyfriend.' She grimaced. 'Don't you hate those squirmy words, "boyfriend", "girlfriend"? So childish.'

He wasn't going to let her off the hook. He would make her squirm, herself.

'Is he a journalist?'

'How did you guess?'

'Wasn't difficult.'

'He is a journalist, yes. And he's sort of my boss.'

Quirke chuckled. It was not a pleasant sound.

'Your sort of boyfriend is your sort of boss. That must be interesting.'

'The point is, and this is the thing you have to understand, the point is that it's not serious. I mean, I'm not serious about him. How he feels about me is anyone's guess. He's English. Undemonstrative is the word.' She gave him a tentative, almost a pleading look. 'Do you mind?'

'Do I "mind awfully", as your boyfriend would say?' He toyed with the cigarette and the ashtray. He didn't know how he felt. 'I wasn't about to propose to you. You're a free agent, and—'

She held up a hand to stop him.

'Don't say it.'

'Don't say what?'

'What you were going to say. The usual clichés.'

'Forgive me, I'm sure, for being obvious.'

They were silent, each looking aside, in opposite directions.

'His name is Adrian. He's the Features Editor.'

'How long?'

She blinked.

'How long what?'

'How long has "Adrian" been your "boyfriend"?'

'Oh, for God's sake! What does it matter.'

'Matters to me, for various reasons.'

They turned back to face each other, and she reached across the table and touched his hand.

'Don't be cross with me.'

'Why would I be cross with you? You've a perfect right to have a lover, and I—'

'Please,' she said, softly but with force. 'Please don't let's fight. Not now, not today, not – not this soon.'

'So it will be all right to fight in – what? A week? A month? What's the waiting period?'

She threw up her eyes and heaved an exaggerated sigh.

'Why do men do this?' she asked herself.

'Why do we do what?'

'Act like babies whose bottle has been snatched away from them. I was trying to act like an adult. I waited to tell you until I judged the moment was right. But of course, no moment is right when it comes to – to owning up.'

She looked down, and rolled a crumb of bread on the table back and forth under a fingertip. The delicate mauve shadows under her eyes seemed to have deepened. Ruth, he thought, Ruth amid the alien corn. The thought occurred to him, with the force of a blow, that he might already be in love with her. Ruth the woman of Moab.

'I'm sorry,' he said, and he too lowered his eyes. 'I've no right to ask anything of you.'

258

She was still rolling the pellet of bread under her finger.

'And if you *were* to ask something of me,' she said in almost a whisper, 'what would it be?'

He lifted his shoulders and let them fall heavily, as if he were setting down two heavy loads.

'I can't—' he said, and stopped. He tried again. 'I don't know what to say to you.'

'You could call me Molly. You know you haven't done it once, not once, even in bed? "Molly". Say it. It's not so hard.' She paused and her eyes took on a glitter. 'Are you afraid you'll get mixed up and call me by your wife's name?'

They sat for a while saying nothing, letting their gazes wander vacantly about the room. Quirke drummed his fingers quietly on the table. He smoked another cigarette.

How like you this? In his head, he heard her saying it. *They flee from me that sometime did me seek.* He had looked up the poem in one of the Oxford books of English verse, and now he knew it by heart in its entirety.

By heart.

He signalled to the waiter, and they ordered coffee. Quirke ordered a brandy, too, and asked Molly if she would like another drink. His voice sounded icily polite, which hadn't been his intention. Molly smiled, but wanly.

'Oh, doctor,' she said, 'are you trying to get me drunk, and it only three o'clock on a weekday afternoon?'

It was the melancholy of the moment that eased the tension between them, banishing itself in the process. Quirke cancelled the brandy, and they left half of their coffee undrunk and walked out together onto the corner of St Stephen's Green. As they crossed the road, a springlike little breeze

259

ruffled the hem of Molly's skirt and made Quirke hold on to his hat.

'Whoops!' Molly cried, and linked her arm in his.

They took a taxi to the little house on Usher's Island, and climbed the narrow stairs to Professor Maunsley's bedroom. It was of a monastic aspect, being narrow and low-ceilinged, not unlike, appropriately, the maid's room in Molly's father's house. Molly drew the curtains. They undressed.

'Christ, it's cold!' Molly said.

She slipped into the bed and pulled the eiderdown all the way up until the edge of it was above her nose. She looked at Quirke with those eyes of hers.

The curtains were blue, and the room was suffused with a muted, bluish glow.

'Put your hand there,' Molly whispered. 'Yes, just there. Ah.' She pressed her head back into the pillows. Her eyes were closed, and the lids trembled. 'What are you thinking of?' she asked. 'Who are you thinking of? Your wife?'

'Which one?' he murmured, his face in her hair.

'Did I know you had two?'

He whispered something into her ear.

'Oh, yes,' she breathed, 'oh, yes, please do.'

A coin of sunlight quivered on the floor beside the bed. The breeze had followed them all the way from St Stephen's Green, and was piping a tiny tune in a chink somewhere.

They sat in the kitchen, which was really little more than a scullery, and drank more coffee. The table was small and rickety, and the Formica top was slightly repellent to the touch. Quirke felt disproportionate to the confined space. He sat wedged into a corner, on a rush-seated Van Gogh chair. He feared he would break something, that the chair would collapse under him.

Molly, wearing a silk wrap, stood leaning back against the sink, nursing her cup in both hands. Shafts of evening sunlight stood in the window like brandished lances.

'This house is damp,' she said. 'The cold seeps into your bones.'

Her elaborate helmet of hair was in disarray. The shadows under her eyes had lightened. Quirke liked to look at them. They were an intimate part of her, at once shrouded and on show. There was a touch of the wanton to her, a wanton with a streak of mischievous amusement. Her warm yet sly, unemphatic humour made him think of Evelyn – made him think of her and yet feel no flinch of guilt.

'Have you any contacts in Israel?' he asked.

Molly sipped her coffee, her shoulders drawn in against the coldness of the little room.

'What sort of contacts?'

'Reporters. Journalists.'

'I have, as it happens. Joel Rozin. He used to be on the *Financial Times*, moved over there and set himself up as a free-lance. Why?'

'I'd like to know a little more about the Lieberman woman, the one we spoke about. Can you contact your friend, ask him for any information he might have on her?'

She thought about this for a moment.

'Have you got access to a telex machine?'

'I think there's one at the hospital.'

'I'll write him a note, and you can get it sent.' She was watching Quirke. 'You still suspect this Kessler fellow?'

'I don't know that "suspect" is the word. He just seemed a bit too good to be true. Your chap Rozin might make a few enquiries about him, too.'

Molly smiled with eyebrows raised.

'The little grey cells telling you there's something fishy there, eh, Sherlock?'

'Poirot,' Quirke said absently.

'Poirot?'

'He was the one for the little grey cells.'

'My, how well read we are.'

Quirke wondered, not for the first time, what it was he was trying to resolve. Something was there, some outline, some pattern, hidden in plain sight. Rosa Jacobs. Shulamith Lieberman. The Kesslers.

When he was a schoolboy, at St Aidan's, someone in his class produced a newspaper cutting of a photograph taken by an American reconnaissance plane. It showed, in black and white, a bleak, snow-covered landscape dotted with rocks and stands of trees. However, if you looked at it for long enough, suddenly the image of Christ's face would leap out at you, the face as it appears in the Turin Shroud.

It was uncanny, and unnerving. The cutting was passed from hand to hand around the school, and led even the worst of the schoolyard louts to bethink themselves and dwell on things of the spirit. The queues for confession were long that week.

As it was then with the newspaper photo, so was it now for Quirke. He had before him a blank space scattered with outcrops, and it was his task to spot the hidden pattern.

There was the young woman murdered in her motor car, there was the German exile on his grand estate, and there was the exile's son. The Kesslers had business dealings in Israel, and in Israel a journalist who reported on the doings of the Israeli armed forces had been knocked down and killed by a hit-and-run driver. All that couldn't be random. It must be all connected. But how?

He knew well the danger of jumping eagerly to neat conclusions. He had not trusted Kessler. Probably deep down he was prejudiced against him, the wealthy foreigner basking in his grand house amid hundreds of acres of one of the loveliest of Ireland's counties. He wanted him to be guilty of something – but was he guilty?

'Hey,' Molly said, and snapped her fingers. 'It's getting lonely over here.'

Quirke lifted apologetic hands.

'Sorry, sorry. I was thinking.'

'Ah, so that's what it was. I thought you had drifted into a trance.' She stretched luxuriantly, arching her arms above her head. The sleeves of the silk wrap she was wearing fell back and he glimpsed her humid, shadowy armpits. 'Love in the afternoon,' she said, and made a thick sound in her throat like that of a cat purring. 'Isn't it wonderful?'

She went to him where he sat, stood between his knees, clasped her hands behind his head and drew his forehead against her breast. He put his arms around her hips. She leaned down and kissed the pale spot on the crown of his head. He closed his eyes and inhaled her musky smell.

Let me not love her, he prayed into the void, *please, let me not.*

He held her hip bones and pushed her a little way away from him and looked up into her inclined face.

'Write that note to your friend in Israel,' he said, 'will you?'

'Oh, Quirke,' she exclaimed with swooning sarcasm, 'you're such an old romantic!'

17

Strafford lay in bed propped against a bank of pillows, looking out through the window at the tops of the trees across the road by the canal. The morning was bright but there was a wind, and the massed leaves heaved and thrashed. They had taken on autumn's grey-green pallor. Some were already brown, and soon they would all turn and begin to fall. The foliage of these trees seemed longer lasting than that of others elsewhere. He supposed their roots deep down must drink from the canal and thus sustain the system. It seemed to him he was quite clever to have thought of this. Though probably it was all wrong. He knew little of nature and her ways.

Phoebe had left early. Quirke would be at the flat, and she was making sure to be home before he was up. She didn't want him to know she had been out all night, even though it was none of his business.

She was an interesting young woman. The worst kind to get involved with, his father would have said. In lovemaking, her natural diffidence became, or came to seem, a kind of swooning languor.

In this respect, as in others, she and Marguerite were utterly unlike. Marguerite made love with fevered intensity, as if she were fulfilling a task unfairly imposed upon her, and which she meant to have done with as speedily as possible.

When they were first married, Strafford had found this

briskness and sense of hurry peculiarly exciting. In his previous encounters with women, few and fleeting as they were, he had always felt that too much was expected of him – too much attentiveness, too much patience, too much *work*. His wife's perfunctoriness was refreshing. In lovemaking, she seemed hardly to notice him, so deep was her concentration on the business in hand. In her arms, he seemed to himself more an onlooker than a participant. He supposed a psychiatrist would diagnose him as a voyeur.

Maybe that was why he had become a detective, to professionalise his incurable inquisitiveness.

Such were Strafford's dark and secret musings, this fine bright blowsy morning.

Quirke had told him of what Molly Jacobs had learned from her journalist friend in Israel, Joel Rozin. She had written to him, and then had spoken to him long distance, on Professor Maunsley's telephone, at enormous cost.

Yes, he said, he had known Shula Lieberman. She was a 'terrier' – his word. She seized on a story and shook it until everything in it had fallen out for forensic investigation. Rozin was surprised she had survived as long as she did, even though she was only in her thirties when she was killed. The military hated her, and he didn't know why they hadn't eliminated her long ago.

Molly was struck by this, and asked if he really believed the army had assassinated her.

Call me paranoid, Rozin had answered, but it seems to me the logical conclusion.

'Tel Aviv is a small place, the Israelis are noted law-abiders,

266

and in this city it would be a rare driver who would not stop after an accident.'

That was all conjecture, Quirke had said. Maybe this fellow Rozin really was paranoid, as he himself suggested.

Molly had asked Rozin if he knew what the project was that Shula Lieberman was working on when she died.

Her abiding project, he replied, the one she had been working on for more than ten years. She had been monitoring Israel's nuclear weapons programme. Her specific focus was to find out how near the country's military scientists were to producing an atomic bomb. This was, he added, extremely sensitive territory. The Defence Force, and Mossad, the intelligence agency, devoted a very great deal of their energies to keeping the nuclear arms project secret, not only from the world but from the Israeli people also.

Did Miss Lieberman oppose efforts to acquire the bomb?

Shula was a patriot, Rozin replied. She would have been the last person who would wish to damage Israeli security. But she believed in openness, championed a free press, and repeatedly pointed out that nuclear weapons are only of use as a deterrent, and if Israel had the atomic bomb, how would it deter Israel's many enemies if they didn't know the Israeli bomb existed?

Did Rozin know of Wolfgang Kessler and his son, Frank?

Of course, Rozin replied. Everyone in Israel was aware of who these righteous Germans were, and the contribution they had made, and were making, to the welfare, security and progress of the State of Israel.

To Molly that all sounded, as later it would sound to Quirke, altogether too good to be true. Rozin had replied that he was only telling her what the Israeli public knew and thought of the Kesslers. For his own part, he agreed with her. But it would be a brave man, and probably a foolhardy one, who uttered the slightest doubt or suspicion about the motives of Wolfgang Kessler and his son.

Had Shula written about them?

Not in anything that Rozin had read. But he would make enquiries, and see what he could find out. It was known that there were links between the Kesslers and the military, but what was not known was the nature of those links.

Could the Kesslers be supplying armaments to Israel?

Rozin thought it unlikely, but if they were, the military or the government were not going to say so – and if anyone did say, retribution would be swift and severe, indeed fatal, if the case warranted it.

Like being knocked down and killed by a hit-and-run driver, Molly had suggested.

Strafford plumped up the pillows and lay back on them again. He really should get up, but he felt lethargic this morning. It was not that his night with Phoebe – it was the first time she had stayed over at his flat – had been particularly taxing.

Their nascent affair, if that was what to call it, was less a thing of passion than of mutual convenience. Its limits were unspoken but well defined. The lovers would not impinge on each other's lives beyond a certain point. This suited them both. Neither was possessive. At least, this was how Strafford saw matters. It was true that Phoebe was something of an enigma to him, but this did not trouble him. Human beings know so little of each other even in their most intimate relations. Look at him and Marguerite. It wasn't even certain that she had left him. She had just gone away and so far had not come back.

He rose at last and made tea and sat with a mug in the lumpy armchair and thought about Quirke.

They had very nearly come to blows that evening at Phoebe's flat.

Strafford had a modicum of sympathy for Quirke. He felt guilty over the death of Quirke's wife, of course he did. It was true that he could not have prevented the woman's death. All the same, he understood Quirke's anger, and his resentment. Grief would demand that someone be held responsible for its cause, and Strafford was the most convenient target to bear the brunt of the blame.

Did Quirke hate him? Would he have hated him anyway, whether or not his wife had died on the floor of that restaurant that terrible afternoon? Strafford was accustomed to animosity. Arrests, investigations, the questioning of witnesses and the occasional issuing of threats against them had over the years thickened his skin.

He was not as vulnerable as he supposed he must seem, to those who didn't know him well enough to understand him. In build and even in disposition he bore no comparison to Quirke, with his bullish shoulders, his bunched fists, his smouldering and so often malevolent stare. Yet Strafford had killed two men, while Quirke had never killed anyone. Surely this should set an unbridgeable gap between them? You would think so, but Strafford could not feel it. It was not a gap that separated them: they might be existing in different spheres, on different planets, even.

Their worlds did not touch. Quirke too must be aware of this.

Despite all that, however, they seemed to share between them an awful, almost a shameful, intimacy.

When Strafford was in his final year at school, a boy in his class had developed a strange obsession with him. What was his name? Stevenson? No, Robinson. David – Davey – Robinson. He was small and good-looking, with dark, deep-set eyes and hair of the same dull no-colour as Strafford's.

It must have been a homosexual crush, probably uncon-scious, that Robinson had developed for him, Strafford thought now, though it had not occurred to him at the time. The boy was drawn to him by a seemingly irresistible compulsion. He lost no opportunity to engage with Strafford, to challenge him, to jeer at him, to denigrate him. Their encounters took place when no one else was there to witness them. Robinson made sure to waylay him in corridors, in classrooms after class, in empty corners of the school grounds. Strafford was baffled by this constant badgering. It was like being pursued by a hapless, tormented lover, one whose love, by being spurned, had transformed itself into a kind of hatred.

When Quirke lunged at him in the doorway of the Mount Street house that night, Strafford had thought immediately of Robinson. There was in Quirke the same kind of neediness and desperation. Was he being protective of his daughter? Was he jealous? Or perhaps Strafford's earlier thought was true, and Quirke simply hated him. There didn't have to be a reason for hatred. Robinson was proof of that.

Phoebe had confided to him how Quirke had abandoned her as a baby to his half-brother and his wife. She was almost

270

twenty before he admitted the betrayal, and tried to make up for it. As if there could be recompense for such a thing. Yet she seemed to have forgiven her father. Maybe that's what maddened Quirke, the having been forgiven.

Quirke's kind love their guilt, Strafford thought, they wrap themselves in it as in a good warm cloak on a stormy day.

He went along the corridor to the bathroom. As he shaved, he was enveloped in Mr Singh's lingering, savoury miasma. Plying the razor, he thought again of Quirke and Molly Jacobs. He assumed they were having an affair. If so, Quirke had certainly wasted no time in shrugging off the shroud of mourning.

Back in his room, he got dressed, in a pair of corduroy trousers and his old tweed jacket with the leather patches on the elbows. He recalled Wolfgang Kessler's immaculate loden jacket, his tailored jodhpurs, his spotless boots. He was convinced, like Quirke, that Kessler was a fake. But what kind of fake?

When he came out at the front door, the wind gusted in his face and frisked about his ankles. He thought of Phoebe, of her cool pale hands, the grave turn of her eyes, of the delicate, milk-blue veins in the backs of her knees. The question of what to make of her, what to make of him and her, could be postponed to another time.

He walked down by the canal to Baggot Street and waited for the Number 10 bus. A tiny woman in a raincoat and an old-fashioned hat went past. She was wheeling a pram in which sat a tiny dog, wrapped in a blanket. Around its neck it wore a white silk ribbon, tied in a bow under its muzzle. He saw the woman often about the streets, with her surrogate baby.

Perhaps he and Marguerite should have had a child. It might have made all the difference. The topic had never been broached. He didn't know how Marguerite managed not to get pregnant, since contraceptives were illegal, and he didn't ask. If he had, she would have pretended not to know what he was talking about.

It was another of her conventions, that what happened between them in bed wasn't what it was. Not that she was a prude. Indeed, she often startled him with a coarse joke, accompanied by an uncharacteristically lubricious, deep-throated chuckle. But the avoidance of all mention of their love life – their love life! – was another aspect of her impatience with the whole tiresome business.

He sat on the top of the bus, at the front. He never felt so much the country boy as when he was up here, leaning forward eagerly on the seat and watching the houses and the shops teetering past, the people in the streets, the traffic. So many lives! He contemplated, yet again, the impenetrable mystery of other people.

At the Pearse Street barracks, the desk sergeant told him Chief Inspector Hackett was having an early lunch over at Mooney's, and winked.

The pub at this hour of the morning had a tired and faintly shamefaced air, after the excesses of the previous night, the usual drinking and shouting and brawling. Hackett was sitting on a high stool at the bar, with a pint and a half-eaten sandwich before him. At sight of Strafford coming in at the door, he tried to hide his annoyance, but failed.

'I thought you were taking the day off,' he said shortly.

Strafford climbed onto a stool next to the Chief.

'Why did you think that?'

'Your office was empty all morning.'

First barb of the day. It was not yet noon.

'I had a late start.'

Hackett made a rumbling noise and shifted his elbows on the bar. He was wearing his raincoat and his blue suit. His hat hung on a hook in the wooden partition against which he was leaning.

'I don't suppose you want a drink?'

'A glass of water,' Strafford said to the barman, who made no reply, only took down a glass and turned on a tap with a disdainful twist of the hand.

'So,' Hackett said, looking into the mirror opposite him, above the rows of bottles, 'what's up?'

It was clear the Chief couldn't care less what was up, or down. He was in one of his moods. Was it only because his mid-morning lunch had been interrupted, or were there other reasons? Hackett's temper was as unpredictable as the skies over Dublin.

Strafford took a sip of water. The pub smells made him feel slightly queasy.

'Quirke told you about Rosa Jacobs's sister, about her phoning her contact in Israel?'

'He told me,' Hackett snapped.

'What did you make of it?'

'What did I make of what?'

'What the man in Tel Aviv told her. About the woman who died over there, the one who was killed, the journalist?'

'A case of hit-and-run, yes. What about it?'

'Bit of a coincidence, wouldn't you say? Two young women dying, one in a motor car, the other hit by a car.'

273

Hackett turned with deliberate slowness and looked at him.

'A coincidence? A girl dies here, a girl dies there. How far away is Israel? Couple of thousand miles?'

'Yes, I know,' Strafford said, keeping his patience. 'But there is a connection.'

Hackett turned back to his pint and his half-eaten ham sandwich.

'And that is?'

'The Kesslers.'

Hackett nodded, but his nod expressed the deepest scepticism. He drank the stout, and with a finger wiped the rim of brownish-grey foam from his upper lip.

'The Kesslers?' he repeated, feigning deep perplexity and slow-wittedness. 'Will you kindly explain to me how they come into the picture? Were they acquainted with this newspaper woman that died?'

'I don't know. Probably not. But they have business interests in Israel, and—'

Again Hackett turned to him, but sharply this time.

'Look, detective inspector,' he said, 'I'm on my lunch hour. I like to eat my lunch in peace and quiet. It's something I enjoy. Time for reflection, for revisiting the past and speculating on the future. Do you know what I mean?'

'The point is—'

'The point is that, as far as I can see, there is no point. So what, if Kessler and his son do business over in Israel? People do business in all sorts of places. Business is business. As for this reporter who was killed, I can't do anything about her. And nor can I see what connection there could have been between her and the Germans. I'm sorry for her, though I

274

know nothing about her, God rest her soul.' Strafford tried to interrupt but Hackett went on implacably. 'For yourself and the good Doctor Quirke, the world is a great big spider's web, and everything is connected with everything else. I, on the other hand, am a simple man, with a simple mind. Things happen. It's chance. Just chance, Mr Strafford, that's all. Now, can I finish my grub here, if you don't mind? The sandwiches are lousy today, by the way, so don't be tempted.'

There followed a long silence, during which Hackett finished his food contentedly and ordered another pint of stout. While the pint was being pulled, he brought out a packet of Gold Flake and lit up. All this as if Strafford were no longer there.

'Grand day,' the barman said, setting the pint in front of Hackett while pointedly ignoring Strafford.

'A bit blowy, though,' Hackett said. 'The kind of day to set the cows running mad.'

Strafford sighed. Hackett was never more irritating than when he was playing the yokel. It was one of his ways of marking the gulf between him and his subordinate, the son of the Big House.

'Chief,' Strafford began, 'I don't want to irritate you and give you indigestion—'

'Glad to hear it.'

'—but I think this is an important point.'

'And what point is that?' Hackett said, winking at the barman. 'I haven't heard you say anything sharp enough to have a point.'

'The Israeli journalist, Shulamith Lieberman, was investigating the Israeli military, and—'

'Oh, she's an investigator, now? I thought she was a reporter.'

'She was working on the Israeli nuclear programme.'

'Would that be a programme on the wireless, now?'

The barman gave a snort of laughter.

'She was trying to find out how close the Israeli military is to developing an atom bomb.'

There was a pause.

'Was she, now,' Hackett said. 'The Jews with the bomb. That's some prospect. Those lads wouldn't hesitate before dropping one of them yokes on the Egyptians, or the other crowd, in Jordan, or wherever it is.'

'Well, yes,' Strafford said, with a small laugh. 'That's the point. Give a weapon like that to a general, any general, of any persuasion, and he'll look for an excuse to use it.'

Hackett nodded.

'MacArthur wanted to drop it on the Chinese in 'fifty-three.' He pushed the pint to one side. 'Here, Jimmy,' he said to the barman, 'give us a small one there, will you? The stout is lying too heavy on the innards.' He turned back to Strafford. 'My brother, over in America, lost two sons in Korea. One was twenty-two, the other nineteen.'

'That was a terrible war,' the barman said solemnly, pouring the glass of whiskey.

Strafford drank more water. It was slightly brackish. Why did people imagine water has no taste?

The atmosphere had turned sombre, from the talk of bombs and the prospect of worldwide annihilation.

He knew he should let the subject go, but he couldn't. The more he spoke of it, and the more he thought of it, the more

276

convinced he became that the death of Shulamith Lieberman was somehow connected with the Kesslers' business interests in Israel. They had dealings with the army, supplying parts – what parts, exactly? he wondered – and she was following up stories on the army's efforts to make a nuclear bomb.

Two young women had died, within weeks of each other. One of them had known the Kesslers, had been invited to their home, had possibly been romantically involved with Frank Kessler. The second one had lived, and died, in a country where the Kesslers were doing business.

'Anyway, detective inspector,' Hackett said, having downed his whiskey and returned to his pint, 'my advice to you is to take a step back from this whole thing. I'll say the same to Doctor Quirke. You've both lost your sense of – what's the word? – your sense of perspective. You're seeing things that aren't there.'

Suddenly, Strafford understood. Hackett had been got to. Someone had spoken to him, someone had said a word, dropped a hint, issued a caution. Who? One of the Kesslers' business associates here? Someone in the government, or in one of the banks? Or the Church? Hadn't Kessler said something about the Church, that afternoon in Wicklow?

He watched Hackett drinking his pint, while the barman, stony-faced, watched him.

Nothing was ever just what it was. Always there was something behind it, and, behind that, other somethings. Layer after layer, web after web.

Yes. Hackett had been warned.

18

'Damn!' The milk had gone off. She had bought it only a couple of days ago, and already it was sour. Maybe her nose was deceiving her? She lifted the bottle to her lips and took a sip. 'Yeuch!'

She looked to the kitchen window and the glossy darkness there. Why did it always seem that the night was trying to get in? It was nine-thirty. What shop would be open at this hour? She would have to do without the big cup of milky cocoa that marked the official end of her day, every day.

But wait. What about that funny little corner shop on Watling Street? Marcus Groceries. She had noticed it because the name over the window struck her as funny. *Hello, I'm Marcus Groceries – how do you do?*

It wasn't far, no more than fifteen minutes there and back. She glanced at the window again. Not raining. She would chance it. She put on her coat, found a headscarf, took up her wallet. Where were the keys? Keys always worried her. Since childhood, she had ever an abiding fear of being locked out. That would be Hell for her, she often thought, to wake up after death to find herself alone on a street at night in the run-down outskirts of an unknown city, all the windows of the buildings dark, all doors shut against her, and no lights anywhere.

The weather was stormy. Since early morning, the wind had been swooping down from the rooftops and barrelling along the streets, driving squalls of rain before it, banging on windows and turning umbrellas inside out. When she stepped onto the pavement, a cold gust struck her full in the face and almost drove her back indoors. She put her head down. That bloody shop had better be open.

It was. Cramped and dim, lit only by a single sixty-watt bulb dangling from the ceiling at the end of a twisted bit of flex, it looked like a place imagined by Dickens. There were shelves on all four walls, stacked to the ceiling with faded cereal boxes, bottled sweets, packets of washing powder and marrowfat peas, and more, much more. Nothing here, it seemed, had ever been new.

The man behind the counter had a sad and weary aspect. Everything about him drooped, his eyelids, his moustache, his shoulders, even the lapels of his tan-coloured shop-coat. She assumed he would be the grocer, Mr Marcus himself. He reminded her of her father.

She asked for a bottle of milk and he gave her a melancholy smile. She couldn't just buy one thing – her shopkeeping fore-bears would not forgive her.

'I'll take a Hovis loaf, please, and' – and what? – 'and a half pound of sugar.'

Why was she buying sugar? She didn't take it in her coffee, and long ago she had trained herself to eat her cornflakes unsweetened.

'That will be one and ninepence, miss,' said Mr Marcus in a deep, soft voice. He spoke the figures as if they were something out of the Bible, a span of days, the age of a tribe. Marcus. Ah yes.

Walking back, she at least had the wind behind her. It

hurried her along like a chivvying parent. She felt it cold against the backs of her knees, through her nylons. Quirke had kissed her there, on his way northwards. For such a burly man, he was surprisingly gentle. He had to work late tonight, doing God knows what. The thought of him in the morgue, or whatever it was called, in his white coat and blood-smeared rubber apron, gave her the shivers. She wished she could be with him tonight. She dreaded the hours still to fill in before she could think of going to bed. A boyfriend, she couldn't remember which one, had told her she was an 'after-hours girl'. And so she was, though it sounded faintly disreputable.

When she turned off Watling Street, there was a lone car parked at the kerb. She glanced at it as she went past. It was low and sleek, like a sports car only bigger. It seemed to her she had seen it somewhere before. She thought there was someone in the driver's seat, but when she glanced back, the light from a street lamp made a yellow glare on the wind-screen, and she couldn't see through it.

The paper bag containing her purchases was flimsy, and she had to carry it with one hand underneath it.

She would leave the sugar for Professor Maunsley. He would be back in two weeks' time. A fortnight, she thought, yes, and then she would be gone. But she didn't want to think about that. She should phone Adrian, but what would she say to him? She tried to picture his face, and was shocked to discover that she couldn't.

The car's lights came on behind her. It made hardly a sound, as it approached. Then suddenly it speeded up. She had taken out the key and was about to insert it in the lock.

She turned her head and looked back along the street. The headlights glared, blinding her. The engine now was making a low growl, like an animal growling at the back of its throat. With a bang and a squeal, the left wheel mounted the pavement. The rounded side of the headlight struck her at the level of her hip. She lurched forward, and her cheekbone banged against the door knocker.

She fell, and as she fell she heard the milk bottle shattering inside the paper bag.

Quirke in his scrubs sat on a metal chair, smoking a cigarette. The light falling on the dissecting room was ice-white and harsh. He didn't know which was worse, that searing dazzle or the neon bulbs' low, relentless buzzing. It was past midnight. Above him, the many-floored hospital was quiet. Now and then he would hear the clang of a trolley, or the squeak of a nurse's rubber-soled shoes on the marble stairs outside.

He was tired. He had done four post-mortems since early evening. The last one had been on a child, a girl of nine, who had died of meningitis. The children were always the difficult ones, no matter how experienced, no matter how hardened, one might be. Children shouldn't die. It always seemed to him the worst flaw, unnatural, unfixable, in the great but defective machine that kept the whole thing running.

The telephone in his office rang. Years ago, when he took over the lab, he had got in an electrician to reduce the volume of the bell tone, but at this time of night it sounded ear-splittingly loud. It was like, he thought, the wails of an infuriated baby clamouring for its bottle. He debated whether to answer it. But on it went, and on, until he had no choice but to silence it.

'Is that you?' Phoebe said.

'Yes, it's me. What's wrong?'

For something must be wrong, if his daughter was phoning him here, at midnight.

'It's your – your friend, Molly Jacobs.'

His heart gave a sort of stagger, as if he had been punched hard in the chest.

'Tell me.'

Molly. Not long ago he had prayed to the eternal nothing-ness that he might not be made to love her, now he begged the same absence that she not be dead.

'Her father telephoned—'

'He phoned you?'

'Yes. I don't know how he got the number. He sounded very distressed.'

'What happened?'

He must know, yet dreaded being told.

'From what I could make out, she had an accident.'

'What sort of accident?'

'I think she was knocked down. By a car.'

'Where?'

'I'm not sure. "At the house", her father kept saying, "at the house". Where is she staying, do you know?'

She was being disingenuous. She knew he knew about the professor's house on Usher's Island, knew he had been there, too.

'Is she hurt?'

'I'm afraid so. She's in hospital.'

'Which one?'

'St James's—'

She was still speaking as he hung up.

The taxi was a long time in coming. The driver was old, and drove so slowly and so timidly Quirke thought he must be half blind. He began to apply the brakes fifty yards ahead of each corner, and stopped at every crossing, even the ones where he had the right of way. He would drape his arms around the steering wheel and lift his backside a few inches from the seat and peer first to the left, then to the right, then left again. He wielded the gearstick cautiously, as if it might injure him. Each gear change required an intricate series of hand passes, the engine roaring as if in anguish since he kept the accelerator pressed as he engaged the clutch.

Quirke's fists were clenched, his palms sweating.

The porch outside the hospital's main entrance was lit by a single lamp with a yellow globe. It juddered in the wind, shedding a scant, shivering radiance. Quirke thought he had never seen anywhere more desolate than this spot.

He entered at a run, letting the door bang behind him. A spectral hush hung in the corridors. The reception desk was tended by a sleepy nun in an elaborate butterfly-shaped wimple. She stared up at him in surprise and began to say he couldn't come in, that visiting hours were—

'I'm a doctor,' he said.

Still she looked doubtful. He gave her one of his special stares, his brow lowered and his bottom lip stuck out. She blinked, and took up a clipboard and ran a finger down the list of admissions.

284

'Gifford, Hennigan, Ivers,' she murmured. 'Ah, here it is. Jacobs, Marian. First floor, St Philomena ward.'

He sprinted up the stairs. The night nurse sat at her desk in a cone of light shed by an angled lamp. She wore bottle-glass spectacles with heavy black frames. A few strands of bright red hair had straggled out from under the band of her nun's veil. At the sound of Quirke's heels on the tiled floor she looked up and wrinkled her nose, so that her upper lip was lifted, exposing two large square white front teeth.

She led him to the ward, opened the door and stood back to let him enter. She did not speak. Hostility came off of her like body heat. Nuns resented consultants. Quirke sympathised. He hadn't much time for them himself.

There were three other patients in the room besides Molly. They were all asleep.

The bed wasn't large, yet Molly looked tiny in it. Her skull was bandaged, and a saline drip was attached to her arm. She had a swollen eye socket, and there were bruises on her forehead and her chin. The flesh over her right cheekbone was as round and red and shiny as an apple. Her eyes were closed, but when she sensed him beside her, she opened them.

'Oh, it's you,' she said. It seemed as if he was the last person she would have expected. Her voice was slurred, because of painkillers, or her swollen cheek, or both. She gave him a timid, almost apologetic smile. 'I must look a sight.'

He drew a chair forward and sat. Her hands lay on top of the sheet. He took them in both of his.

'Darling,' he said.

The unaccustomed word rolled awkwardly over his tongue. She squeezed his fingers.

He asked if she was in pain. She said her hip was sore – 'that's where the car hit me' – and that she had a crashing headache.

'What happened?'

For some seconds she said nothing, gazing up at the ceiling. Then a tear overflowed and ran down her temple and disappeared under the bandage on her skull.

'Oh, Quirke,' she said, 'they tried to kill me.'

He didn't want to press her for details, but she was eager to talk.

She told him how she had gone out to buy milk. She described the dim little shop, and the mournful shopkeeper, said how dark the streets were, how strong the wind had been. She paused, swallowed with difficulty, and went on.

'The car was parked at the corner of the street, at the other end from where the house is. I wasn't even sure if there was anyone in it. I walked past, and I was just letting myself in at the front door when' – she swallowed again, he heard the effort her throat muscles made – 'when it started up and came along very fast and mounted the pavement and hit me.' She looked up at him with her great round eyes. 'They were trying to kill me. I thought, when I fell, I was going to die.'

He gripped her hands more tightly.

'"They" – you said "they". Did you see them, did you get a glimpse of them?'

'No, the lights were shining in my eyes. It might have been just the driver.' She turned her face aside. She was crying in earnest now. 'I don't *know*!' she softly wailed. A woman in one of the other beds murmured something in her sleep. Molly turned back to Quirke. 'I don't know,' she said again, this time in a low, urgent whisper.

The night nurse came in then, and checked Molly's pulse and laid a hand on her forehead to judge her temperature.

'You shouldn't stay long,' she said to Quirke. She had a Cork accent. 'She needs to rest.'

'I'll go shortly,' he said.

The nun was about to say something more, but changed her mind and moved off to tend the other beds.

Quirke relaxed his fingers and slid both his palms under Molly's and leaned forward and kissed her on the forehead. He caught a whiff of her hot and swollen flesh.

'The car,' he said, 'did you get a look at the car?'

'Yes, when I passed it by at the corner. I didn't look very closely. I thought I had seen it before, maybe parked in the street some other time.'

'What make was it? What colour?'

The nun had finished with the other patients. She went to the door, and paused there a moment and gave Quirke an admonishing look. He nodded to her, mouthing some bland, temporising word. It didn't do to annoy the nursing staff, as he knew from bitter experience.

'I don't know what it was,' Molly was saying. 'Low, like a sports car. And some dark colour, blue, I think. Dark blue.'

19

Quirke flung open the door with such force he might as well have kicked it. With Strafford at his heels, he fairly plunged into the poky little office. They were in the upper reaches of the Pearse Street barracks. Hackett at his desk looked up in alarm. It seemed that if there had been another door, he would have leapt to his feet and fled. He held up both hands, showing the two men his palms.

'All right, all right,' he said. 'Don't start shouting at me.'

He knew what had happened to Molly Jacobs the night before. A squad car on the prowl had found her collapsed across the doorstep in the darkened street. He had sent a couple of detectives up to Usher's Quay first thing that morning to investigate the scene. They were rookies, the two of them, and were unlikely to come back with their hands full of clues.

The cramped little room seemed suddenly smaller still. Quirke's anger was like an expanding gas, pressing against the walls and the small square window behind Hackett's desk. Even Strafford was scowling. They were both wet and dishevelled. The storm that had started in the night was still raging outside.

'She was damn near killed,' Quirke said, breathing heavily. 'You do know that?'

'I know it,' Hackett growled, 'I know it. Sit down, will you, the two of you?'

There was only one chair. Strafford sat on it, while Quirke paced the floor as if it were the floor of a cage.

'It has to be the Germans,' he said, punching his right fist into his left palm. 'They have to be behind all this.'

'Listen, doctor, calm down. There's not a shred of evidence to—'

'For Christ's sake!' Quirke exploded, stopping and planting his hands on the desk and looming at the detective, his forehead turning livid. 'Three young women – one dies in her car, one is killed by a car, and now Rosa Jacobs's sister is run down by a car. How much evidence do you need?'

Hackett was peeling the cellophane wrapper from a packet of Gold Flake.

'Have a smoke,' he said.

'I don't want to smoke! I want you to haul in Kessler and that son of his and sweat the truth out of them.'

Strafford was watching him. Despite himself, he was impressed. He had never seen the man in such a transport of rage. It was exhilarating, even for one as sceptical of the man as Strafford was.

They had met in the day room. Quirke had come striding in from the street, and without a word had flipped up the counter flap, ignoring the desk sergeant's startled eye, and mounted the stairs, taking the steps three at a time.

Strafford, following in the wake of this whirlwind, was relieved. He and Quirke had not seen each other since the disastrous evening at Phoebe's flat. He had been wondering uneasily what they would say to each other when they did meet. Now, with all this drama, there was no need to say anything. And even when the drama was past, they would be able to pretend that scuffle on the doorstep had never taken place.

Hackett was lighting a cigarette and taking his time about it. Quirke still stood there, leaning on the desk and breathing angrily down his nostrils.

'A coincidence is not evidence,' Hackett said, blowing a cloud of smoke at him. 'What reason would I give for bringing these people in? A girl dies in her car, a girl is killed in Israel, a drunken driver knocks down the first girl's sister. All right. But the word, Doctor Quirke, is "coincidence".'

Quirke let his shoulders fall, and stepped back from the desk.

'Will you at least go down to Wicklow and question Kessler,' he said in a level tone, controlling himself with an effort.

Hackett looked up at him calmly. The doc was sweet on the Jacobs girl, that was plain to see. Had they done the business yet, the two of them? Tut tut – and he a widower of only six months' standing.

'What sort of questions would I ask him? Can you tell me that?'

Now Strafford spoke.

'This all can't be a coincidence,' he said. 'There are just too many pieces – there must be a pattern. Somebody has panicked.'

Quirke turned to him.

'What do you mean, panicked?'

'The two deaths are connected – Rosa Jacobs and the woman in Israel – and if these deaths in turn are connected with the attempt last night to murder Miss Jacobs's sister—'

'Who says they're—' Hackett began, but Quirke made a chopping motion with the edge of his left hand to silence him.

'Go on,' he said to Strafford.

'The connection must be Israel,' Strafford said. 'The Kesslers do business over there. They have dealings with the military. The young woman, what's her name, the journalist, Lieberman, she was doing stories on the race to build an atom bomb. And—'

'And I,' Quirke said, 'I got Molly Jacobs to phone her friend in Israel and ask about Miss Lieberman and how far she had got and how much she had found out. And last night a car ran her down in the street.'

He stopped, and set off pacing again. The room was so small it took no more than three paces to cross it.

'What strikes me,' Strafford said, 'is the clumsiness of the thing. That's what I meant by panic. If someone, the Kesslers, let's say, are behind all this violence, they're doing it out of desperation. Something has gone wrong. Secrets have been revealed, plans have been disrupted.'

'It has to be the Kesslers,' Quirke said. 'There's no one else.'

Now it was Hackett who erupted angrily.

'What the bloody hell do you mean, there's no one else? How do we know what's going on over there in Israel? Anybody could be up to anything, with that crowd. What would they care about some girl here in Ireland? – who, by the way, was of their own persuasion. Do you think they'd send someone over here to do her in?—'

He stopped, his forehead darkening. He had remembered, too late, that someone had been sent to Spain to cause mischief, as a result of which Quirke's wife had died. Rain clattered against the window behind him.

Now Quirke spoke.

'No, I don't think they would send someone to kill Rosa Jacobs. There were people here who could do it for them.'

Hackett was shaking his head.

'This is all in your imagination, Quirke,' he said. 'You must see that.'

'I see no such thing!' Quirke responded angrily. 'You haven't met Wolfgang Kessler. I have. He's not right – he's not what he's pretending to be.' He turned to Strafford. 'You felt that too, didn't you, the day we went down there?'

Strafford, sitting on the chair with his legs crossed, looked aside with a faint shrug.

'I suppose so, yes,' he said.

Quirke looked at Hackett again. No one spoke. Outside, the wind raged.

'Listen to me,' Hackett said, sounding weary, 'I can't bring that man in here and question him without something to show that I have grounds to suspect him of committing a crime. I can't do it.'

He kept his eyes on Quirke. *It's fine for you,* he was thinking, *you're well off, with your big salary from the nuns at the Hospital of the Holy Family. You don't have to worry about your pension.*

'All right,' Quirke said with a sigh, 'all right.'

He turned and walked heavily to the door. Hackett and Strafford exchanged a look. Strafford stood up from the chair.

'Doctor Quirke,' Hackett called, as Quirke's back disappeared from the doorway, 'tell that young woman in the hospital I was asking for her.'

20

The Stephen's Green Club was unusually busy. A waiter led Quirke to a table in a corner of the ornate dining room. Dick FitzMaurice was there already, looking at the menu. He wore a dark suit, a white shirt and his signature bow tie. Today it was dark red, with white polka dots. He rose, and they shook hands.

'Good to see you,' Dick Fitz said.

'Sorry for the short notice.'

'It's fine. As it happened, I was free this lunchtime, and wondering what to do with myself.'

'I'm glad to have solved that problem for you, then,' Quirke said.

They sat.

'How are you managing?' Dick asked. 'It must be tough, even still. How long is it since—? Six months?'

Dick FitzMaurice was the Minister for Justice, having been re-elected and given that post after the last election. He it was who had dealt with the repercussions here of the debacle in Spain. Retribution had been visited upon the people who had been responsible, if indirectly, for Evelyn's death. Quirke supposed he should have derived some comfort from that, but he hadn't. The meting out of vengeance would not bring her back.

'I'm all right,' Quirke said.

Dick Fitz regarded him with sympathy.

'Is it getting any easier? The grieving, I mean.'

Quirke considered.

'It changes,' he said. 'It evolves. I no longer burst into tears in the street. Now it just gnaws.'

'I can't imagine what it must be like. If I were to lose Margaret—'

He shook his head. Dick's wife was a Dwyer. One of her forebears had fought in the Battle of Vinegar Hill in 1798. More recently, her father had been in the General Post Office in 1916, shoulder to shoulder with the leaders of the Rising. This meant Dick was 'well got', as the saying had it, which was the reason he was able to get a number of liberalising laws onto the statute books. De Valera had been a firm friend of the late and much lamented Malachy Dwyer.

'Would it be bad taste to offer you a glass of champagne?' Dick asked of Quirke.

'Depends on the vintage,' Quirke said. These days, he made a point of putting people at their ease as regards Evelyn. His grief was nobody's business but his own. He would cry on no one's shoulder. 'But I'd prefer wine. The bubbly stuff gives me a headache.'

'Right you be,' Dick said. He shook out his napkin and spread it over his lap. 'So, what are you up to?'

'Work, as usual. I took some time off when I came back from Spain, but idleness didn't suit me. Left me too much time to brood.'

He could see from Dick Fitz's look what he was thinking. What sort of a man would seek distraction from bereavement in a dissecting room? But Quirke had long ago given up trying to explain what he felt and didn't feel about the cadavers that were delivered to him and his scalpel every working day. Death is an abstract concept. It's not an experience in life – where did he read that? He believed it to be true. The ones left behind, it's they who do the suffering.

They ordered roast beef and roast potatoes, carrots and sprouts. Dick Fitz asked for mustard – 'English, not French' – and smeared it thickly on the meat.

'What about wine?' he said. 'Shall we treat ourselves? It's on the Department of Justice.'

He ordered a bottle of Cheval Blanc.

Quirke looked at his plate and lost heart. He rarely ate like this at lunchtime. In general, he had lost interest in food, and hardly noticed what he was eating. Mostly, these days, it seemed he fed on grief.

The wine, though, was superb.

'I drank this last month in Paris,' Dick Fitz said, holding his glass up to the light and admiring the purplish tint. 'Conference on capital punishment,' he explained. 'Our position same as usual: hang 'em high. But my God, the food! Better than before the war, I believe, and that's saying something.'

Quirke pushed a carrot this way and that on his plate.

'Speaking of which – the war, I mean – have you come across a German here by the name of Wolfgang Kessler?'

Dick was busy with his food – no slackening of his appetite, it was clear.

'Yes, of course,' he said. 'Why?'

The waiter came and refilled their glasses. He wore a morning coat and pinstriped trousers.

Quirke drank his wine and was silent for some moments. He was venturing onto uncertain ground here. As a politician, Dick Fitz was known for his courage, even for his daring. He didn't bother to conceal his disdain for his party's old guard, the Fianna Fossils, as he called them. But his powers, like the powers of everyone in government and out, were limited. One misplaced word, one lapse of judgement, one ill-advised démarche, and the most glittering career could be cut short in an instant. And Wolfgang Kessler, Quirke knew, had friends at the highest levels of public life – and life here, public and private, was ruled over by the Church.

'Do you know,' he asked, 'about that young woman who was found dead in her car in a lock-up garage next to the Pepper Canister church?'

'Rosa Jacobs. Yes, I have a report you have on it from the Commissioner. A bad business.'

Quirke heard clearly the note of wariness that had come into the Minister's voice.

'Yes, very bad. I presume it's in the report you have that she was most probably murdered?'

'The Commissioner mentioned it. Mentioned you, in fact, now that I think of it. You didn't believe it was suicide.'

'No, I didn't. And don't.'

Dick Fitz pursed his lips and speared up another morsel of beef. Quirke tried not to look at the pinkish slice of flesh with its bilious yellow smear of mustard.

'You mentioned Wolfgang Kessler,' Dick said, chewing. 'Why is that?'

Quirke lifted his glass. It really was delicious wine, perhaps the finest he had ever drunk. Expenses must be lavish at the

Department, even if it was the Minister who was doing the spending.

'Let me ask you,' he said. 'What do you know about Kessler, and his son?'

Dick Fitz was thinking. It was clear he didn't like the direction this conversation was going in. A murdered young woman and a rich German horse breeder, that was a potent combination.

'He's a businessman,' he said, 'with interests all over – Europe, America – Russia, even.'

'And Israel,' Quirke said.

Dick Fitz looked up quickly from his plate and regarded him with narrowed eyes.

'Yes, Israel too,' he said.

He was a good-looking man, tall, slim, with an elegant, somewhat languid manner. His father, in his time also a minister, had been a dedicated ladies' man, and so was he, by all accounts. Margaret, his wife, was a famous beauty, or had been when she was young. It was said her life was a misery due to Dick's tireless infidelities; nevertheless, she kept up an unfailingly placid front. It was known that he went to her for advice in times of crisis. Yes, the FitzMaurices, husband and wife, were a formidable pair. If Dick asked her, Mrs Fitz would advise him to exercise the greatest caution in any matter involving the Wolfgang Kesslers of this world.

'The dead woman's sister,' Quirke said, 'her older sister, is here. Molly Jacobs. She's a journalist, based in London. She came over for the funeral, and stayed on for – for a while.'

'You know her, then, do you?' Dick enquired mildly.

Was that a knowing glint Quirke detected in those hand-some grey eyes fixed on him across the table? Dick made it his business to be well informed. There wasn't much that happened in this city that he didn't know about.

'Yes, I met her through David Sinclair,' Quirke blandly lied. 'He used to work with me at the hospital. Went off to Israel, now he's back.'

Dick Fitz was still fixed on him, and slowly nodded.

'Israel, again,' he said. 'Coincidence.'

'Not really. I have a strong feeling, a very strong feeling, that Israel is the connection between the killing of Rosa Jacobs, the death of a journalist in Tel Aviv, and the attempted murder last night of Molly Jacobs.'

Dick stopped chewing, and stared.

'Where was this?'

'Usher's Island. She's staying in a house up there, lent to her by a friend.'

'What happened?'

'She went out to the shop for something, about half nine. When she came back, a car drove up onto the pavement and knocked her down. She was lucky, she got away with bruises and a banged-up face.'

'Did the driver stop?'

'No. A couple of Guards in a squad car found her uncon-scious on the pavement. She's in St James's. They'll release her in a day or two. Amazing nothing was broken. She's badly bruised, but she'll be all right.'

Dick Fitz had eaten half the food on his plate but now seemed suddenly, like Quirke, to have lost his appetite. He had the air of a man slowly realising that he has walked himself unwittingly into a trap.

'Is your friend Hackett looking into it?' he asked.

'And Detective Inspector Strafford.'

'Strafford. Is he the one who was with you in Spain when—?'

'Yes.'

Dick Fitz signalled to the waiter that they had finished the main course.

'Bit of cheese?' he said to Quirke.

'I've had enough.' The waiter had cast a fisheye over his plate and the food he had hardly touched. 'Maybe a brandy.'

'You'll forgive me if I don't join you.' He looked at his watch. 'I've a committee meeting this afternoon.' He turned to the waiter. 'I'll take a spoonful of Stilton, Michael.'

Dick always knew the names of those who waited on him.

'Anything to drink, Minister?' Michael enquired. 'Drop of port, with the cheese?'

'Thank you, no.'

'Just the brandy, then,' the man said, and went away.

Quirke was sure the waiter knew his name and had deliberately not addressed him by it. He found the nice distinctions made by servants a continuing source of fascination and amusement.

'I'm sorry, Quirke,' Dick Fitz said, making a point of looking again to his watch, 'but I'll have to go shortly.'

'What about your cheese?' Quirke asked drily.

Dick smiled his smooth smile.

'Tell me what it is exactly you want me to do,' he said.

There was an inch of wine left in the bottle, and Quirke divided it between the two glasses.

'To be honest, Dick, I don't know. As I say, something is going on, involving Israel, Wolfgang Kessler and his son, and these two deaths and the attempt last night on Molly Jacobs's life. But I've no idea what it is.' He leaned closer. 'What's the nature of Kessler's business dealings in Israel, do you know?'

'Heavy machinery, I believe. And something to do with land reclamation. He has a lot of interests in a lot of projects.'

'Weapons?'

Dick blinked.

'What do you mean, weapons?'

'The journalist who was killed in Tel Aviv was working on a story, or a series, or something, on Israel's nuclear programme.'

All expression drained from Dick Fitz's face.

'Has Israel got a nuclear programme?'

'I believe they're busy making a bomb.'

'And you think—?'

'I wonder, I just wonder, if Wolfgang Kessler's heavy machinery plant might be supplying the Israelis with something other than buckets and spades to reclaim the desert with.'

The waiter came with Quirke's brandy, and the plate of cheese.

'Sorry, Michael, my man,' Dick said to him, 'I shouldn't have ordered it, I haven't time.' He dabbed his mouth with the napkin and laid it down beside his empty wine glass. 'Must go.'

Quirke stood up, and the two men shook hands.

'Will you ask around about Kessler?' Quirke said. 'Two young women were murdered, Dick, and a third one might have been.'

Dick's eyes had taken on a look at once evasive and impatient.

'Let's see what Hackett and your man Strafford turn up, shall we? My civil servants are very busy at the moment.' He lowered his voice and glanced about. 'You know de Valera is dead set against any kind of European union? "We didn't free ourselves from the British," he says, "only to be taken over by another gang of freebooters." He's priceless, that man.'

'Goodbye, Dick,' Quirke said.

Dick lifted a finger to his forehead in an ironic salute, and walked away. Quirke sat down and looked at his brandy. He knew he shouldn't drink it. But when he had, and it was gone, he would most probably order another. He knew himself too well.

Dick suddenly appeared again, set one fist on the table and leaned down to speak close to Quirke's ear.

'One thing,' he said. 'About Kessler. That's not his real name.'

'It's not?—'

'Shh. No, he was originally called something else.'

'Sit down for a second.' Dick again looked about at the other tables, then sat down on the edge of the chair. 'What was he called?'

'Don't know. Can't remember. Anyway, the passport he had was false. We let it go – he had a lot of money to spend when he landed here. And he was in thick with the sky pilots.'

'Which ones?'

'McEvoy, the bold Bishop Tom.' He smiled. 'See who you're dealing with? Keep asking the questions you've been asking me, next thing you know you'll be hearing from Drumcondra.'

Quirke didn't have to ask what he meant. Drumcondra was where Archbishop McQuaid had his palace. A telephone call from him to the head of the board of the Hospital of the Holy Family, and Quirke would be packing a bag and on his way to London or America to look for a new job.

'Tell me more,' he said. 'I know there's more.'

Dick Fitz tapped a finger to the side of his nose, shook his head and smiled.

'If there's more,' he said, 'you'll have to get it from someone else.'

He stood up and walked away from the table, and this time he did not come back. Quirke downed the glass of brandy in one go, and signalled for another.

21

Strafford was dreaming. He was in an old-fashioned steam train, luxuriously appointed in art deco style. The seats were upholstered in wine-red plush, and above them there were framed photographs of *fin de siècle* cities, London, Paris, Vienna. Between the photographs were mirrors, framed also, in gilt, with lilies and long, undulating leaves painted around their edges. Oddly, although in the dream it seemed not odd at all, the carriage was not travelling over tracks, but was floating along smoothly in some soundless medium, water, or perhaps just air itself.

Something was wrong, however. There was danger, or an emergency of some kind, for in the distance an alarm bell was ringing, ringing and ringing. At last it stopped, but was succeeded after an interval by an insistent knocking close by. It was as if someone were outside the train, knocking to be let in. He heard his name called. But who could know he was here, travelling in this carriage, in this floating or flying express train?

He woke up.

'Mr Strafford! The phone! It's for you!'

Groggily, he threw back the covers and got out of bed. He switched on a lamp, and stood blinking. He was dizzy from the dream.

'Mr Strafford!'

He put on a dressing gown and opened the door. Mr Claridge was there, wearing a heavy black greatcoat over his pyjamas. He was in carpet slippers, and his legs were bare. What was most startling in his appearance was his hair. Usually heavily oiled and brushed flat, it now stood on end. He looked, Strafford thought, exactly like the actor who played Mr Dick in the old *David Copperfield* picture.

'I was beginning to think you weren't in,' he said crossly. 'Do you know what time it is?'

'No,' Strafford said thickly.

'It's nearly two o'clock.'

'I don't understand.'

Mr Claridge's eyes bulged. He looked almost apoplectic.

'What don't you understand?' he cried. 'The phone, man, the phone! Someone wants to speak to you on the phone!'

Strafford followed him to the head of the stairs. The light was on in the hall. Mr Claridge pointed an angry finger.

'The phone, see?' he said. 'There!'

He turned and strode away, muttering. Strafford put a hand to his forehead. He went down the stairs.

When he picked up the phone, the line was dead. He stood and listened to the buzzing for a while, feeling stupefied. He wasn't fully awake. At last, he replaced the receiver and went back to the stairs. When he was halfway up, the phone began to ring again. He hurried down to it.

'Yes, yes,' he gabbled, 'who is this?'

'I'm sorry,' a man's voice said, 'I ran out of pennies, I had to go to the car and—'

'What? What are you saying?' Strafford rubbed a hand over his eyes. 'Who is this?'

'It's Frank Kessler. I—'

He broke off, and there was a hoarse, choking sound. He was weeping.

The night was damp and cold. Scraps of mist drifted on the shiny black waters of the canal, and the street lamps had fuzzy haloes. All the roads roundabout were empty. Everything seemed to be holding its breath.

Frank Kessler was sitting on a metal bench on the towpath. Above him was the broad canopy of a sycamore, through the leaves of which the street lights shed a feeble, flickering glow.

When he saw Strafford approaching, Kessler jumped to his feet and took an uncertain step forward.

'I'm sorry,' he said. 'Forgive me, I know it's late.' He wiped his nose with the back of his hand and drew in a shivery breath. 'You were the only one I could think of.'

By now, Strafford had reached a state of almost hallucinatory clarity, that he knew was not clarity at all. Everything around him was starkly sharp-edged and unnaturally solid, imbued with an inevitability only encountered in dreams. Was he still asleep, and none of this real?

'How did you know the phone number?' he asked.

For the moment this seemed an issue of paramount importance, which must be cleared up immediately.

'What?'

'The number,' Strafford said, raising his voice, and gesturing towards the Claridges' house across the road. 'How did you know it?'

'I called the Garda station. I said I must speak to you, that it was an emergency.'

Jesus Christ! Strafford thought, *they gave out my phone number to somebody calling at two o'clock in the morning.* It could have been anybody. It could have been a lunatic, or someone his evidence had sent to jail who was out now and bent on vengeance. First thing in the morning, he would find out who the desk sergeant was tonight and by God!—

'I'm sorry,' Kessler said in a small voice, and hung his head.

He wore a transparent plastic raincoat over his suit. The knot of his tie was crooked, and his shirt collar stuck up at one side. He looked as if he had been in a scuffle. At every movement, the plastic coat creaked and squealed tinnily. There was a shiny black splash of something down one side of it. Was it paint? Strafford almost laughed at the madness of it: the fellow had been painting, in the middle of the night!

'Where have you come from?' he asked. 'Where were you?'

'From my father's house.'

The words had a biblical ring, uttered as they were with such gravity and, as it seemed, out of such a depth of sorrow.

'You came from there tonight, now?' Kessler nodded, and said something that Strafford didn't catch. 'It's very late. It's the middle of the night.'

Strafford didn't know what to do. Kessler was plainly in extreme distress. He was breathing rapidly, almost panting, and at intervals a violent shudder ran through him, making the plastic coat crackle like a fire of thorns leaping up.

'Forgive me,' Kessler said, and held out both hands in an abject gesture.

'Let's sit down here, on this bench,' Strafford said.

He was shivering from the cold. He had put on a pair of

308

trousers and a jumper over his pyjamas, and had wrapped himself in his raincoat, but nothing, it seemed, could resist the insinuating, rank misty air.

They sat down. Their breath billowed about them like clouds of ectoplasm.

'I killed him,' Kessler said, suddenly but matter-of-factly. 'I shot him, with his own pistol.'

'Who did you shoot?' Strafford asked, though he knew the answer.

Quirke was right. It had been the Kesslers, all along.

They sat there on the bench for a long time. Either something had happened in the air to warm it, or they had got used to the chill. Now and then a car went past on the road, the head-lights sweeping whitely through the mist. No one was about, except, briefly, a couple, whose footsteps rang steely on the pavement. They were having a fight. The woman was intent and bitter, the man hardly responded, sounding embarrassed when he did. Soon they went dejectedly away. There was an occasional rustling in the sedge that bordered the water, and a splash or two. Moorhens stirring in their sleep, Strafford thought, or rats on the prowl.

'What shall I do?' Kessler said.

It was less a question than a spoken thought. The agitation of earlier had been replaced by a kind of lifeless calm. It was as if he were a long distance off, looking back reflectively, and in vague wonderment, at the strange circumstances in which he found himself.

'Let's think about that later,' Strafford said. 'For now, tell me what happened.'

'I told you. I killed my father.'

'Why?'

Kessler turned his head and stared at him, then softly laughed.

'Where should I begin? How far back should I go?'

'Just talk about tonight,' Strafford said.

But Kessler seemed not to have heard him.

'Always he despised me, always pushed me to the side. *"Mein kleiner Schwächling,"* he used to say to people. Look at him, my little weakling, *mein kleines Mädchen*. He could never accept me as I am.'

Strafford stole a glance at his watch.

'*Tonight*, Mr Kessler,' he said. 'Tell me what happened *tonight*.'

Kessler made an impatient gesture, crossing and recrossing his legs. The noise of that plastic raincoat was beginning to get on Strafford's nerves. Maybe he should shut this fellow up and haul him down to the station by the scruff of the neck and let Hackett shake the truth out of him.

'You know he had that young woman killed?' Kessler said.

'Rosa Jacobs?'

'What?' Kessler stared at him again. 'No, no – the one in Israel, the journalist.'

'How do you mean, had her killed?'

'He went to his friends in Mossad. I can hear him talking to them in his commandant's voice. "She's going to destroy everything, you'll have to shut her up, you'll have to get rid of her."'

'Are you saying the Israeli secret service assassinated Shulamith Lieberman?'

'Oh, they wouldn't do it themselves, just as my father would not do it. There are always people who can be hired, gangsters, murderers, petty thieves – even in virtuous Israel, where everybody is supposed to be a hero, or a fearless soldier, or a tireless kibbutznik.'

'What had she found out, the Lieberman woman, that made her so dangerous?'

Kessler leaned back on the bench and extended his arms along the top rail. Strafford remembered Wolfgang Kessler doing the same thing, sitting at his ease on the sofa in his house in Wicklow.

'She had learned,' he said slowly, 'that my father was supplying Israel with important components for the manufacture of an atomic bomb.' He leaned his head back and looked up into the dense and faintly crepitating foliage above him. 'That story could not be allowed to come out.'

Strafford had a sudden longing for a cigarette. This was ridiculous, since he didn't smoke. Was it warmth he wanted, or just something to do with his hands? He supposed that was the reason people became addicted to cigarettes. Cigarettes were companionable; with them, one need never be entirely idle.

'Would a newspaper in Israel publish something so explosive?'

Kessler laughed again, quietly.

'That is a very bad – what do you call it? – a very bad pun.' He glanced up once more into the leaves. 'She had contacts at the *Manchester Guardian* – you know this newspaper? Left wing. Had she been allowed to finish her searches and write the story, they would have printed it. Maybe. There are many rich and powerful Jews in Britain, as everywhere else. Even still.'

A lorry went past, wheezing and rattling. What business had anyone to be out in a lorry at – what was it now? Christ, it was almost three o'clock! All this was unreal.

'Did you really do what you said you did?' Kessler nodded, almost pettishly, pushing out his lower lip. 'And is that why you did it? Because of Shulamith Lieberman? Did you know her, in Israel?'

'No. I never met her. But there were people who knew what she was doing. Tel Aviv is like Dublin. Everyone knows everyone else's business. On the other hand, there are so many rumours you do not know who or what to believe.' He paused. 'I like the Jews, you know, I admire them. But they make fantasies. They talk and talk and talk and you have to try to separate what is true from what is a dream.'

'If it wasn't the killing of this woman, then what?'

Kessler looked about. He seemed distracted. He hummed a tuneless tune under his breath. He picked at the buttons on his plastic coat.

'My father was a very wicked man. Very wicked – more than you could imagine.' He stopped, and gave yet another little snort of laughter. 'Even his name was false, did you know that? No. No one did. Wolfgang Graf von Kessler – ha!' He bent and picked up a shard of gravel from the path and threw it out over the canal. It fell into the unmoving water with a comic little plop. 'Hitler's name should have been Schicklgruber – did you know *that*? His father was the bastard son of an Austrian slut, *his* father unknown. Little Adolf spoke all his life like a Bavarian farmhand – *dodle dodle dodle* – and never had proper German. "Graf von Kessler" liked to pretend he was an aristocrat from the Bavarian Alps.

The truth is, he was born in a Munich slum. As a child he was sent to work for nothing for an uncle, up in the mountains. He lived in a shed, like one of the farm animals.' He laughed softly. '"*Die Hütte*". Ha.'

Strafford was tired, his brain was fogged. He was still wondering what to do with this strange young man who not long before, if he was to be believed, had shot and killed his own father. What would become of him? Maybe he could plead insanity, but to spend the rest of his days in a madhouse would surely be worse than serving a life sentence in jail.

As if he had heard these thoughts, Kessler asked now:

'What will happen to me?'

'I don't know,' Strafford answered. A thought occurred to him. 'Was it you who ran down Rosa Jacobs's sister in your car?' Kessler nodded, and bit his lower lip with his upper teeth, like a naughty child. 'Why did you do that?'

'Because my father told me to. She had been talking to another journalist in—'

'I know.'

Kessler glanced at him with genuine interest.

'How much *do* you know?'

What should he answer? He had decided that the man sitting beside him was mad. Perhaps they were both mad, father and son. Frank Kessler was capable of anything, not out of wickedness, in his case, but anguished desperation.

'We know a great deal,' Strafford lied. 'We have all the pieces, we just need to fit them together. You can help us.'

Kessler put on a sulky face.

'Why should I?'

'Isn't that why you came here, to me – to confess?'

'I came because I thought you would – I thought you would understand me, and what I did. You know we look alike? Have you noticed it? If I were some years older, we could be twins. Don't you think?'

A pleading note had come into his voice. Strafford felt he had never before encountered someone as lonely as this young man. He recalled that day in the Hibernian Hotel, as they walked together through the doorway of the lounge. He almost felt again the strange little tremor that had gone through him at the accidental touch of Kessler's shoulder. But had it been an accident?

Mein kleiner Schwächlin, mein kleines Mädchen.

'Tell me what happened,' he said again.

Kessler expelled a long, unsteady sigh.

'He told me I must find a way to stop that woman, Molly Jacobs, to stop her for good. He mocked me, called me *ein Stümper*, a – what do you say? – a bungler, because I failed to kill her that night, with the car. "Next time you must do it right," he said, "if you do not want to lose the tiny bit of respect I have for you."' He turned to Strafford and laid a trembling hand on his arm. It felt to Strafford as if a live electric wire had touched him. 'Don't you see now why I had to do it? Why I had to shoot him.'

'No, I don't,' Strafford said mildly. 'My father was like that, and—'

'I knew it!' Kessler exclaimed, and his grip on Strafford's arm tightened convulsively. 'I knew we were brothers, of a kind, kind of – *Wie heißt das?* – of a spiritual kind. Brothers in spirit. Don't you feel it, too? Surely you must.'

Strafford freed his arm, and put his hands in the pockets of his raincoat. He was cold again, yet hot, too, hot with embarrassment, and a strange kind of shame.

'I'm sorry,' he said, hardening his voice, 'but you came to the wrong person. I'm not your brother, or anything like it. I'm a detective, investigating the murder of a young woman, and the attempted murder of another.'

'I didn't kill her,' Kessler said.

'Who?'

Kessler looked at him almost pityingly.

'Rosa Jacobs – who else?'

This made Strafford sigh. What was the point of lying, at this late stage of things?

'Then who did?'

'How should I know?' Kessler responded haughtily, with a toss of the head, and for that moment he was unmistakably Wolfgang Kessler's son. 'Probably my father had one of his people do it for him. He wouldn't hesitate, if he felt himself and his interests were under threat.' He let his shoulders slump, and began to pick at the side of his left thumbnail. 'I'll tell you what was the final insult, the final betrayal, and the reason I had to kill him,' he said, in a strange, musing, faraway voice, as if someone else were speaking through him. 'Do you know what is the Mabahith Amn El Dawla? No? It's Arabic. It is the name of the Egyptian security service.'

He picked up another stone, and threw it into the water. There was a sharp movement among the reeds.

'I learned, during my recent time in Israel,' he went on, 'that my father was conspiring with them, with Nasser's spies. This was told to me by my father's partner in crime out there.'

'Teddy Katz?'

'How do you know of him? Well, it doesn't matter. Even as he was selling parts to the Israelis for their bomb, he was betraying their atomic programme to the Egyptians. You see, he hated the Jews, would have them exterminated. In the war' – he swallowed, making a gulping sound – 'in the war he—' He put his fists together and pounded them slowly on his knees. 'I can't,' he whispered. 'I can't say it.'

'What did he do in the war, your father?'

'No no, I can't. Don't ask me, it's not fair.' He stood up, and went to the edge of the canal and stood there motionless for some time, with his back turned. A church bell chimed, a single peal; it reverberated through the darkness as if to announce the passing of a sentence.

'Your family's secrets are of no interest to me,' Strafford said.

Kessler wasn't listening.

'You were one I thought I could trust,' he said, without turning. 'That day, in the hotel, I almost—'

'Almost what?' Strafford asked, although in truth he didn't want to know.

'I could have loved you,' Kessler said, still with his back turned, and so softly that Strafford wasn't sure he had heard correctly. 'But it's too late.'

Now he wheeled about. He was holding something in his hand. It was a pistol – Strafford recognised it as a Luger. Slowly, he stood up from the bench.

'Give that to me,' he said, holding out a hand.

Kessler shook his head very rapidly from side to side.

'Don't be frightened,' he said. 'I won't hurt you' – he smiled – '*Bruder mein.*' He looked up into the darkness. The

316

moon was there, peering through the mist like a single, fat white eye. '*Hier ist Erlösung.*'

He smiled once more at Strafford, and put the barrel of the gun into his mouth and pulled the trigger. The report was oddly muted, an offhand sort of sound, as Strafford would think of it later. Kessler fell back slowly, as if in a swoon, and the water flew up around him in graceful cascades.

That stain on his coat. It wasn't paint, of course. It was his father's blood.

22

Some days later, along the same stretch of the canal, Quirke walked with Molly Jacobs, in the rain. Molly's left arm was in a sling. The bruise on her cheek, over the bone, had turned blue-grey with sallow patches. Quirke held aloft a wide black umbrella over them both. He felt as if he were following a funeral cortège. The rain was heavy, it fell straight down through the still air with vengeful concentration. The towpath was muddy. Why were they walking here, when they could be in a café, or a pub?

He knew what was going to happen, here, today, shortly. He didn't know how he knew, but he did. It *was* a funeral, of sorts.

Already he had told her about the Kesslers, father and son, both of them dead. He had gone down to Wicklow, with Hackett and Detective Inspector Strafford. There was a different driver this time, a fat, cheerful young Guard who kept up a continuous, low and tuneless whistling that set Quirke's teeth on edge. There was rain that day, too, but not rain like this. It was more a kind of absent-minded mist that drifted slantwise across the moorlands. Sheep huddled in the lee of thorn bushes, or just stood unconcerned, methodically nibbling the thinning autumn grass.

Wolfgang Kessler's body lay under a tarpaulin at the foot of the front steps, which he had descended to greet Quirke and

Strafford, the first time they had come here. He had been shot in the back of the neck. Another bullet had punctured his spleen, but would probably not have been fatal. He must have been fleeing from his son, fleeing for his life. Quirke remembered how the rain-light had shone on the tarpaulin. It reminded him of something from the far past, he couldn't think what.

'Have they found out who he really was?' Molly asked.

Quirke had already warned her that her shoes would be ruined, in this rain, but she wanted to be outdoors. A public funeral, then.

'Hackett is in contact with the German police,' he said. 'There was talk of sending Strafford over there, but a veto came down from on high. Old business, old crimes. The Israelis will say nothing. Their German benefactor might not have existed, as far as they're concerned. I imagine they'll have to scrap everything and start again on their bomb. As for the Egyptians – well.'

They passed by the sawmill, on the far side of the canal. There was the scream and stutter of a chainsaw ripping through timber. The smell of sawdust drifted on the air, despite the rain.

'Poor Rosa,' Molly said, 'caught up in all that.'

'She had courage.'

Molly set her mouth in a tight line.

'Only the stupid are brave,' she said bitterly. Then she dipped her head. 'My foolish, heedless sister. Typical of them to kill her with gas. Heaven knows, they had plenty of practice.'

They walked on, sloshing through the mire.

'I imagine Kessler must have been involved in the Holocaust,' Quirke said.

'The Shoah.'

'What?'

'That's what we call it. Someone else came up with the word holocaust. Shoah means catastrophe.'

They were at Baggot Street bridge.

'We could go up and look into Parson's,' Quirke said. 'I could buy you a book.'

'What book?'

'Any book.'

The rain drummed on the umbrella. Quirke's arm was going numb from the weight of the thing. *This is absurd*, he thought, *standing here in the rain, in the sad rain of autumn, waiting for the end*. She must have sensed what he was thinking. She said:

'I think I need to go back.'

'But you have the house for another week,' Quirke said, 'more than a week.'

He heard how petulant he sounded. Like a little boy who has been told his holiday is to be cut short.

'Yes,' Molly said, 'but I need to go – home.'

'I see. Right.' He shifted the umbrella from his right hand to his left, and silvery fat drops cascaded from the brim. 'I could come over and see you. For a visit, I mean. The odd weekend. We could go for a trip, Paris, maybe, or—'

'Quirke.' She touched a middle finger to the back of his hand. He recalled her doing the same thing, in the bedroom at Buswells Hotel, that first day, when he held the lighter flame to her cigarette. Soon it would be only memories. Soon.

'I wish you'd stay,' he said.

'Yes, I know you do. And I wish I could. But I can't.'

321

'Why not?

The little boy again. *But Mammy, Daddy!*—

'Because I can't. Just that. I can't.'

A bus thundered over the bridge, like an elephant, rearing on the up slope, plunging forward on the down.

'I thought we could – I thought we might make something, between us.'

'I thought so too,' Molly said. She looked at her shoes. 'You were right. They're ruined.'

'Molly—'

He fumbled for her hand, but she drew it away.

'Don't,' she said. 'It's no good. You know that as well as I do.'

'What if I said I need you. That you've become part of my world – part of me.'

She smiled up sadly into his face.

'I wouldn't believe you,' she said gently. 'Nor would you, believe yourself. You're like a wounded animal, Quirke.'

'I am a wounded animal.'

'Yes, but I'm not the one to put you out of your misery.' She stood on tiptoe and kissed him lightly, fleetingly, on the lips. *Dear heart, how like you this?* 'Don't hate me,' she said, smiling again.

She stepped back, out of the shelter of the umbrella, and turned and walked off along the towpath, bare-headed in the rain.

They flee from me.

Epilogue

She shouldn't have threatened me. I took a lot of grief from her, but this was the limit – beyond the limit. And I wouldn't tolerate it. How dare she. I took her on, her and her damned Irish Jews, did all I could for her, launched her on what was a promising career, highly promising. And how did she thank me? First she said she'd go to the Provost and tell him I had forced myself on her. Then she changed her mind – she'd ring up Deirdre and reveal all. Jesus. I hardly care to think what Dee would have done.

Why am I so afraid of that bloody wife of mine? I've thought about this a lot, and decided it's her single-mindedness that scares me. She sails through life like one of those Arctic ice-breakers, clearing all in her path. Never entertains the slightest doubt about herself and her opinions. Got that from her dad, the Master of the Ministry. Sir Ralph Ponsonby Wheeler. No hyphen, mark you. Puffed up with pride like a bullfrog after fifty years of lording it over the civil servants under his command. It was contempt at first sight between him and me, the Magnificent Mandarin and the working-class upstart from Up North. Has a particularly active cancer now, to keep him company in his retirement. Good old Mother Nature.

What was I saying? Deirdre, yes. Should have given her a clutch of kids, that would have slowed her progress. She didn't want them, made that clear from the start. 'Don't think I'm going to bear your brats, Ronnie my love. I've better things to do with my life.' Probably just as well. Imagine having my Dee for a mother. And imagine having me for a father.

The funny thing is – though it's not funny at all – the reason we got engaged was because she thought she was pregnant. When she found she wasn't, it would have been bad form on my part to break it off. Spent our honeymoon in Paris. I got food poisoning. 'Trust you,' Deirdre said, and went off to buy a hat. So began our life of wedded bliss.

My trouble is, I've always had a weakness for the girls. You might say, I might say, who could blame me, but in that regard I'm honest. I could be married to Marilyn Monroe and I'd still be a skirt-chaser. Oh, the Mabels and the Queenies and the Antoinettes, and all the others whose names I've forgotten, what fun they were! Nothing bucks a man up like a bouncy new sweetheart tucked away discreetly somewhere.

How have I got away with it for so long? That's a question that often has me awake in the night, in a cold sweat. Dee I wouldn't mind losing, if she found me out and it all went crash, but the Ponsonby Wheeler money, now, that's another matter. I've been living the good life for nigh on twenty years. Think I'd be content, scratching along on my Trinity salary? Not to be contemplated.

Anyway. It's pleasant sitting here, in the watches of the night, scribbling in my little black book. It's risky, I know. I suppose that's part of the pleasure. But when Dee turned thirty-five last year, she took to poking around in my things. What she thinks she'll find, I don't know – any secrets I have I keep locked away in a filing cabinet in the office. I shouldn't leave the diary here at home. What if one night I were to forget and leave it out on my desk for her to find? That's another prospect I'd rather not contemplate.

It was nice, with Rosa, at first. Or no, 'nice' is not the word. Rosa wasn't nice, which was what attracted me to her in the first place, I think. Never met anyone like her, before or since. She had Deirdre's energy and untiring self-regard, but there the comparison ended. Poor Dee hasn't a brain in her head, though she hides the fact behind a bossy manner and that cut-glass Ponsonby Wheeler accent. 'Itt will nott doo, Ronald, itt simply will nott doo!' Yes, m'lady, of course, m'lady, put your dainty foot up on this pouffe so I can kiss your shoe.

Bloody woman. See how I keep circling back to her? It's like the moth and the candle.

But Rosa, now. God, she was exciting! I was dazzled, dazzled by her darkness. She had a man's ruthlessness, a man's way of cutting through the nonsense, the lovey-dovey stuff, and getting down to basics. She was a demon in bed – a demon. There was nothing she wouldn't do, nothing she wouldn't have done to her. I'd never known anything like it. After a session with her I would flop over on my back, grinning and gasping, then five minutes later I'd feel those fingers of hers on me again. She couldn't get enough of it. In the army I used to hear fellows talking about ones like her, mill girls, shop assistants, factory workers, who were anybody's for a Woodbine and a bottle of Bass. I thought it was just talk, the stuff of wet dreams. Then I met Rosa.

At first, I could hardly believe my luck. What did she see in me, a working-class lad from Stockport who had pulled himself up by his bootstraps and could only get himself a university chair in Ireland, of all places? Also I was a lot older than she was, and married to a termagant. I had a bald spot, and a bad knee from the war. I wasn't even circumcised, for Christ's sake! But she took one look and set her hat at me.

I know, I know: it couldn't but help that I was Lecky Professor of History at Trinity College Dublin. As I say, Trinity is hardly Oxbridge, but it has a noble history, as the college grandees never tire of reminding you. Founded by Good Queen Bess in the year dot and so on and so forth. And what, after all, was Rosa Jacobs? A huckster's daughter from Cork, and a Jew into the bargain. I'll give it to her, she didn't put on airs or try to buff up her origins. Though she had her pride. She came of an ancient race, she would say, the race of Maimonides and Spinoza, of Rahel Varnhagen and Simone Weil, blah blah blah. My eyes would glaze over after two minutes of that stuff.

Oh, she was a crusader, she certainly was. She talked in placards. Ban the Bomb! Women's Rights! Abortion for All! House the Tinkers! You couldn't shut her up. I learned to let it all wash over me. In breaks between our exertions she would sit up in bed, with her skinny shoulders and her little pointy tits, smoking like a chimney and going on and on, a cross between the Communist Manifesto and Mary Wollstonecraft, until I ran a hand up her leg and off we'd go again. I sometimes thought that for her, lovemaking was politics by other means. She went at both with unstoppable force. What a girl.

We used to meet in her room in the Rubrics. I had to go carefully there. Wouldn't do for the Lecky Professor of History to be seen creeping into a doctoral student's quarters. But oh, those afternoons! The light like muslin, and the tops of the trees swaying in the window, and in the distance the *pock!* of ball on bat and the little figures in white loping at their gentlemanly leisure over the plush green grass of College Park. Whatever I may say to the contrary, I have a certain fondness for the old place.

I miss her. I miss Rosa. I know how absurd it is to say so, but I do.

We managed one away match. A disaster. I told Deirdre I had been invited to a conference in London, at King's. It would be a dreary affair, I said, she'd be bored silly. I promised to bring her back a jumbo box of chocs from Fortnum & Mason. She groused a bit, but gave in eventually. She had been with me to conferences before, and they had been no fun.

Didn't want to fly – what if the plane crashed and Rosa and I were found dead in each other's arms in the wreckage? – so we went on the ferry, in her car. Nice little motor, with a canvas roof that could be rolled back should we have been going to Italy, say, or the Côte d'Azur. The south of England was wet that weekend. We had driven to Rosslare and crossed to Fishguard, then set off up the long curve towards London. And promptly ran into trouble.

On the approach to Carmarthen, the clutch cable snapped. Nothing daunted, I got to work with pliers and trusty pen-knife. My old dad would have been proud of me. We limped into the town, and put up at a pub straight out of *Under Milk Wood*. Whiskey and sandwiches in a bar lit by a gas lamp, and then a bedroom with a floor sloped at about forty-five degrees. Next morning, we found a mechanic who promised he'd have the job done by noon. It took three days. By then, tempers were frayed. I saw another side of Rosa. A spoilt child whose party had been rained on. Christ, how she sulked. By the time we got the car back, we had run out of weekend, and it was time to go home.

Nothing was quite the same, after that calamitous jaunt. She wouldn't even give me credit for patching up the car so we didn't have to walk into bloody Carmarthen. She started to look at me in a new way. I would catch her doing it, that sideways, narrow-eyed glance from under her hair, her mouth pursed and the tip of one ear showing through those wiry curls. And to be honest, for my part I was getting a bit tired of her. A man can put up with only so many harangues about unmarried mothers and the iniquities of the Catholic Church. I mean to say.

I thought I had my excuse when I saw her one evening meeting a man under Clerys's clock. I was tootling by in the Morris Austin. Deirdre was in the car – can't remember where we were going – otherwise I might have stopped. We were waiting at the lights at the corner of Abbey Street when I spotted her. She was wearing her blue raincoat and the black beret that made her look, I used to tell her, like a gamine in one of those new French movies. The man she was meeting was youngish, on the tall side, stiff-backed, with limp pale hair. Did I recognise him as a German? Probably not.

When Rosa and I next met, I confronted her with what I had seen. I felt like a Victorian father demanding to know of his daughter who the fellow was he had caught her dallying with under the lime tree by the lychgate behind the tennis court. She put back her head and fixed me with one of her long looks, then gave a sardonic laugh.

'For a start it's none of your business, and furthermore, he's not interested in girls. Not at all – you understand?'

330

Frank Kessler, he was called. She used to know him, years before, when he was a student first at Trinity. I enquired, mildly, how and why had he come back into her life. Again, that stare. Who she chose to meet was none of my business, she said. I pressed her. I pressed her quite hard, I can tell you. I think she thought I might hit her. Which I might have done, had she kept on resisting me. It was the first time she had seen what a temper I have, when I'm seriously annoyed.

It turned out that the fellow's father, one Wolfgang Kessler, was the real focus of her interest. A wealthy Kraut, with a big place in Wicklow. She was doing a bit of snooping on behalf of a pal of hers in Israel, a woman journalist who suspected that Kessler *père*, who had some sort of business going over there, was up to no good. I laughed, of course. It was like something out of one of those spy pictures Ealing Studios have been churning out since our glorious victory over the Nasties.

'When are the Jews going to stop being paranoid?' I asked her.

I thought she would take a swing at me.

'You'd be paranoid, if the Germans had invaded England and carted off millions of English people and murdered them.'

Oh, here we go, I thought. Why couldn't I keep my mouth shut?

'Let's go to your room,' I said.

She looked daggers at me. No canoodling for Ronnie, not that afternoon.

It was about that time when she got it into her head to go to Israel. The plan was to join her friend Lois Lane of the *Daily Planet* in her quest to foil the evil plot being hatched by the Gauleiter Wolfgang Kessler to cause mayhem and bring down the Jewish state. Would I lend her – no, would I *give* her the fare to Tel Aviv? I told her not to be ridiculous. Then she would ask Frank Kessler for the money, she said. That afforded me a genuine laugh.

'You're going to get the son to fund your crazy campaign against his own father?'

She scoffed. Frank Kessler hated his father, she said. Frank was a good man, who wished to atone in any way he could for the crimes the Germans had committed against the Jews.

Pull the other one, I almost said.

Time went by. I could see she was brooding. I was barred from her room – nix on sex. I languished.

I was alarmed, too. I got it into my head that she was working up a plot against me. I had fallen below the high standards she had set for herself, and therefore for me also. I would have to be taught a lesson.

I bumped into her one windy evening, crossing Front Square. She was clutching her raincoat around herself, and her beret was pulled down over her ears. It was funny: she looked just like a figure in one of those photographs of her people being herded onto the cattle trucks going East. I asked her what the matter was – I was concerned she might be sick. A sick girlfriend would be no fun.

'I'm pregnant,' she said.

Just like that. I nearly fell over.

Now, I never understand why men are always astonished when their girls tell them they're up the duff. I mean, they've been shagging away for months in gay abandon, blithely confident that the girl being shagged will have protection in place, even though no sign of it can be seen or felt. Do we think she offers up a prayer to the Virgin Mary, or summons up a voodoo spell, while she's taking off her clothes, and that's all that's required and everything is safe as houses? How can we be so self-deluding?

I said nothing, only blundered past her and walked away, leaving her huddled there on the shiny cobblestones in the rain. I was in a rage, an absolute blind rage. How could she? *How could she?* A freezing trickle of rainwater got under my shirt collar and raced down my spine.

This required bold initiatives. I went up to O'Neill's and sat in a corner over a hot whiskey and considered my position. It was not a good position. Indeed, it was a very bad position. An image of Deirdre's face hung before me on the air like the head of Medusa in that painting by Caravaggio.

There would have to be an abortion. No question about it. If necessary, I would take hold of those delicate and very breakable wrists of hers and drag her over to London and shove her into some struck-off doctor's premises down a back street in Hackney, or Paddington, or wherever such people operate. There was the question of money. I could afford it, certainly, but Dee kept a harpy's eye on our finances, her pater being a significant contributor to them, and she would want to know how and why a chunk of cash had gone missing. And what did an abortion cost, anyway? Fifty pounds? Seventy-five? These were matters I decided I could leave to deal with later. One hurdle at a time.

I got a letter, it was pushed under my office door one evening. I had stayed on late to correct some papers, and nearly stepped on it when I was leaving. How long had it been there? Anybody could have picked it up. She hadn't even sealed it properly!

She assumed, she informed me, in that barbed-wire scrawl of hers, that I would leave Deirdre and get 'a place of our own', she and I and the child. Jesus Christ Almighty! This was madness. I really did think, as I sat down with that sheet of paper fluttering in my trembling hand, that she was unhinged. Was this what girls turned into when they got pregnant, this imperious, crazed and self-deluded harridan?

It was in this letter that she threatened to denounce me to the Provost. When next I saw her in her room – I had to whisper a pack of smarmy lies, my mouth pressed to the panel of her locked door, before she would let me in – I begged her to spare me. My memories of that night are a little hazy, but I believe I actually got down on my knees before her and pressed her hands in mine and pleaded with her for mercy. I offered to give her the money for the trip to Israel, as much as she needed. No go. *But my life will be ruined!* I cried. Hers, too, I added. Into the second part of that plea I inserted the faintest hint of menace. Two could play at blackmail.

She caught it, the hint, but it only made her set her face more coldly against me. She turned away, walked slowly to the bed, sat down on the edge of it with her hands folded in her lap. Some moments of silence elapsed. Then she informed me in a quiet, perfectly controlled and toneless voice that in that case – in what case? – she would call round to my, to Deirdre's and my, house on Sandymount Green and inform my wife that she, Rosa Jacobs, would in seven and a half months' time be delivered of her husband's, Mr Armitage's, illegitimate

334

son, or daughter, as the case might be. 'Maybe it'll be twins,' she said, and gave a nasty laugh.

I pause. I have a confession to make, dear diary. I know you'll be tolerant, that you won't condemn me, old friend.

She wasn't the first. Rosa was not the first. Long, long ago, in the Stockport days of my youth, there was a girl, another girl. She too informed me, one wet and windy night, that she was with child – with *my* child. Her name was Doreen. She was a grand girl. She ended up under the wheels of the London to Edinburgh express. It was a tragic incident. There were mutterings about foul play. The rozzers questioned me, and young though I was I gave a superb performance. What an actor the world has lost in me! Anyway, not a shred of evidence was found against me or anyone else, no witnesses came forward, and eventually the case was closed. Her parents tried for years to get it reopened, without success. Doreen became a statistic.

Now back to more recent matters of life and death.

I planned it all with the greatest care. So meticulous was I, in fact, that when I consider the thing at this remove, in the late-night tranquillity of my comfy, locked and shuttered room, I can't but wonder as to the state of my sanity. Why did I think I had to go to such elaborate lengths? It's not difficult to push a girl from a deserted platform onto the tracks in front of a speeding train. Should I not have been content with something equally simple, clean and final, this time round?

But no, I had to devise a plan of such maniacal intricacy that even the great Agatha C. herself would have considered it a bit much.

I pause for a moment. How strange – now that I've got to the sticking point, I suddenly find myself regarding the whole

335

thing as both tawdry and tedious. I'm no monster of depravity, I'm no Crippen, no Christie, and certainly no Gilles de Rais. An average fellow, your regular man in the street, a dull and plodding scholar, yet I am – or at least I was, briefly – a meticulously calculating fiend who saw the very foundations of his life threatened by a dirty little Jewess and acted decisively to save himself.

I got the stuff from a former student. Once a young man of promise, he had gone to the bad. He asked me what I wanted it for. I said I had a sick cat whose sufferings I wished to put an end to, but didn't want to give the poor thing into the uncaring hands of a vet. He didn't believe me, of course, but I insisted. He was in my debt, over an old matter of a pass mark rather than a fail – I knew that favour would come in handy one day.

I even derived a crumb of worried amusement from the affair, when I phoned the fellow whose lock-up was for rent. I disguised my voice by calling up my former talent as a boy soprano in the Manchester Cathedral Choir. I was surprised to find I could still do a passable falsetto – passable over the phone, with a handkerchief over my mouth. Anyway, it must have been convincing, since the idiot fell for it.

When I put the phone down, I had to laugh. At that stage I still had myself convinced I was just indulging in a bit of harmless fun: a thought experiment, let's say. If I were to be forced to eliminate her, this would be a way of doing it. But once the thought had occurred, a momentum set in, a momentum I couldn't resist.

Ironically enough, I got the idea from her. She had been looking for a place to keep her motor where it would be out

336

of the weather and protected against vandals. She loved that little convertible, it was one of her weaknesses. I told her I had found just the place, and that morning she drove up with me to Herbert Lane. What's-his-name the garage man had left the key under a stone. In we went. Rosa loved to show off her skill at reversing – she was the mistress of the three-point turn. However, she started to get suspicious when I shut the double doors while we were still in the lock-up, but by then it was too late.

I won't pretend I didn't experience a moment of animal exultation when I was shoving the handkerchief into her mouth. What did T. S. Eliot say, in that ridiculous attempt he made at writing a Greek verse drama? Wait, I'll look it up. Yes, here it is:

Any man has to, needs to, wants to
Once in a lifetime, do a girl in.

I was surprised to discover how strong she was. She fought me like blazes, and managed to deliver me a good clip on the side of the head with one of those sharp little fists of hers. My ear was still ringing for half an hour afterwards. But the stuff I had put on the hankie was fast-acting and in seconds she was under. I kept having to sprinkle more drops on the gag as I was rigging up the hosepipe and sealing the windows – wouldn't do for her to come round and start fighting me again. I worried about the canvas roof, but reasoned that if it was tight enough to keep out rain, it would surely keep in the exhaust fumes. I was right, as it proved.

She didn't suffer, and I was free.

337

Open the door, have a quick look along the lane – wouldn't do to be spotted at this final, fateful moment! – then stroll off down to Merrion Square and catch the Number 10. Bob, I can definitely say, was my uncle, that day. I was euphoric. Nothing like decisive action to put a spring in one's step. One can learn a lot from Metternich. I certainly did.

Did she lie to me about the pregnancy? There was no mention of it in the newspaper accounts of her sad demise. Not that there were many, and all of them were markedly short on detail. They said she had died by accident – they don't report suicides, over here, because they believe it's a sin, I suppose. I did get a start when that chinless wonder with the hoity-toity accent turned up at college that day to grill me about Rosa. He was oh so diffident, but I wasn't taken in, oh no. What was he called? Stafford? I put him on to Gauleiter Kessler and his queer son. That was a brainwave, if I do say so myself. Both dead now.

The thing worked out so sweetly, you'd almost believe there was a hidden pattern behind it all. Or shall I just put it down to native genius? A man in trouble is capable of working wonders.

So that's that. See me dust off the hands, adjust the tie, slick down a forelock, and saunter off, whistling.

All the same, I do miss her.

Author's note

My thanks as ever to Raymond Bell, Gregory Page and Barry Ruane.

Also by John Banville

Snow

The first Strafford and Quirke mystery

'The body is in the library,' Colonel Osborne said. 'Come this way.'

Detective Inspector St John Strafford is called in from Dublin to investigate a murder at Ballyglass House – the Co. Wexford family seat of the aristocratic, secretive Osborne family.

Facing obstruction from all angles, Strafford carries on determinedly in his pursuit of the murderer. However, as the snow continues to fall over this ever-expanding mystery, the people of Ballyglass are equally determined to keep their secrets.

'Superb.' *The Times*

'Outstanding.' *Irish Independent*

'Exquisite.' *Daily Mail*

'Hypnotic.' *Financial Times*

faber

Also by John Banville

April in Spain

The second Strafford and Quirke mystery

When Dublin pathologist Quirke glimpses a familiar face while on holiday with his wife, it's hard, at first, to tell whether his imagination is just running away with him. Could she really be who he thinks she is, and have a connection with a crime that nearly brought ruin to an Irish political dynasty?

Unable to ignore his instincts, Quirke makes a call back home and Detective Inspector St John Strafford is soon dispatched to Spain. But he's not the only one en route: as a terrifying hitman hunts down his prey, they are all set for a brutal showdown.

'Deeply atmospheric.' Mick Herron

'A joy to read.' *Sunday Times*

'The ultimate page-turner.' *Irish Independent*

'Utterly absorbing.' *Daily Mail*

faber